STAR DREADNOUGHT
BISMARCK
THE VOID WARS – BOOK 1

MICHAEL G. THOMAS

2nd Edition

Copyright © 2022 Michael G. Thomas

All rights reserved.

ISBN: 979-8423631093

CAPITAL SHIPS ENCYCLOPAEDIA

REPULSE
Renown Class Battlecruiser

Length: 2150m
Crew: 1720

RODNEY
Nelson Class Battleship

Length: 2210m
Crew: 1850

PRINCE OF WALES
King George V Class Battleship

Length: 2600m
Crew: 2150

HOOD
Admiral Class Battlecruiser

Length: 3000m
Crew: 2800

BISMARCK
Bismarck Class Star Dreadnought

Length: 2910m
Crew: 3000+

STAR DREADNOUGHT BISMARCK

PROLOGUE

While Vrokan's infantry was unmatched on the battlefield, the Vrokan battle fleet remained a mystery. Few ships were ever seen, their efforts apparently spent on secretive, rarely seen deep-space hunters. Classified as Jaeger ships, these powerful vessels would appear alone from the void, disabling transports and warships and then fleeing before they could be engaged in battle. With Commonwealth ships diverted to protect massive convoys, an opportunity presented itself. For the first time the Vrokan Empire could unleash its most powerful weapons into space, and soon all eyes would turn to the product of Vrokan's labour; ships of a size and power never seen before in battle.

Masimov's Guide to Fighting Ships

Commonwealth Light Cruiser 'Dauntless', Convoy 221
1,881st day of the war

The long, sleek shape of the cruiser moved effortlessly through space. Blue light flickered from her jump engines as she led the massive convoy of almost a hundred transports through the cold void of space. The craft were separated by hundreds of kilometres, though in space it was essentially point-blank range. Two other cruisers were mixed in with the formation, as well as five destroyers, each positioned around the periphery to create a mass of ships that occupied more than ten thousand square kilometres. One by one they passed through the next waypoint, each unable to change their course as they hurtled through space at impossible speeds. That was moment the vast field of interdiction mines detonated without warning. The array of mines instantly created a pulse of energy that rippled outwards to damage and disable the systems of any ship caught close enough to its blast. Over half of the convoy managed to escape the pulse and continued onwards, but forty-three ships were caught in the energy wave as their jump systems failed, and they returned to normal space.

Dauntless burst out into normal space, with clouds of white scattering around her hull as though she was burning. Ensign Graham Gilroy lay in his pod as the alarm sounded. He was completely, still, his body in a state of partial hibernation as he rested following yet another marathon tour. The lights blinked gently inside, and then the device started to become brighter. He'd been inside for more than a week, and still his body craved more rest. He waited there for a full five seconds, utterly still and unable to comprehend quite what was happening. The waking process was supposed to be carried out over thirty minutes, instead of a matter of seconds. In an instant, he felt weightless and a little sick. The onboard life support unit dumped a cocktail of drugs via his drip feed and into his bloodstream. The anti-nausea drugs acted quickly, as did the additional shot of adrenalin that pumped through his body.

"Alert...Alert!" said the voice in his head, "Emergency crew activation sequence underway. Jump sequence aborted."

What? Emergency activation?

"Breathe slowly. This will not take long."

Ensign Gilroy wanted nothing more than to jump up, but as he lay there, it all flooded back to him. Entry to the pod, the cool air, and then relaxation. He had no idea how long he'd been there, but he knew the process couldn't be hurried. And so he waited and did as ordered, keeping his eyes closed. He felt dreadful, though with a mild drug-induced sense of elation.

The last two weeks had granted him a rare moment of deep sleep and relaxation, and even as his mind wandered towards whatever emergency it was, it still managed to drift back home, and to thoughts of standing on solid ground with real gravity. And in the background was the unending din as the klaxons continued their call.

"Open your eyes."

Ensign Gilroy opened them slowly and found himself looking to the pearlescent pod that enveloped his body. He could see the crew quarters and the people moving about, but not in any details. The hazed effect of the pod made it impossible to make out more than shapes. Two handles on each side of the pod blinked red, and for a second, he was tempted to pull on them, to blast the canopy clear and escape. But his training forced him to remain calm.

"Pod opening."

A hiss filled his ears, and his breathing rate increased as he witnessed the confusion all around him. People floated past, as well as plastic storage bins and pieces of clothing. But that wasn't the worst. Instead, he could feel something in his gut, something about the ship. Little did he know that the cruiser had been forced into normal space, and away from so many of the transport ships that continued forward without protection. The computer's voice was then followed by the angry shouts of the vessel's captain.

"Action stations. Dauntless is under attack! To your stations immediately! I repeat; we are under attack. This is not a drill!"

"Move it!" shouted a nearby voice, "You heard the Captain. Action stations!"

Ensign Gilroy's eyes opened even wider as he looked out at the others moving around. The ship was a hive of activity, causing him to almost choke as he inhaled and tried to swallow at the same time. His throat was parched; made worse by the dry, stale air that pervaded the interior of the six-hundred-metre-long ship.

"What...what is going on?"

A man pushed past him, and then vanished directly above. Gilroy watched him go, and then looked back to see the others racing off to their stations. There was extraordinarily little space, the light cruiser being small and cramped inside. It was designed for short duration missions and unsuited to these months' long operations. The bunk space was so small that even in zero-gravity there was no space to move without striking metal. Without thinking, he undid the harness holding him inside his slip, a thin, fully transparent sleeping bag attached inside the pod to stop him from touching the cooler metal of the pod's housing, and then floated from the bunk.

"Gilroy, you slacker!" said another of the crewmen, "Thought you'd decided to go back to bed."

"Johnson," he said, struggling to remember the man's name, "What's going on?"

"No idea. It's serious, though. Peters said the jump engines are down."

"Down? As in we're stuck at sublight speed?"

Johnson shrugged, and then pushed away and floated off towards another of the bulkhead doors. Others floated about nearby as they pulled on their overalls or uniforms. The crew quarters were one of dozens of similar positions fitted throughout the ship so the men and women could sleep near their stations.

"No time for that," said a junior officer from the open bulkhead door, "We've got incoming. Get to your stations. I don't care if you're naked and with your arse hanging out. Tactical needs you, now!"

Gilroy nodded while struggling to pull his clothing into position. A woman floated past with nothing but her underwear on and vanished through the doorway. She was slowly rotating while pulling on her shirt. He knew he should be getting ready, but all his attention locked onto her half-naked form just as the entire ship shook. His vision blurred, and he was thrown hard against the nearest internal wall. The woman slammed into his leg, and then spun away, leaving a trail of blood floating about in the craft. Gilroy reached for a grab handle just as something tore a hole nine metres wide along the length of the port-side of the ship. Armour plating, shattered bulkheads, and dozens of crewmembers vanished out into the coldness of space as secondary explosions wracked the vessel. He watched open-mouthed as the half-naked injured woman was sucked out into space a second before the internal bulkhead doors snapped shut.

"We're under attack. Vrokan ships spotted on approach."

Gilroy froze is horror at hearing that.

"They're here?"

"Get to your stations!" Lieutenant Harbridge said as he

floated next to one of the hatches, "The next few minutes will decide who lives…and who dies. Our drone scouts utterly failed. And now we've been caught with our pants down."

He made it halfway through and then looked back as a device on his wrist pulsed. He tapped it and imagery and diagrams appeared.

"Goddammit. Not good."

He looked up as the crew moved away to their normal stations throughout the ship."

"Ensign, not you. You're needed in the command centre. They need fresh blood. Now hurry!"

Something else slammed into the ship, and this time he felt the impact through the shock waves carried through the ship's internal atmosphere. A helping hand reached out and grabbed his, pulling him clear and to a narrow hatch leading to the main passage running through the ship. It didn't take long to reach the heavily armoured command centre where dozens of officers and crew strapped themselves in.

"Ensign, here!" called out the ship's XO, a grim, dour-looking woman called Commander Abbot. She floated about inside the command centre, barking orders to the crew, "Man the dorsal gunnery batteries."

"Sir!"

Gilroy tried to stay calm as he moved through the open space and past the debris floating about inside. As he reached the consoles, he almost vomited. There in front of him were two junior officers, both still strapped into their seats, and killed at their stations. Dark patches marked where small fragments of metal had punched through their clothing and into their flesh. There were numerous gel-sealed puncture marks on the inner wall, a reminder that not even a military vessel was safe out here. The bridge looked almost deserted as more and more personnel floated into position. Two-thirds of the stations remained unmanned, as was normal during long-range transits, though with each passing second, more people settled into position. The interior lighting had already shifted to dark red, instantly reminding them they were on full alert. Proximity alarms then sounded, causing Gilroy's throat to tighten. He felt the fear in his body and almost dreaded looking to the glowing panels before him.

I can do this. Just remember your training.

He moved his hands over the panels as he readied his station for combat. Dauntless was an old ship, one purchased from the Titanians as a desperate measure to protect the convoys. While modern ships had automated weapons systems, she still carried much more primitive systems that were reliant on manpower over technology.

"Heavy Transport Star Alpine reports they are under attack by three unidentified vessels. That puts them approximately forty-thousand kilometres," said Commander Abbot, "Lay in an intercept course."

"Aye, Commander," said the helmsman, "Course laid in."

Alarms sounded, but this was a vastly different sound. It was not a call to battle, but a warning that the main drive was about to be activated.

Commander Abbot tapped the device attached to her wrist and spoke calmly.

"This is acting captain Abbot. We are moving into position to protect our transports. Brace for acceleration in…ten seconds."

Gilroy nodded to himself as he double-checked his harness. At the same time, the gimbal-mounted seat and display shifted to point in the direction they would be travelling. He turned his attention to his station, doing his best to ignore everything else. The displays showed a wealth of data both with regards to the weapon systems and to the targeting matrix. He could see the markers for the three ships, but no tactical information of any kind.

"Commander, I'm seeing no data on the targets."

"The computer can't track them. But we have impact and debris markers. Just keep your eyes open. You may see what the computer cannot. Remember your training and focus on the target zones."

"Yes, Commander."

The countdown ended, and a gentle shudder shook the entire ship. Gilroy felt as if he was being forced into his seat, and still the pressure increased. One moment he was weightless, and the next he was back home and subject to gravity. It didn't stop, and after twenty seconds he began to cough.

"One point six," said the Commander, "Hold on, this is going to get worse a lot faster than normal."

Gilroy's vision began to blur as he experienced a mild blackout. The cruiser was one of the fastest in the fleet, and though old she was able to out accelerate many newer ships at sublight speeds. Gilroy fought against the forces acting on his body even as his vision narrowed down into a tiny slit. He could hear what the others were saying, then without warning the sound of the alarms stopped, and the pressure on his body eased to something almost bearable.

"Range?" asked the Commander.

"Closing fast. We have three damaged transports within thirty thousand kilometres. Twenty-nine, twenty-nine point five," said Lieutenant Baxter, the ship's tactical officer, "Where are those bastards?"

Gilroy focussed on his display, as though squinting or leaning in closer would yield information hitherto hidden from him.

"Passive scanners show nothing, Commander," said Lieutenant Baxter, "No heat signatures, no magnetic...wait."

He looked at the screen carefully, moving his right hand up and around several shapes. At first it looked like no more than a few flickering stars, but then he spotted a shape blocking out much of what was behind it. It wasn't the shape of a ship, but something much bigger that was growing in size while simultaneously reducing in density.

"What is it, Ensign? Talk to me."

"There." He pointed to an area of space not far from the damaged ships, "Can you see it? The moving shape in space."

Lieutenant Baxter looked to his own displays and zoomed in on the tagged areas.

"I don't see much of interest, Ensign. Keep at it, though. Nothing gets through."

Gilroy shook his head several times.

"No, Sir, you don't understand. There's something out there, and it's not natural. Look again."

Baxter sighed but did as suggested. He continued to shrug as he looked on.

"There's a cloud. It's like a mist in space."

"Exactly, Sir. And if you look more closely, there's a denser part as though the mist is being pumped out from somewhere else."

"Show me."

Lieutenant Baxter tagged the area, and then sent it to the Commander's station. She leaned in closer, her eyes running along the multiple displays attached to her own gimbal seating. "Interesting. It's like a dust cloud, and our sensors cannot penetrate it. You think it's a debris field?"

"Perhaps. Or maybe something else, maybe to mask or cloud our sensors."

"Now that is interesting. An inert dust cloud, perhaps made up of a specific compound to confuse our sensors."

He then rubbed his chin.

"That would be the perfect place to hide ordnance, mines…or even something larger."

Gilroy then gasped as he spotted movement on his display. It pushed through the dust cloud to create a narrow wake and moved quickly.

"Sir…Something just launched from the cloud. It hit the transport."

Each of them looked to the tagged area as the ship's powerful optics adjusted and then zoomed into the area. It was difficult to make out due to the range and the strange visual artefacts caused by debris and clouds of dust around the ship.

"She's gone," said the Commander, "Cut to pieces."

She rubbed her forehead and looked back to Gilroy.

"You definitely spotted weapons fire from the cloud?"

He nodded and ran his finger over the display to show a timeline. He then moved back several seconds, showing the tagged events and markers.

"Yes," said Lieutenant Baxter, "I see it, too. It's subtle, but there. Looks like gunfire alright. The scanners didn't pick it out. Good eyes, Ensign. There's still a lot to be said for the mk1 eyeball."

Gilroy smiled at the praise, but it didn't last long. As he looked back, he noticed the blood splatters where the droplets of fresh blood had been forced back into the ship during acceleration. They lefts stains on the bulkheads, serving as a grim reminder of what had happened, and potentially what was to come.

"Okay," said the Commander, "We can't let the convoy fall like this. Tactical, target the cloud with a plasma spread."

The tactical officer tagged several stations, including the dorsal battery now commanded by Gilroy. Multiple targets areas were flagged, though as Gilroy looked on, he could still see nothing but the clouds. He licked his lips as he moved his hands over the panel, and for the first time in his life, activated the station. He couldn't see the weapons as they deployed, but he could feel it as the turrets rose from their internal spaces and moved free of the ship's hull.

"Plasma coils are full power," he said confidently, "Dorsal batteries charged and ready."

"Good work," said Lieutenant Baxter, "Fire on my mark."

Gilroy focussed his attention on the target as he made small adjustments. The computer then sent the data to the array of gun batteries fitted along the upper side of the light cruiser; consisting of the four massive gun mounts, each fitted with a pair of rapid firing 420mm linear accelerators, the same weapons fitted as secondary batteries on battleships and starcarriers.

"Fire!"

Gilroy activated the guns, and the ship shuddered as they

fired in sequence rather than simultaneously. It spread the impact along the hull to avoid it being thrown off course. He watched in fascination as the doughnut-shaped pulses instead of solid slugs of material flew to the target. It took almost four seconds, and then as they struck the clouds of dust, they exploded in colourful flashes of lights.

"Tactical, report," said the Commander.

"Uh…No signs of debris or damage, just the energy dissipation from our weapons."

"There's got to be something."

Gilroy adjusted the targeting matrix, but nothing changed, only the resolution of the noise in the cloud. And then without warning he saw it, a long, dark shape with barely discernible features. One moment it was there, and then it disappeared back in the cloud.

"Wait…I saw something."

"Tactical. Activate scanners. Find that damned ship."

"On it, Commander."

A loud pulse echoed through the compartment as pulses of energy were sent forwards to the cloud. The sound from the computer marked each pulse, but it took many seconds for the anything useful to come back.

"Okay…we've got something in that cloud. Approximately seven hundred metres long, and it's…"

He stopped and then gasped.

"It's coming for us."

Gilroy could barely breathe as he spotted the shape moving out from cover. It was big, much bigger than he'd ever expected. The hull was only a little smaller than his ship, but it was almost impossible to make out any features. It looked like the low-slung superstructure was far to the rear and the engines were slung far back in pods. The fog appeared to move with it as it shifted its course and then turned away as though fleeing a predator.

"Yeah, you can run," muttered Gilroy, "We're gonna find you."

That was the moment the threat alert sounded automatically.

"Something else is targeting us," said Lieutenant Baxter, "That's an active radar track. I think we…"

Gilroy spotted the danger and called out.

"Incoming torpedoes. They just activated their engines."

"Stealth weapons," said Lieutenant Baxter, "This is going to be a close one."

"Brace for impact," said the acting captain, "We're under fire."

Gilroy watched in horror as multiple pintle-mounted automated turrets activated. They were small calibre point-defence systems, fully automated and capable of hurling thousands of flak projectiles. Streaks of white dots reached out into space, with no sound save for the vibrations that could be felt through the metalwork of the ship. One flash marked a detonation, and those on the bridge cheered at the success.

"We got one!" said Gilroy happily.

He focussed on his screens and adjusted the tracking of his guns a little to starboard, to where he expected to see the enemy ship. But the displays shut down for a brief moment, and then all power vanished from the ship as another slammed into the underside of the cruiser.

"We've been hit!" called out a voice.

"Deploy countermeasures," said Lieutenant Baxter.

He then looked to the Commander who simply gave him a nod. It was all he needed to put the vessel on a war footing. Another series of dull vibrations shook the vessel as anti-tracking measures activated. The most significant was a spiral of decoy drones, each of which burst away when emitting a series of white-hot flares and electromagnetic pulses to simulate the innards of a ship. They scattered in a widening ring around the ship to confuse thermal, radar, and optical tracking technologies.

"Switch all weapons to image scanning only and go hot. If it's a threat, burn it to ash."

A sharp impact rocked the ship from near the stern. Gilroy would have been thrown from his seat had it not been for the harness. A moment later the lights were back, as well as multiple fires now burning inside the hull.

"Report!" called out the Commander.

Gilroy cancelled out the shouting, and instead looked towards the bow of the enemy ship as it slowly emerged from the dust cloud. It shimmered and pulsed while moving, confusing not only Dauntless' sensors, but also his eyes. Without being given orders, he adjusted the attitude of his main battery and tracked in front of the ship.

"I have a firing solution," he said calmly.

"Then fire!" Lieutenant Baxter said.

Gilroy held his breath as he activated the guns and watched as the pulses of lights struck around the target. With both ships moving, there was little they could do to avoid such high-speed weapons. Three of the eight shots missed, but five scattered near its bow, enveloping it in fire and flashes of energy.

"Good shooting, Mr Gilroy. Keep it up."

A smile spread across his face as he turned all his attention to the target. It was closer now, and he felt almost privileged at seeing one of the Vrokan ships for the first time. He lined up for another volley.

I can't believe it. A Vrokan stealth ship!

He aimed again and fired. This time the sequence shifted, with the turrets firing in pairs. It allowed him to strike the target with focussed groups of shots. Most of them landed, but as they began to cheer, they were stopped by Lieutenant Baxter.

"Two new contacts, bearing five-five. They're in visual range."

"Change course!" cried the Commander, "And give me a full burn. We need to shake them!"

Thrusters roared, but they could do little but alter the ship's attitude. The ship continued on exactly the same course as it moved towards the clouds, and the first enemy ship.

"Main drive...fire!"

The main thrusters roared with power, quickly shifting onto a new trajectory while still moving ever closer to the first target. The three ships were now close enough they could be monitored and tracked by eye with relatively little difficulty.

"They are big," said Lieutenant Baxter, "Each one a floating torpedo platform. Let's see how tough they really are. Switch to kinetic slugs."

Gilroy nodded as he made the adjustment. The change of ammunition type would reduce his rate of fire, but also massively increase the potential damage he could cause.

"Incoming warheads. Point-defence weapons online."

Lieutenant Baxter looked to Gilroy and Ensign Erikson, both of whom commanded the gunnery controls. There were five stations in total at the tactical officer's station to command the ship's vast array of weapons. Between them they commanded all the ship's offensive and defensive weapons.

"Erikson, focus on the pursuing ships. Gilroy, weapons keep hitting the one in front."

"Yes, Sir," they replied in unison.

"Fire at will. Let's punish them."

The guns opened fire immediately, with the numerous gun batteries opening fire on the two pursuing ships. Gilroy's eyes opened wide as he watched the streaks of light and heavy metal slugs thundering towards their target. Many of them struck home, and he gasped in relief as small explosions wracked the vessel's hull. And then it responded. For a moment it looked like his own fire, but the stream connected with Dauntless and ran along the armour. Tiny holes opened up in the internal compartments, as kinetic rounds punched through the outer armour and deep into the ship.

"My God!" Erikson muttered. She looked to Gilroy as a slug burst through her chest. The round continued out through her back and into the computer panels behind her. Gilroy felt deep pain in his arm and turned to his left to see two of the fingers on his left hand were gone. Blood pumped from the wounds, with the minute globules of blood floating about like small red worlds.

"Help!" he screamed, but nobody was paying attention. Tiny holes continued to pepper the interior, and half the systems were already offline.

"Eject the distress beacon," said the Commander, "Maybe Command can use the data we've uncovered. These stealth hunters have never been seen, let alone recorded before. The data could..."

"Commander!" said a stunned Lieutenant Baxter, "We've got boarding pods coming this way. ETA twenty seconds."

The ship rocked again, and more holes appeared inside the hull. The Commander was hit in the chest and slumped down in her seat. Two more shots hit her, and then a massive booming sound echoed throughout the ship. Security alerts sounded, and when Gilroy looked to his displays, he could see the danger, and watched as streaks of white dots from the point-defence guns hammered away at the approaching pods. Two were ripped apart, but the other made it through, albeit it with heavy damage and struck the ship. The thud of them making contact with the damaged hull could be heard with little effort.

"They're inside the ship," said Lieutenant Harbridge, "Arm yourselves."

Gilroy sat there, unable to move or even comprehend what was happening. He thought they'd been winning, and now it was all falling apart. A marine drifted past and handed him a weapon. He took it, and then looked down at the body. It was a Kousar T9 assault carbine, specifically designed for use aboard the ship. Rectangular in shape, short, and with a pistol grip that swept back, and then extended to the butt of the weapon with an angular back plate. A small synthetic front grip hung down, and a holographic sighting module sat atop the housing. As his hands touched the pistol grip, a light blinked towards the rear as it activated. It was then he remembered his missing fingers, and the blood still pumping away.

"This can't be happening. No way." He reached to the pouch attached to the side of his seat and ripped away the medical pack. Inside was a small syringe gun filled with a clear liquid. He tapped the side, and it began to warm. He pressed the tip against his wounded hand, and a wide spray of foam covered the stubs, causing him to cry out. The blood flow stopped immediately, and just seconds later the pain had subsided.

"Ensign. Pass that over here!" called out one of the marines.

He tossed it towards the man, and it spun about as it moved through the zero-gravity environment. The man caught it and gave him a thumbs up. Gilroy then looked to the right and spotted the Lieutenant working away on the ship's computer. Moments later he heard words that chilled his very soul.

"Self-destruct sequence activated. Thirty-minute countdown."

"Lieutenant!" he called out in horror, "What are you doing?"

The man looked back, and Gilroy recoiled at seeing the injury to his shoulder and neck. The officer held a trauma pouch to his neck while shaking his head.

"They cannot take Dauntless. Standing orders. If we fall, the ship goes with us."

He then released his harness and floated away, holding a carbine in his right hand. He moved effortlessly with a skill and ease that could only come from years of experience.

"Find what cover you can," he said as confidently as he could manage, "Fight to the last man! Do not let…"

Three red holes appeared in his body, and he flew backwards from the impact, crashing into computer displays. Gilroy pulled on his harness, dragging himself behind the displays as he took aim with the weapon. The optics were crystal clear, and a small red reticule glowed gently inside. He took aim and moved his finger to the trigger. A single shape drifted into the command room, and for a second, he assumed it was another body. But then the black armoured shape rotated and opened fire. Another followed behind as they sprayed slugs throughout the open space.

Gilroy pulled the trigger and fired, bracing himself against the gimbal mount his seat and computer panels were attached to. Shots came for him, but he ignored them and continued shooting as more of the black-clad warriors entered the ship. They looked like demonic entities, with their bodies fully encased in armour. One spun away after being hit numerous times, causing Gilroy to feel a moment of relief, all until gunfire raked his station. Sparks flew as the seat and gimbal were smashed, and then slugs struck him, one in the arm then two more to the torso. He tried to breathe, but blood gushed from his mouth.

"Bastards!" he spat as he lifted his carbine.

Two of the enemy soldiers were close now, and he could see their faceless helmets for the first time. They were utterly devoid of humanity, with an armoured respirator, and glossy black visor covering the eyes, nose, and forehead so that no skin was exposed. They could just as easily have been machines. One took aim, and Gilroy fired again, the last of the bridge crew still alive. It was his last futile gesture, and the slug struck the enemy soldier in the arm before he was hit by return fire. Silenced by a single shot to the head, he spun away and struck the inner wall, and then there was silence.

CHAPTER ONE

The Commonwealth had few friends, and even fewer allies in that bitter tenth year of the war. It started with banners flying and hopes high, as the Grand Alliance went to war against the might of the resurgent Vrokan Empire and its allies, but those days were long gone. The empires of the past were gone, fallen in the first years of fighting to the lightning strikes of the insidious Vrokan and its brutal legions of indoctrinated soldiers. The remaining powers chose peace over war, all but the Commonwealth. They remained alone and defiant; to face the wrath of an unstoppable and relentless enemy as they awaited invasion and inevitable defeat while engaged in ground battles on a dozen different fronts.

History of the Void Wars

Occupied Torugan Space

Pulses of white gas flashed from small manoeuvring thrusters, as the fighter made subtle course adjustments and began to angle upwards from its previous position. The high-speed reconnaissance fighter passed through the faint wisps of colour in the nebula, leaving a small, barely perceivable wake behind it. The fighter rolled almost thirty degrees to align it with the next waypoint projected over the cockpit's forward canopy. Lieutenant Fury looked forward carefully from inside the cramped interior of the fighter, checking for any signs of trouble. The thick armoured glass of the canopy slightly distorted the light through its angular slabs, causing him to almost squint off into the distance. Satisfied all was clear, he moved his hand slowly over the controls.

And now a little boost.

Fury pulled on the main thrust control, moving it towards him with the precision of a surgeon working in a silent operating theatre. Blue light extended from the engines to the rear of the craft, and it began to increase its forward velocity away from its previous course. After ten seconds, he cut the thrust, and the fighter continued forward. Only then did he look down at his charts on the navicomputer.

Nothing out here today in Torugan space. Just like last time.

He sighed and shook his head in frustration. He hated these missions that took him away from the safety of the major shipping lanes, and to the conquered planet and moons of Torugan. He looked to the map of the area and gulped at seeing the names of so many failures. Torugan had fought for four long months but had still fallen in the second year of the war, even though supported by numerous allied ships and divisions of soldiers.

Another of our many failures. How many more can we stand?

Torugan wasn't the first, but it had been one of the most surprising debacles that had seen the insidious newcomers continue their string of conquests. And now Noruega was a particularly dangerous problem due to its proximity to the Commonwealth's Core Worlds, making it a constant thorn in its side. Fury thought back to the stories he'd heard of the fighting and shook his head in frustration.

Whoever thought fighting the Vrokan on their home turf should be shot. We take them on in open space. It's our only chance. Every time we engage them on the ground, we end up their prisoners.

Though he tried to remain confident, it wasn't easy with the war going so badly. He knew that routine reconnaissance missions like this was a job that had to be done. But that didn't mean he had to like it. The war had been ongoing now for close to four years with nothing but a string of massive defeats for the allies. Any attempt to engage the enemy in battle near his own territory had ended in catastrophic failure. Fury might be an experienced pilot, but even he'd only encountered the enemy once so far, and it had not been pretty. Since then, he'd spent his time escorting convoys from the independent colonies to the Core Worlds of the Commonwealth, and not once had he encountered anything more than a few ion trails.

They could be right on top of me, and I wouldn't see them.

Just thinking that sent chills through his body. The ghostly hunters were by now infamous. Nobody had seen one long enough to broadcast any details, but many had seen what little remained after one of their attacks. The burnt hulks of the transports were a common sight, and one that was hard to forget. Fury tapped the controls once more and boosted the engine as he reached the next waypoint on his pre-planned route.

All clear so far. Just a little longer and I can leave this graveyard.

He tried to adjust his position in the seat, but there was no give, and the straps kept him locked securely into place. His PR25 Valkyrie was a small spacecraft, one of the newest designs in service with the fleet. The craft was built around a narrow cockpit, fitted above the stubby, rakish nose leading down to an integral weapons bay that normally carried the fighter's main armament. The wings were short, extended out, and then bent downwards to a pair of jettisonable drop tanks. Just behind the canopy was a wide armoured upper panel that stretched back to a pair of upward angled tail winglets. The engines looked huge and oversized, one on each side of the rear fuselage and hanging down like paniers. Flashes of red and white marked out the various panels, while the wings sported the insignia of the Commonwealth Navy.

Wait…what was that?

His attention shifted to the square display panels fitted in front of him below the canopy. Most showed status indicators for the various internal systems, but one was for the attached electronic warfare suite. To most, the countered waveforms might be little more than noise, but as he looked at the peaks and troughs, he was taken right back to his last convoy mission.

I've seen that before. There's something out here.

He looked directly ahead, but forward visibility was down to less than a hundred kilometres due to the thin clouds of gas that littered the occupied territories. A decade ago, this had all been clear space, but now it hung around star systems, providing a deadly screen that rendered most of his sensors useless. He tapped the buttons fitted in panel around the display to adjust the noise filters. The passive scanner matrix shifted in range as the computer focussed on closer targets. At first there was nothing, but then a single indicator began to flash.

"What?" he muttered.

He looked up and gasped in horror as the massive wreck burst into view. Fury pulled on the controls and boosted the manoeuvring thrusters. It was almost too late, and internal warnings sounded as he struggled to move above the wreckage.

Towers and the large upper decks whooshed on by as he spun away. The fighter started to spin too rapidly, and it took a few seconds to right it. By the time he'd brought the craft under control, he could see his heat signature had increased fivefold and now flashed red on his threat warning display.

Dammit, I need to get the temperature down…fast!

He tapped the button next to the main display, and at once the interior lights, displays, and status indicators either dimmed or switched off. Another button caused the main drives to shut down, leaving the small spacecraft effectively dead in space, save for the power remaining in the primary capacitor. He glanced back to the status indicators, but they still showed his fighter was emitting far too much heat, and in the cold vacuum of space that would make him stand out like a beacon.

"Screw it." His voice made him jump after being silent for so long, "Time to go dark."

Unlike the standard F25A version of the fighter now used as a space superiority fighter, this model was designed specifically for photographic reconnaissance rather conventional combat missions. The average person might think that simply meant fitting it with cameras, but the reality was the fighter had been rebuilt into an almost completely new craft. Instead of an ability to engage and defeat enemy fighters, it was now much more important to increase the craft's agility and acceleration to get out of trouble fast, as well as to make it much more difficult to spot and track. All of this meant significant upgrades to the engines, as well as numerous features to reduce the radar cross-section, as well as to deflect as much heat as possible. The fighter carried numerous systems that would shield or vent heat from the warmest parts of the craft. The added complexity and weight rendered the craft useless as a fighter, so all its weapons were gone to free up space and to reduce anything that could make its exterior easier to detect.

And now we button up.

A large metal cowling extended up over the front of the fighter, blocking off his view ahead and sealing the canopy, cockpit, and most of the sensors. The metal was layered and spaced away from the craft's hull, all part of the design to keep heat as far away from enemy sensors as possible. These additional components were unique to the reconnaissance variant and part of its stealthy design. With his forward view now blocked, Fury had to look down to the small display showing a videofeed from one of the forward cameras.

I need to get some metal between me and the shipping lane.

With the main drives offline, and the entire craft quickly turning into chilled metal, he knew he had to hurry. The main capacitor had already lost five percent, and he hadn't even touched the thrusters. A few puffs moved the craft laterally as it slid sideways and towards the broken remains of a massive common tower. Fury tried to ignore the carcass and treated it as little more than broken metal. Two more boosts of power, and then he slowly approached the surface of the ship. Skids extended out from below his fighter, and a moment later they made contact. The collapsible pistons compressed slightly, and the mag-clamps activated to secure him to the wreckage. It took a moment for the onboard system to confirm the connection, and he waited in silence until finally they blinked positive.

That'll do.

All it took was a few more taps to disable the remaining systems, other than the bare minimum levels of life support he would need to stay alive. Fury could survive on relatively little oxygen, but the heat was the big problem. The fighter was small, and with the systems offline, it lost heat quickly. He would be able to manage just minutes before the cold began to affect him, and shortly after that he would be rendered helpless in the craft. As he waited, he made one final adjustment to ensure that power continued to the camera bank fitted in place of the main nose gunnery system, and the warning system beeped loudly, making him jump.

"What!" he yelled accidentally, and then lifted hand to his mouth as though hiding his voice from another person. He chuckled to himself and then looked back to the display and to the wreckage that littered the place.

There's no sound in space, you fool. They cannot hear you.

His eyes focussed on the grainy view from the camera and found his attention drawn to the massive holes in the hull of the Commonwealth warship. They were not the explosive hits from missiles of plasma weaponry, but the massive puncture wounds from super-heavy calibre main guns. As he looked to the entry points, he wondered what the damage would be like inside the ship. He thought sadly.

Poor lady. Set upon by two of their battleships. You never stood a chance.

As he looked to the damage, something moved, a subtle shift that could mean little if he was back home on solid ground. But space was infinitesimally small, and when something moved, it was always worthy of his attention. His eyes narrowed as he concentrated, and for a second it seemed no more than a piece of wreckage. But then he noticed the thin coloured mists circling around the shape as it moved closer and closer, and then came a subtle course correction, something only an artificial object was capable of.

I can't believe it. That's a ship! One of ours, maybe?

He tapped the camera controls and switched the lens out from a 17mm wide angle to a stabilised telephoto lens that quickly snapped into focus. He half-expected to see another Valkyrie, even though the odds were incredibly small. The more he looked at it, the more he could see it was something quite different. The shape was dark and various shades of grey. It could quite easily have been little more than clouds, but then he saw one of the mighty turrets, an instant indicator that this was something much more significant. This was no fighter, and it was definitely not a freighter or long-range passenger liner.

A Vrokan warship! They've finally decided to break free and head out into space. This is a problem…a big problem.

Excitement slowly turned to dread as he realised it was heading in his direction. The range estimated from the passive sensors showed it was only sixty kilometres away. In capital ship terms this was point-blank, and he was sure his ship must be visible to them.

Okay. What do we have? Visual estimates show significant size, approximately…two thousand, no, three thousand metres in length!

His eyes opened wide in surprise at that number. He'd never seen anything like it, save for some of the decrepit transports used to haul ore from the asteroid belts.

"She dwarfs every ship in the Commonwealth fleet. Well, except for Hood. Nothing else even comes close to her. She's a big one alright."

For a moment he took heart as he thought back to the mighty Commonwealth warship. She'd plied the shipping lanes and flown the flag at a hundred different ports over the years. Friends and foes alike knew her often simply by her reputation. The jewel of the fleet, and by many accounts the most beautiful ship ever built. Images flickered on the display, and Fury turned his attention to the schematics. The computer took numerous high-resolution stills images, but as he looked at them, he could see they were hazed and lacked detail. The more he looked, the more he could see the shape of the ship looked as though it was shimmering, making it difficult to pick out specific details.

"What is that? Some kind of jamming or countermeasures?"

He tagged the buttons next to the display and activated two passive scanner modes. The computer combined data collected by the various cooled sensors to try and build up a better picture. All ships could be tracked to some extent by their electronic and magnetic emissions.

"Alright, then, computer. Who is it?"

The display pulsed in response to his question, and then silhouettes of known ships that had been previously spotted appeared, though none were close to this vessel's size. There were surprisingly few, a testament to how little the Commonwealth knew of their foe. Each type and configuration carried an identifier code and a codename.

"Target is not in our database. More input required."

"Come on. More input? What do you want me to do? Fly right up to it and knock on the front door. Check again. What is it?"

He looked back to the videofeed and changed the settings so that it overlaid a wide-angle feed to the right of the close-up. With each passing second, the computer was able to construct a three-dimensional model. Now he could make out the armoured hull, her massive engines, and the four massive weapon array, each filled with colossal turrets with barrels extending out into space.

"Wait," he said just as the computer caught up with him, "Isn't that one of their star dreadnoughts?"

He almost choked as he rotated the model about with one finger sliding along the display. The imagery and data were incomplete, and much of the last third of the ship, including all of its stern a jumble due to the fog, but he already had a picture of a long, and incredibly bulky vessel, strewn with secondary turrets and weapons, as well as her primary weapon batteries.

"That's got to be one."

The image stopped rotating, and then a designation appeared as the system finally identified the target.

"Well, I'll be damned. I just spotted a brand new Vrokan warship."

The computer then displayed details and names for the known ships in the class.

"A two ship class, perhaps more. It can be either Tirpitz…or Bismarck."

He tapped the buttons and a new list appeared.

"Let's have a closer look."

He brought up the imagery of the ship on the database and grimaced as he tried to make sense of it all.

Hm. Fragmentary. Two vertical photographs from a reconnaissance bird and some heat signature scans. Not much to go.

Then something caught his eye, the odd arrangement of the superstructure, and when he looked back, he noticed subtle difference between the ship he could with his own eyes, and those on the scans.

That's not Tirpitz. She's definitely the Bismarck. Wait...she? I thought the Vrokan called their male warships he.

He angled his head to the left and then shook it.

This is the Commonwealth. We have our own traditions...and we've had them a damned sight longer!

He rolled his shoulders as he grinned to himself.

"Bismarck, you old bastard. I found you, and the doughnut."

The smile as his own joke quickly vanished as the grey, pulsating shape moved away and slipped into the mist. Fury turned his head and watched it go so intently, he didn't notice the smaller and sleeker-looking warship moving right behind it. An alert flashed on the warning display, and as his eyes shifted to the right, he gasped.

"What!"

The computer tagged and identified the ship immediately, adding a suffix to the code to mark it was the third such vessel so far identified and added to the database.

"Vessel PR223 C. Classification light battleship or heavy armoured cruiser."

It looked quite similar to its larger cousin, though almost half its displacement. A long ion trail extended from its main drive as it chased after the star dreadnought, and then they were gone, both leaving a wake that swirled about in the coloured mist. Like the Bismarck, it was fitted out with its turrets in the old style, arrayed along what could be considered the upper hull, a concept that meant little in space.

"Prince what?"

Fury scrolled through a list of known names for the ship.

It might seem excessive, but command had constantly reminded him that he needed to obtain as much data as possible, including the class, condition and name of any vessels he encountered.

"Okay...We've got the Admiral Hipper, Blücher, Prinz Eugen, Lützow and..."

A red outline flashed around one of the models in the database as the scans confirmed the mast and turret layout to a probability of almost a hundred percent.

"Prinz Eugen...That will do. The old field marshal, huh?"

He tapped the entry and pulled back to get a better view of the tagged starships. A single massive star dreadnought and a heavy cruiser that matched the mass and firepower of some of the Commonwealth's recently scrapped light battleships.

"All this time wandering the void, and now I've got something. Finally."

Fury looked on in silence and then reached to activate his communications substack, before bringing his hand back.

Fool. You'll never get a signal out before they find you. Stay slow. Stay silent.

Remaining there, completely still and unable to fight or flee was that last thing Fury wanted to do. He was a fighter pilot, skilled in aerial combat, long-range interception, and everything else that might be expected of a member of that elite group of men and women. But sitting still and waiting it out proved to be even more stressful to both his body and spirit. He spent the next minute gazing out at the brutalist design of the ship that remained partially shrouded in fog. It wasn't ugly, but that in part was due to its nature as a warship. With no requirement for atmospheric flight, the ship lacked any form of aerodynamic shape, with sections of superstructure exhibiting long flat plates and extended towers that would have torn off during planetary re-entry. Even the primary and secondary guns were left exposed to space, with the bulky and heavily armoured barbettes extending out from the hull, providing them with complete coverage of one side of the ship. Tall antennae extended out from the superstructure, with many more pointing directly ahead from the hull like spear points.

"They might be powerful…but God they're ugly."

The ship was now directly adjacent to his position, and he was forced to swivel the camera mount around. It took a moment, and by the time it had brought up the stern of the ship, it was already moving away and through the mist. As he watched, he was sure he could see some of the mist escaping from the flanks of the ship, as though it was dumping the mist into space as a smokescreen, or similar. And then the pair was gone, just as quickly as they had arrived. Fury remained still, his eyes moving over his systems as he checked, and then triple-checked that they were not coming back.

"Readings are nominal. Somebody at Admiralty is going to want to hear about this, and fast."

He deactivated the cooling shrouds, and after nearly a minute the plates were fully retracted, leaving his engines, thrusters, canopy, and other sensors clear and free to operate. Sensing danger, he looked again, half-expecting to see another ship lurching out of the fog at him.

"Time to get back home. Do I have a story to tell!"

CHAPTER TWO

For generations, the great armoured behemoths of a hundred worlds provide the military muscles of numerous war fleets. While frigates, cruisers, destroyers, and gunboats proved useful, none could ever match the range, survivability, and firepower of a fully armed battleship. Some believe that their day has gone, and that it now belongs to the starcarrier, and its array of fighter-bombers that can strike far from the battlefield. Are battleships now relics of the past, armoured hulks soon to be forgotten? Or is the starcarrier a novel innovation that will vanish as quickly as it has arrived?
The rise of the starcarrier

Alba Transit Station, Alba V, Core Worlds
Captain John Leach watched the slowly changing view as the elevator moved higher and higher above the planet.

"Rotation in ten seconds. Please remain seated for your safety," said a pre-recorded voice. Some of those onboard sounded nervous as they checked their straps, but not Leach. He continued to look out at space and the grand curvature of the planet.

"Rotation will now commence."

Leach could already feel the change in g-forces as the elevator slowed towards the end of its journey. Unlike the others, he knew how fast they'd been travelling, and the consequences if they didn't begin their rapid deceleration now. There had never been an incident with the space elevator, but if there were, it would spell their deaths, and probably all of those aboard the tethered station.

"It's okay," he said as a child started to cry, "We're nearly there."

Of all those aboard, he was the only member of the Commonwealth Armed Forces, made obvious by his standard service uniform. He wore smart black trousers, piped with gold, and a tunic with shoulder boards denoting his rank, as well as a red line running down from the chest to the flanks. The gold piping continued around the collar, as well as a pair of coloured bands above the elbow of the right arm.

"Look!" The child pointed to his arm and spoke to his parent, "A ship."

On his left shoulder was the patch of his command, the brand-new battleship Prince of Wales, and on his left the insignia of the Commonwealth Navy, the largest and most powerful fleet among the Terrans. He smiled, knowing full well that just seeing a Commonwealth ship was the dream of so many children on the planet below.

"Deceleration will end in thirty seconds. Please continue to remain seated," said the voice as before.

The space elevator seemed so vast on the outside, and yet there was only enough space for two-dozen people inside the hexagonal car taking them higher and higher. Looking down, he could make out the planet that was currently sheathed in darkness. Faint patches of white marked the massive cities that covered much of its surface, while the large dark area were clearly the oceans and seas. Moving shapes were aircraft crisscrossing the skies, while small rockets and shuttles periodically launched up through the atmosphere.

There were four other people in the car, and none said a word as they watched the remarkable journey from surface to space. It was a silent trip, with the car making no sound or even shaking as it rose hundreds of kilometres directly up. Captain Leach looked up and watched as the flashing light came closer, and then the car entered the underside of the station, moving through a series of locking plates to detach from the shaft. Before he could even rise to his feet, another car began its descent down to the surface. In seconds it was moving at hundreds of kilometres an hour, and still increasing. The doors then hissed open, leading to another set of doors where naval staff were waiting.

"Welcome to Alba Transit Station. Please follow lit signage to your transit vessels."

Three of the other passengers exited and made for the computer displays, but not Leach. He stepped out and waited as his body adjusted to the odd sense of gravity. It was quite close to planetary normal, but a man as experienced as him could tell the subtle changes. His inner ear and stomach told him more than any computer could, and once comfortable, he moved towards the waiting station crew.

"Captain. This way," said a woman waiting at the doors. She wore Marine Corps uniform, though without body armour or helmet, and carried just a sidearm in its secure plastic holster at her flank. Waiting just behind her was a Marine guard who looked on impassively. He wore light body armour and a red-visored helmet that mostly hid his eyes from view. He carried a carbine in his hands that partially hung from a two-point sling attached to his armour.

"Thank you."

Captain Leach didn't bother looking at the signage as he stepped out and passed two more bored-looking officials. He'd been here more than enough to know how everything worked, even if it was one of the most awe-inspiring engineering feats in the Commonwealth. He continued forward from the central section of the station into a ring-shaped lobby that wrapped around the main shaft leading down to the planetary anchor. Tall displays showed images of transit shuttles, transports, and even one of several docked heavy liners designed to ship large numbers of people throughout the Commonwealth. One ship caught his eye. It was clearly visible through the massive concave windows that were easily five metres tall and rose from vertical to a steep curved until they met a wide metal ring. Next came a large partially transparent dome, with a tower extending upwards and to yet another mooring ring.

Star Spirit. One of the fastest cargo clippers ever built. What a beauty.

Though in a rush, he still found the time to move to one of the observation platforms fitted around the exterior of the ring where numerous people looked out at the impressive sight around them. Most looked down to the glittering shape of the planet below, but others found their eyes drawn to the scores of vessels moving back and forth from the space elevator and its attached transit station. Captain Leach's attention focussed on that one ship, with its long rakish bow and monstrous engines. The thing was long, much like a predatory pike, with a barely visibly superstructure and no discernible weapon mounts.

"Captain," said a voice to his right.

He turned and found a military contractor waiting there, along with two technicians. They wore the patches of Sigma-Armstrong Corps, the corporation responsible for building many of the Commonwealth's largest and most powerful ships. The woman feigned a smile and nodded to one of the large vertical panels with a rolling news story and update.

"Yes?"

"I'm sorry, but I've just heard a ship my sister-in law was on was attacked and been reported as lost in action. Convoy 221. I need answers."

He sighed as he listened to her. Convoys were hit all the time, and he was not privy to strategic data on the whereabouts of ships. It was a closely guarded secret to provide as much protection as could be offered.

"I'm not the man you need to speak with," he said sadly, "I suggest you contact fleet command. I can put you in touch with them if that helps."

The woman shook her head and lifted her communicator device. It projected a flat panel showing still images of wrecked ships.

"How did you get that?"

"Haven't you seen? It's on the public channels."

"That's dammed irresponsible," he muttered.

"Please. Her ship was hauling food from the Union. Where are they? What's happening out there?"

She moved closer, and one of the waiting guards spotted the potential problem and began to move closer. Captain Leach saw him and shook his head. The guard stopped but remained nearby and with a wary eye on the woman. Leach looked back to her as he considered the question, knowing full well he lacked much of the data, as well as not being in a position to speak to the public. He was a naval captain, not a public relations officer.

"I've just come from Cauthen City, and I've seen first-hand the difficulties the Core Worlds are facing. My own family are struggling with the rationing."

"We should try and negotiate," said the woman, "We can't win this. There's just no…"

"We can win, and we must win. The Vrokan blockade is their attempt to starve us out of this fight. It is a sign of their weakness. If they were as strong as they say they are, they would already be here."

He could see the woman had little interest in strategy, but her suggestion of surrender and negotiation rankled with him. He knew that such talk could result in arrest, or worse. Public opinion was one thing, but it could quickly turn to unrest and even revolution. If they were to win, they first had to unite against the common foe.

"If the Vrokan succeeds, we will be forced to come to terms, and that means they'll have a free hand to move through space. They will not stop until they have enslaved every populated colony."

"But my sister. She then pays the price while you're safe aboard your battleships." She moved in even closer, "Where is she? I need to know what happened."

Captain Leach shook his head. He reached forward and moved his hand in front of her device. It blinked as he passed his contact details onto her. She didn't notice at first, but then she lowered her gaze to look at the information.

"Captain Leach?"

"Yes. I am the captain of the Prince of Wales. I will see what I can find out. I can't make any promises other than to find out what I can."

She reached forward and grabbed his hand.

"It's worse than we ever thought. Food rationing, police on the streets, and the public are nervous. They know we're in trouble."

He could see the fear and doubt on her face as she tried to explain.

"They are right to be uneasy. An unseen enemy threatens to enslave all of humanity. Few will dare stand against them, but the Commonwealth will not yield."

"It is madness. To stand alone."

"If we do not, then who else will?"

"The Union?"

He shrugged at the mention of their unreliable ally.

"One day, perhaps, but not today. Until then, we must fight. And the Navy is our bulwark…"

He strained as he tried to make out her glowing nametag pinned to her chest and the name of her corporation.

"Ms Kowalski? You work for one of the largest and most powerful military contractors in the Core Worlds. Your work is what builds our ships and keeps them fighting. Without you and me, the enemy will run rampant through open space."

A light blinked on the nearby doors where his shuttle awaited him.

"I am sorry, I must leave. But please, keep doing what you're doing. I will reach out to you if I find anything. But believe me, the work your sister does is critical. She has not been forgotten, nor will she be."

Kowalski tried to speak, but her voice had vanished, and her eyes swelled up red as she fought to control her emotions. Captain Leach moved from the observation area and towards the waiting shuttle. The place was big, perhaps as large as a battleship, though it was nothing more than a transit lobby for people arriving or leaving Alba V. A series of large glass doors blocked his path, and he waited patiently as his credentials were checked for the second time since arriving. There were more guards at this point, with two carrying heavy support cannons as they blocked access to the final airlock doors. As with the others, they sported red visors on their helmets, and their grey body armour and plating gave the station a militaristic feel.

"Your shuttle is ready," said a guard as he stepped aside, "Watch the step on the way through."

He indicated over his shoulder towards the smaller pair of transparent doors, and the airlock and umbilical that connected out into space. There was a low ridge on the ground where the umbilical connected to the station. He grimaced, and then stepped forward. The doors hissed open just enough for him to step through, and then closed again in sequence. The umbilical sounded more fragile than it actually was. It was more like a narrow passage aboard a ship, but with transparent sections on its sides and wide metal rings every few metres. It could be retracted back into the transit station as required.

He moved to the craft, settling down into a seat on the left side. It didn't take long for it to detach. It then rotated and moved away, leaving the station visible in the upper left quadrant. Leach looked back to the space elevator that connected directly to the ring-shaped station. It was much smaller than a naval base and operated as a way station for shuttles and transports moving throughout the Commonwealth. Three heavily armed cutters waited a short distance away, their navigational lights blinking brightly in the blackness of space. Further back two light cruisers were ready and waiting, should an enemy appear in the system.

Times have changed. Six years ago, there would have been one cutter, now there's an entire taskforce in orbit.

He turned his attention to the Scapa Naval Station while shaking his head. The craft continued its elliptical course away from the station, moving away from the space elevator and its attached transit station. The shuttle was a small craft, little larger than two fighters joined together end to end, and with enough internal space to seat eight passengers. It was designed for short-ranged transit only, incapable of planetary entry or even travelling more than a day in any direction. There was no pilot or crew; just a passenger area, armoured hull, and engines, making it feel more like a pod than a spacecraft.

He sat there quietly as his shuttle took almost an hour to complete the journey to the largest of the planet's moons. Only then did he leaned closer to the small window to get a view of the series of massive drydocks, quays, and replenishment bays that covered much of the moon's surface. Large metal spars extended out to offer partial protection against impacts, but also as braces and mounts for metallic shields and screens to hide the vessels from prying eyes. There was little left to show it had once been the largest natural satellite around the planet Alba V, the second largest planet in the Commonwealth's Core Worlds.

One floating dockyard was positioned a significant distance from the moon, and as he moved past, he was able to get a better look inside the lattice of metal barriers. Snuggled inside like a fly caught in a spider's web, were two ships. One was a frigate, and next to it and much larger, a heavy cruiser, her stern missing and great holes in the side of her hull. Captain Leach felt sadness close to the emotional loss of losing a loved one. It was Elektra, one of the Commonwealth's most recent losses in the unending war with the Vrokan. The floating dockyard moved away, and there before him was the fortified starbase, military shipyard and bastion of this sector, the legendary Scapa Naval Base.

There they are.

All thoughts of defeats and ship losses vanished, as he leaned across to the narrow viewport on the starboard side of the shuttle and looked on with pride at the array of ships. As always, there were scores of military transports, shuttles, tugs, and small ships travelling around the planet's moon, but this was the first time in over six months since he'd seen these two very different ships together. On one side was the aged, but renowned battlecruiser Hood, a ship from another time. He looked to her long, elegant lines, partially retracted main battery, and array of secondary guns. She remained the largest and fastest gunship in the Commonwealth fleet, as well as the oldest.

"She looks as ready as ever."

A smile spread over his lips as the shuttle continued past, circling around the next bay, heading towards one of the many hangars. He kept his eyes locked onto the aged ship and exhaled happily. There was no vessel more famous in the Commonwealth Fleet, perhaps any fleet than the Hood. Named for the long-admired Admiral, she had visited every colony in the Commonwealth over her long career, with hundreds of thousands of people having visited her and stepped inside her armoured bulkheads. She was more than just a ship. She was the flag and symbol of every city, colony, and world in the Commonwealth.

"What a ship," he said proudly, "There's never been a ship like her, and likely never will again."

He then looked on with interest as his shuttle moved over the second ship. Much of the stern was hidden behind an array of metal gentries that wrapped around her like a spider's web. From these gantries moved scores of robotic drones, beavering away on her exterior. They were tethered with fine cables providing motor control and power.

"And there's my command," he said as though announcing the name of some holy relic. The metal lattice frames ensnaring the ship served as a reminder of how far behind schedule they were, "And she's still not ready."

The ship was shorter than the battlecruiser, but that was where any similarity ended. While Hood was an agile hunter, this ship was quite different. Her hull was much bulkier, and two thirds of her main batteries were shifted forward of the primary superstructure where the turrets housed the latest 720mm pulse cannons; a brand-new development of the venerable bombardment cannons used on earlier ships. She carried engines almost the same size as those fitted to the battlecruiser, and able to match her in acceleration and agility. Hood represented the past, of the old days of Commonwealth power and glory. Prince of Wales was very much a ship of today. Built to be all things to all men, and cheaper to both build and to operate. She was smaller, though with better armour and less powerful, but higher velocity main guns.

While there was only one Hood, there were five ships of

the King George Class battleships in various stages of completion. The shuttle circled around her stern, and then made directly towards one of the main supply hangars built into the hull of the ship. As the shuttle approached, the outer doors opened, revealing flashing lights and marker beams for the autopilot to follow. The landing was smooth, and by the time Captain Leach had moved to his feet, the door was already opening. Cool air washed inside, and he could instantly pick up the scent of cleaning fluids, burnt electrical cabling, and smoke.

"I'm home."

CHAPTER THREE

How could an impoverished people like the Vrokan move from a backwater to the most powerful empire seen in a century? The start of her rise to power can be seen not in machines or war leaders, but in the economic collapse of the pre-war years, a period that left the population starved and broken, a people waiting for a hero, a messiah to lead them to prosperity. Few at the time noticed the darkness surrounding those new heroes, and the terrible crimes they would inflict both at home and far away on now forgotten worlds.
Fascism, war, and the Rise of the Vrokan Empire

Commonwealth Battleship 'Prince of Wales'
Scapa Naval Station

There was something about a battleship that inspired confidence. And even in this state of completion the ship still looked like a monster to Captain Leach as he inhaled the cool air. It has been weeks since he'd last been aboard but looking out at the vastness of the internal hangar space put a smile on his face.

"Captain," said a voice directly ahead.

"Commander Percy, it's been too long."

He moved down the ramp and through a cloud of steam to find two lines of men and women, all smartly dressed and waiting at attention. They looked as though they were waiting for a detailed inspection, though far fewer people than he would have expected to see. Behind them, and partially covered in plastic cladding, were four Walrus search and rescue craft. Their engines and retractable wings were barely visible under the sheeting. Bulges along their flanks marked the position of gun emplacements, a reminder that these spacecraft were designed to be able to defend themselves. Stacked next to them were dozens of heavy containers, most of which were still sealed.

"Welcome home, Captain. We weren't expecting you so soon."

"It is good to be back." He moved across the metal deck, "Events conspire against us."

He moved closer while glancing towards a hole in the ceiling where a bulkhead spar had ruptured. As he looked more carefully, he could see up several levels where the bulkheads were in a state of partial repair. Several workers were inside, sealing new beams in place, along with drones helping with the heavy lifting.

"That's new. What happened?"

"Welding problems on three shafts."

Captain Leach stopped for a second. "How far spread is it?"

"Just this section," said the Commander, much to his relief, "There was a technical fault for three days of construction, and it's been isolated to this one location. It required three decks to be opened up, but we can't take the chance."

"And that is going to set us back further, is it not?"

"Every two steps forward are leading to one back. We're in such a rush there just isn't time to finish things as they should be. I tell you; we need to slow this down."

"In a perfect world, perhaps. But have you seen the reports?"

Percy shook his head.

"Convoys are in trouble. Everything with engines is being sent out to protect them. Destroyers, cruisers, and even battleships waiting to be scrapped; even some of the Revenge Class battleships are being patched up."

"Really? They're even older than Hood." Percy shook his head as the news sunk in, "So that probably means us soon, then. We're the newest ship in the fleet."

Captain Leach gave him a curt nod, and then looked down to his polished boots and the grubby deck. He could instantly feel the difference from the shuttle and the transit station. There was gravity here in the shipyard, by virtue of the moon's significant mass. It was very low, little more than a third planetary normal, but changed the way he walked significantly. As he moved forward, his feet tapped smartly on the plating below.

"I can see the cleaning crews haven't moved in yet."

Commander Percy looked positively embarrassed as he looked at the floor. It wasn't dirty, per se, but rather the discarded pieces of plastic trunking, metal powder, and dust lay all around, made worse by the scores of boots that had trodden through it all.

"My apologies, all hands are…"

"It's okay. Right now, it's all about the work. Better to have sealed and operational bulkheads that can take a broadside than a dust free deck. Functionality comes before form these days. Aesthetics come later…if there is a later."

"Aye, Captain. Always the if."

The two continued along the deck, and as they walked ahead, Captain Leach found his attention drawn to some of the newly fitted components. Grab handles and ladders were fitted into places that looked impossible to reach in a world of standard gravity. Even stranger were the signs dotted about the ship, some sideways or slanted so that they could only be read from certain positions. To a newcomer it might seem rather poorly designed or even pointless, but for a crew that lived most of their lives in zero-gravity it made perfect sense. One sign in particular continued to flicker until a contractor struck the plating with a rubber hammer. It flickered once more and then stopped.

"How is the work progressing? I've been looking over the reports, but it's not easy trying to get a picture of her state."

"Well, we're making better progress than the other ships, that's for sure. Duke of York, Anson, and Howe are all anything up to a year away from completion. But we're still not ready."

"Go on."

"This entire class wasn't supposed to be ready for combat for years. Everything is a rush. The guns have never been tested. The mounts are not within tolerance, and there are problems with the wiring looms. And that's just getting started on the ship...let's not forget the personnel."

"You don't have the numbers, still?"

"Oh, we've got the crew allocated, but most of our people are fresh out of the academy simulators. The veterans are in space already, on cruisers and older battleships. The Admiralty won't waste veterans on ships stuck in drydock."

Captain Leach rubbed his temples as he gave that more thought.

"I said a month ago this work should be continued in zero-g. There's more space for the drones and…"

"That would have helped, but it's just not possible. All available orbital shipyards are being used for mass production of escort ships. In any case, the contractors are still stress testing the hull and bulkheads, and for that they need the ship right here. It's the only reason we found the stress fractures in the bulkhead spars." He smiled as he tried desperately to put a positive spin on the whole thing, "But we're still on schedule."

"That was the old schedule. Yesterday's report is mind-boggling. You would not believe our convoy losses."

He tapped his wrist, and then showed his number one the chart of losses.

"Five escorts lost, and twenty-four transports destroyed or crippled over three days. It would have been double that if not for the escorts."

"Can we sustain those losses?"

"In the short term, yes. But another year of this will see us on our knees. Viral bombings have killed off food stocks, and we simply cannot build armour, infantry weapons, and ground vehicles fast enough. If the Vrokan break through and land their transports, it will be over."

Commander Percy nodded.

"And that's why we need to keep the transports coming. The Admiralty wants our heavy capital ships launched as quickly as possible. Those convoys need protection."

"We're all working as fast as we can, I can promise you that, Captain."

"I know you are, and I would expect nothing less."

The two walked along in front of the crew, each of whom

looked directly ahead and utterly still. Captain Leach was something of a legend in the fleet and having him aboard meant they were one small step closer to launching.

"I've been reading through your progress reports. The original plan was at least another year before trials. We're making impressive progress, but it sounds like Prince of Wales could do with another three months in dock. At least?"

"Three months is pushing it. She was transferred here before her weapons were even installed. We're going as fast as we can, but corners are being cut everywhere to get her ready. We've learned a lot from King George, and we're not making the same mistakes. But I'm still having to cut corners wherever I can."

"Then you've got enough to do without me breathing down your neck."

He stopped and looked to those waiting at attention.

"Forget the formal inspection and get them back to work."

"Captain? I've got them ready to…"

"You're already doing all you can, so keep at it. I'll see if the corps of engineers can rustle up more personnel. Based on what I've seen, we need as many ships in space as we can muster."

"Good luck with that. Every request I've made says they're being diverted to the carriers. Even Hood's upgrades have been pushed back indefinitely."

"Tough times. Six years ago, we were in an unprecedented era of peace. The Vrokan appeared from nowhere, and now they occupy territory on all sides. Their legions are victorious everywhere."

"Everywhere but here," said Commander Percy.

He bit his lower lip, and his expression became more serious.

"If you need anything else let me know. Personnel, hardware, drones, I'll do what I can."

"There's nothing left in reserve. We need the new colonies' help, and fast."

"Good luck with that. They still want to stay out of this one. Just the same as the republics in the Voronoff Union. I hear most of them are talking of siding with the Vrokan to avoid war."

Commander Percy's eyes opened wide.

"Together they would be unstoppable."

"I know. They are fools. Voronoff has no fleet to speak of. If we fall, they will be next, and they can do nothing to stop it."

He rubbed his chin, and then did his best to look confident.

"The eyes of the galaxy are on us, old friend. Friend and foe alike know we have reached the point of no return. The war is out of our hands. All we can do is be ready for what is to come. Just get my ship ready for battle."

"I'll do all I can." The Commander lifted his hand in salute.

"I know you will."

Captain Leach answered the salute, and then before either man could say another word, the Captain was gone, moving quickly through the ship he knew like the back of his hand. Though the ship had never left her shipyard before, he'd spent hundreds of hours moving about her via the virtual reality hardware used to train new cadets. The passages were half filled with storage bins and containers, and he had to step aside numerous times as robotic loaders moved past with their heavy loads.

She's not ready, not even close. If we go into battle like this, we'll be lucky if we can get any of our guns to fire.

He moved so quickly most of the crew had no idea he was there. He appeared on the massive engineering deck without warning, causing the crew to leap to attention as he brushed past. It was a multi-layered area, with consoles and their attached seating fitted to gimbals that could move once the ship was underway. He removed his hat and shook his head, moving quickly past them and towards the large ring-shaped compartment guarded by another two marines. They saluted with their left hands across their chests due to carrying their carbines, and then stepped aside to let him through the double-layered security barrier into the heart of the ship. Once inside, he stopped and looked ahead to the array of tall, liquid cooled reactors laid out in two long rows of four. Massive blast barriers partially blocked off each pair in case of damage or leaks. Beyond them were four huge turbines, each vastly larger than the reactors, and surrounded by heavy metal protective shells.

"Captain," said the Chief as he as spotted his commander.

He moved towards him and wiped his forehead with an oily rag.

"Chief. I can see you're in your happy place."

"Aye, it would be if it were all working."

"Working? I've seen the progress reports. What's happened now?"

"She's just not ready, Captain. These turbines might be

state of the art, but they've never been installed on a battleship before. Half the connections severed when we started her up, and the crawl space is too small to get near them. I've got hundreds of Sigma-Armstrong Corps engineers and contractors working around the clock to get it working the way we need it."

"The war is not going well. Everything is being rushed out the door. I've heard two cruisers still have work crews aboard on their first patrols."

"Well, that's one way to run a shakedown cruise," laughed the Chief, "Nothing gets a ship fixed up than necessity."

"Perhaps. But Admiralty is concerned that we're operating with a fleet of antiquated ships. We need these ships ready, and we need them fast. At least tell me we have operational engines."

"I can give you engines. But with the unreliable turbines we might be forced to run on back-up generators if they fail. We've still not completed internal air tests, ventilation tests, internal door seals, fuel management, or gunnery. She's a new class of ship. This usually takes months, sometimes years."

Captain Leach's communicator unit flickered, and as he lifted it, he was greeted with a red warning indicator.

"Looks serious."

"I need to get to the bridge."

He turned to move away and then looked back to the Chief.

"We've got command controls and comms, right?"

"Aye, that's something we do have." The Chief knew that tone only too well and raised an inquisitive eyebrow, "Problems? More transports lost?"

The Captain licked his lips, and then nodded.

"A lot worse."

The Chief looked surprised to hear that.

"I'm not sure what else could be worse."

"One of their star dreadnoughts has been spotted."

"In port?"

"No. Leaving occupied space. Command believes Vrokan capital ships are breaking out into open space."

"Good God. Let's hope not. That one ship could cripple our convoys and end the war in months. Our escorts can do nothing against it."

The Captain considered that for a second, and then began to move away.

"Run triple shifts if you have to. Strip men from everywhere you can find and get this fighting lady into shape. We may be needed before we're ready. And no matter the state, Prince of Wales will enter the fray with her colours flying."

"Aye, Captain. She'll be ready."

As he moved away, he lifted the device on his wrist.

"Number one. Meet me in the command centre as soon as you can."

"Problem?"

"Just a little."

"I'll be there in ten."

* * *

Captain Leach struggled to move inside the ship's command centre as he pulled himself through the door. Metal trolleys heaped with computer equipment made progress difficult, made worse by the reels of cable partially unwound on the floor. A marine saw him arrive and helped pull two large plastic cable housings free to let him inside.

"Captain."

"Sergeant. This place looks like a bomb hit it."

The marine grunted in agreement.

"It's looked a lot worse, Sir."

That put a smile on Leach's face. The marines were a tough bunch, perhaps the toughest fighters in the entire Commonwealth. While the Army was responsible for the bulk of the major battles, the Marines went wherever the Navy went, so they found themselves in action throughout space and in a million different scenarios. They were always ready, first into action, and almost always outnumbered. Leach moved past him, and into the command centre. Though it might not be obvious from there, it was one of the most heavily protected parts of the ship, with the internal citadel armour extending around it.

"Captain on deck!" said a voice to his left.

It was impossible to see who it was due to the containers, but as he moved further inside, he found himself facing off against two naval officers and five contractors.

"As you were."

There was a moment of hesitation, and then they returned to work. Cables hung down from the ceiling, and many of the computer systems were still not even connected up even though they were installed and in the correct place. Some were still covered with protective plastic sheeting to protect them from dirt or damage. It was a relatively cramped rectangular space, with gimbal-mounted stations on both sides for the officers. On the right an open doorway led to the war room and its planning table and array of flat displays.

He carried on as the space opened out into a wider space,

with further stations along each side. At first glance, the place looked incapable of being used, but as he ran his eyes past the various stations, he could see that most were connected and operational. The science and engineering stations, along with helm appeared finished, though the weapons stations were not. In the centre a spherical projection space currently showed a floating model of the ship. He walked around it, soaking in the detail of his new command. Prince of Wales was the second of the Commonwealth's latest generation of warship, but she would not be the last. He reached out to touch the ship's bow, and it instantly distorted as his fingers blocked the path of light from the projectors.

"Captain."

He turned back and there was Commander Percy. The man was a little out of breath where he'd clearly been running through the ship. He moved in closer, past the mess filling the space, and stopped alongside the model.

"I came as quickly as I could."

"We've got a problem, a really big one. To the war room."

The Commander raised an eyebrow as he followed Captain Leach back through the command centre, and to the slightly narrower compartment that led into it. Between the primary bridge and the secondary area was a substantial triple-layered security door. There were massive metal pistons partially external on both sides, showing where they closed like the jaws of a great beast to seal off the senior officers from the rest of the crew in an emergency. The stations on the one side were devoid of people, and even the door to the war room was left open for anybody to access. Leach moved inside, and Commander Percy followed. Once inside, Leach moved his hand over the panel. The inner door half closed, and then made a grinding sound before struggling to move further.

"Does anything work on this ship?"

Commander Percy grimaced.

"Everything important is in position, installed and ready. But we've got a lot of testing and shaking down left to do. She's a brand-new ship, fresh off the line."

Leach placed his head in his hand, and then looked about the room to see what was functional. A holographic projection space took up a fair amount of space in the middle, with cylindrical projector mounts positions so that information could be presented no matter the orientation of the ship. He tapped the controls fitted to the gimbal mount and the unit sprung to life. He checked over his shoulder to be sure they were alone, and then tapped his wrist device.

"Imagery from one of our reconnaissance fighters. It detected two ships, a super-heavy cruiser, and a star dreadnought moving out of occupied space."

"Once they're clear of the star system's grav wells, we'll never have a chance to find them."

"Exactly."

He tapped the unit to bring up a strategic map of the Core World and the shipping lanes used by the convoys to reach them.

"Once in open space, they will move in to strike the convoys from any number of attack vectors."

"Then we have to stop them before they can escape," said Commander Percy.

"Exactly. Admiralty has sent two heavy cruisers into Occupied Torugan Space to hunt for the ship, but it's a lot of space to monitor."

"That's a tall order. The odds of them finding the ships are almost zero."

"That's why I called you in. Prince of Wales and Hood have been activated."

"Wait. Did you say activated?"

"I did. Can it be done?"

"How long do we have?"

Leach licked his lips, clearly uneasy with the information.

"First thing in the morning. We have to block...."

"No. Just no. We're simply not ready."

"We're the only ships anywhere near close to launching. Other vessels are being recalled, but if the Vrokan make it to open space, then it's already over. I need engines and basic gunnery. We can work out the rest as we go."

Commander Percy kept shaking his head, but deep down he knew he had little choice.

"I'll need to keep the work crews onboard for the entire trip. This grand old lady needs a lot of work to make her ready."

"Whatever you need, you will have it."

"I can't believe it," said Percy as he resigned himself to taking the ship out into battle, "We're really doing this?"

"Aye, we are."

"And Hood is coming with us?"

The Captain nodded, putting Percy at least a little at ease.

"That's something. The mighty Hood is nothing but reliable. With half our systems being worked on, we'll need her more than ever before."

"Then get to work. I'm recalling the crew. The rest will join us in space. We can't take chances with this one. Fingers crossed our scouts find them before it's too late."

"We'll be ready for a fight, if I have to stand outside and manually guide the guns myself."

"From what I've seen over the last hours, you might just have to do that."

Commander Percy tried to make light of that, but he could see the worry in Leach's eyes. The man knew they might be going into battle, and soon. And their ship was nowhere near ready for what she might be expected to do.

STAR DREADNOUGHT BISMARCK

CHAPTER FOUR

The Mighty Hood was a ship known throughout the Void and admired by all that saw her. In the peaceful years before the Vrokan War the Hood travelled far and wide, flying the flag for the Commonwealth, and reminding all that she remained the largest, fastest, and most powerful warship afloat. Even as newer ships travelled for the first time, the grand old lady of the Commonwealth still carried enough firepower to cripple half a battle fleet should it ever come to war.

Masimov's Guide to Fighting Ships

Commonwealth Heavy Cruiser 'Norfolk', Kamineso Nebula, 15 hours later

Lieutenant Alethea Madeline concentrated her gaze as she looked at the computer displays. As tactical officer, she was responsible for much more than merely managing the ship's weapon systems. She was also in charge of the ship's numerous sensor arrays and targeting equipment as they hunted for signs of the enemy. One display showed a series of horizontal bars that displayed the composition of various elements at distinct levels in the vast nebula.

"Boring," she muttered to herself, "Another cloud of nothing."

Her attention shifted to the second monitor, and to their twin travelling nearly a thousand kilometres away and directly above their dorsal guns. She increased the magnification and waited until the ship moved into focus. Normally, it would be easy to see a ship in open space, but the Kamineso Nebula shrouded a vast region of space around occupied Torugan territory, making it the perfect area for enemy ships to pass through on their way to their hunting grounds.

Suffolk. Now you are an ugly spud, aren't you?

She knew the silhouette of the ship only too well, though as she squinted, she found it kept fading in and out as if travelling through fog. The ship was perhaps not the prettiest ever built and looked much like planetary skyscrapers placed sideways, the decks laid out vertically along her hull. She was very well armoured for a cruiser and bristling with heavy guns fitted along the flanks only. In battle, the ship could simply rotate along its axis to bring both sides online at once to provide maximum coverage from all its weapons. She smiled as the navigation lights blinked, as though answering her own thoughts. And then the entire ship moved from view, only to reappear seconds later.

Hello again.

The entire front was slab-shaped to provide maximum protection for the crew areas, as well as to be thick enough to provide the space for the numerous decks from front to back; for when engines were active and the crew able to walk about rather than float through the ship. The superstructure remained relatively blocky, much of it consisting of thick amour plating and right angles present all over the ship.

"I can barely see a thing."

A few taps changed the visual scanning mode, but they showed nothing but the Commonwealth warship and the wake she created moving through the fine clouds of particles. She shook her head, and as she moved away, her finger tapped the panel, swinging the camera around to directly behind her own vessel. She leaned in to change it back, but then spotted something.

Wait a moment.

Alethea was no rookie, but a woman with three years' experience at her station. Her eyes and ears were highly attuned to the peculiarities of space, especially inside the curious phenomena encountered inside nebulas. As she looked at the area of space, fresh data arrived from Suffolk, the other heavy cruiser out patrolling with them. One area in particular appeared to have caught their attention, but they could find nothing more than traces of naturally occurring radiation. It was noteworthy, but certainly not what they were out here for. She moved her fingers to the displays and made a series of adjustments to the filters to assess what they'd seen. The ship was already moving away and quickly flagged the data as anomalous.

Hmm. I don't know about that.

She stripped away the bands of colour, and then brought some of them back as she struggled to identify different clusters of chemicals. It took time, but nothing was going to stop her as she ran a series of level tests and enhancements. Only then did she lean back to get a better overview of what she was looking at.

That doesn't look right. That's interesting.

Alethea rubbed her chin twice, and then nodded.

Cross check with any of our ships in the area.

It didn't take long to track the route each of them had taken, and then to overlay the new data to see if they were in any way responsible. As she finished, she simply sat there, staring at the long line making its way through the nebula.

"Commander…Can you take a look at this for me?"

The man a short distance away turned in his gimbal seat and looked across to her.

"What have you got, Lieutenant?"

"I'm not sure, but it shouldn't be out here. Suffolk picked up something in the marked quadrant. I've run statistical checks on it and put it through all known filters."

"And?"

"It's not much more than some random ion clouds."

"It happens."

"Perhaps. But they match up with two other readings I've taken."

He raised an eyebrow but said nothing.

"Commander. If you project all three onto our tactical map, we get a curved line through three-dimensional space. It follows a Bezier curve perfectly."

"As if a ship's course change?"

"Yes, Sir. I believe so. There is another point fifty-four kilometres back that shows a flat trajectory. They pulsed their engines to move five degrees off their original course."

"Send it to me."

"Sir."

The imagery appeared on his three large panels, and he looked at it for a number of seconds before looking back to her.

"And this is timestamped as of three minutes ago?"

"Yes, Sir."

"Lieutenant...I think you've just found our prey."

"Prey?"

He then smiled at her and turned away to speak with the Captain. As he did so, she looked back to her own display. The imagery was undeniable. A ship had come through here in the last hour, and at some speed. With the ever-changing nebula, and the myriad of dangers hidden inside, it could mean only one thing. A ship with a commander that knew the area well, and a commander that didn't want to linger for too long.

"No," she said, much to the amusement of the Commander. As she looked back, he was staring right back at her.

"I think we've got the scent of our prey."

"Prey? What are we looking for?"

At that very moment, the lighting inside the ship darkened. The displays became dimmer, with a subtle red shift occurring so as to allow them to see them clearly in the lower light and at lower brightness levels. At the same time, the internal speakers crackled. She looked over her shoulder and to the position of the ship's Captain next to the Commander. She could hear him clearly without the need of the speakers, but if they were being used then she knew it was important. Captain Phillips' voice was slow, calm, but assertive. And she could tell immediately that something significant was about to happen.

"This is the Captain. We've picked up the scent of our prey. Thanks to the crews of Suffolk and our own ship we've located traces of a Vrokan battleship of incomprehensible size and power."

Alethea's eyebrows rose as she realized the enormity of what she'd just heard.

"This ship and its escorts have breached our blockade of the Vrokan's ports and is heading for open space. If they make it out and are able to attack out convoys at will, it could bring about our fall."

He paused, and as she watched him, she could see he was checking reports on his displays.

"I can now confirm that ships have already been released from Scapa Naval Station and The Rock to block potential routes."

He nodded slowly, and then looked to the men and women present in the command centre.

"We and Suffolk will give chase and trail them. No ship can safely power up a jump drive if under risk of attack. We are that threat. And so I call on each of you to do all that you can to see this done. The ship is codenamed Bismarck…and we will not return home until she is a burning hulk. Captain out."

He placed the intercom unit back into its mount, and then turned to speak with his executive officer. Alethea glanced across to the other officers as they turned their attention to their stations. At the same time, the ship's thrusters activated to move them onto a new heading.

"Main drive powering up in twenty seconds," said the helmsman, "Brace for drive shunt."

Alethea double-checked her harness, and the others did the same as the countdown continued. A gentle warning noise sounded throughout the ship, telling each of them to prepare for what was coming.

"Four…three…two…one!"

It started gently, and then the force pushed her down into her seat. The gimbal shifted so that she was now technically facing the side of the ship. It was an odd sensation, and for the first few seconds she felt a little nauseated. But as it subsided, she was able to enjoy the normal respiratory feelings as once more she could feel her own body.

"All eyes on station," said the Captain, "Visibility in this nebula is poor. The last thing we want is to run right into her guns. Trust me…Bismarck is a monster."

Imagery appeared on her display, and then she gasped. The vessel shown on the database was unlike anything she had ever seen before. It was vast, though much of its form was incomplete due to missing data. Some parts were detailed and others little more than a haze.

"I've never seen her kind before."

"None have." The Commander looked across to her, "Admiralty believes the Vrokan have at least two ships of her class, perhaps more. And she's not travelling alone. Bismarck is three kilometres of solid metal and covered in a blistering array of weapons."

Alethea gulped nervously. Until now she'd felt quite safely ensconced inside her heavy cruiser. There was nothing that could cause them much damage outside of a larger warship, and they could always count on their speed and agility to escape. But no more. If the information on this enemy ship was correct, they were now facing a threat like no other.

"And the cruiser?"

"Yes. It's Prinz Eugen, an Admiral Hipper Class heavy cruiser. Identified by the scout that spotted her. You know what to do?"

"Yes, Sir. We'll track them down. Both of them."

"Good," he said with a nod of grim determination, "And

when we find her, we'll call in the heavies to burn them to their keels. The Vrokan may control battles on the ground and in orbit, but in open space we're in command."

* * *

Commonwealth Battleship 'Prince of Wales'
Six hours later

Captain Leach settled into his seat and ran his eyes over the screen in front of him. The naval station was long gone, as was Alba V as they streamed away from the Core Worlds and to the assembly area. A series of tramlines showed their projected course, along with anticipated time of arrival, as well as markers showing the position of other ships already out there. He found the unmoving image of space to be quite enthralling. They might be moving ever faster as they moved away from the gravitational forces of the Core Worlds, but from where he sat, it was as though nothing moved.

"Space...none ever appreciate the vastness until they travel aboard a jump drive equipped starship."

He turned about on the spot to look to the rest of the men and women aboard the command deck. Commander Percy was already there and looking to his displays. When he looked back, he did his best to look confident, though his nerves were impossible to hide.

"Moving past the second waypoint, Captain. So far everything is looking good. Main engines are performing as expected."

"The Chief has done the impossible."

"He always does, Sir."

"Indeed, he does. Indeed, he does."

"And my ship. How is she doing? Are the contractors on schedule?"

"She's as ready as she'd ever going to be. We will just have to fix any issues as they arise."

"Good…Very good. Let's take a look, shall we?"

"Navigation bridge?"

"Yes."

"Yes, Captain."

The two released their harnesses and moved to a single armoured bulkhead door fitted to the side of the command deck. The door hissed open, and both moved through, travelling a short distance to where a spherical room awaited them. It was not particularly big and had been completely dark as they approached. Now the internal lights activated to reveal three gimbal-mounted seats, as well as a ring of metal plates along the one side.

"Let's take a look outside."

Both men moved to the seats and pulled on the harnesses. Once in position, the gimbals adjusted and rotated about so that the officers were facing in the direction the ship was travelling. For any watching from nearby, it was as though they were now looking up to the ceiling. The change in forces on their bodies was quite pronounced. One moment they were able to walk about on the deck, the next they were looking directly forward, and being pushed back down into their seats, like the crew aboard a rocket during launch.

"Open them up."

The massive articulated metal shutters slid away, and there

before them and directly in front of the senior officers were a series of narrow windows, each well protected by thick metal ribs running between each pane. The protective metal barriers were layered and only partially retracted. They could easily be moved back into position. Out on the other side of the glass was unfiltered space. Both watched in awe as they took in the blackness and the infinite array of twinkling dots and colours filling open space.

"It's quite something, isn't it?"

Commander Percy gazed out into space, and for the first time in days, he actually smiled. Not the forced smile of agreement in front of another, but the natural expression at seeing something truly extraordinary.

"It's like a drug. Only those that have seen it could ever understand."

"I didn't bring you here to look at the stars," said the Captain with a smile, "Not that one can ever truly bore of seeing them. I need to talk to you about the crew."

"I see."

"Are they ready for what's coming? You and I have been here before, but most of them are green. The price of having the biggest navy in the galaxy is you rarely get to use it. The Commonwealth is the best at patrolling the great shipping lanes of space…but combat." He sighed as he tried to imagine what a fight might be like, "We've not fought a major engagement since the days of the Grand Fleet. And even then, the fight was inconclusive."

"Well. They were forced back to port, and we continued control the shipping lanes. I'd call that a…"

Commander Percy stopped at seeing his captain and

friend was simply making a point.

"This is a first for us in an exceptionally long time. How are our people? Should I be worried?"

"No more so than any captain should be. They are all professionals. They know what they have to do. It's not the people. It's the ship."

"Thank God we have Hood with us. Else I think we'd still be back in the dock."

He nodded towards the distant white light far ahead of their position. It was impossible to make out any details, save for the bright glow from the old battlecruiser's ion drive as she hurtled ahead.

"Over a hundred years old, and she's still faster than we are…"

"Faster, perhaps. But we've got the armour, modern command and control, and high-velocity cannons. It's not so one-sided. Now…" He stopped as an emergency alert sounded on his communication unit. He lifted it and looked on open-mouthed at the report, "We've got her."

"Got her?"

Captain Leach looked to his executive officer and smiled grimly.

"Heavy cruisers Suffolk and Norfolk have spotted Bismarck and are trailing the ship. Apparently, the Vrokan ships are accelerating away, but our ships are staying just close enough to follow the trail."

"They've been spotted?"

"Unknown. But now we know where they're going. And we're the nearest ships in the area. Victorious is still training her new pilots, and Ark Royal, Renown, and the others are several days away."

Captain Leach nodded, and then tapped the controls. His seat moved back, and soon they were back on the command deck proper. They returned to their stations, and Captain Leach rubbed his brow before speaking. As he opened his mouth, his communications officer called out.

"Captain, incoming priority message from Hood. It's Vice Admiral Holland."

"Put him on throughout the ship."

"Captain."

Imagery appeared on every display through the ship, with the audio coming through via the internal speaker systems. Captain Leach looked to his own bank of screens and nodded as the image of his superior appeared.

"Captain Leach. Is Prince of Wales ready for a scrap?"

"Ready we are, Admiral."

"Good. Our cruisers are trailing the pair of ships through a major debris field within the nebula. It appears the Vrokan ships are trying to slip past our sensor nets by using the nebula. They cannot jump until they clear the nebula, but the same is true for us. Tracking is not easy, but doable."

"What if they turn back?"

"Because they're arrogant, Captain Leach. They believe they are undefeatable. Once clear, they can jump at will. We must act, and fast. Do you have the new jump coordinates?"

Captain Leach turned to his helmsman.

"We have them, Captain. It will place us approximately fifteen hours away from their expected position."

Captain Leach turned back to his screens.

"Admiral, we have the course locations, estimated

positions of the enemy vessels, and their projected course."

"Very well. We will rendezvous with a light destroyer flotilla already en route just outside of the Kamineso Nebula. We will proceed with a full war council upon arrival. I want a battle plan that gives us the best chance of engaging and defeating this force sooner rather than later."

He looked to his antique silver-plated watch before looking back into the camera.

"If all goes as plans, it will be their battleship and heavy cruiser, and a battleship and battlecruiser of our own, plus another two cruisers and the destroyer flotilla."

"Not exactly a fair fight, Admiral."

He chuckled.

"All's fair in love and war, old friend. And this super dreadnought of theirs is an unknown. I'm taking no chances. Five to one sound like the kind of odds we need. Make sure everything is ready. Failure is not an option. The Commonwealth, nay, the entire galaxy's future now rests with the outcome of this battle."

"Understood, Admiral. We will be ready, and we won't let you down."

"I know you won't. My best wishes to you and your gallant crew. Admiral Holland out."

The two men saluted, and the videofeed cut. Captain Leach looked to the star map and the new course, finally speaking to those around him.

"Lay in the new course and follow after Hood."

As he spoke, he could see Commander Percy looking right back at him.

"It's happening," said Percy.

"Indeed, it is. The time for talk is over. Now we will see what this ship really is made of."

He gave a nod, and Commander Percy began calling out orders to the senior officers. It didn't take long before warning alarms sounded as they began the slow, meandering process of changing course. Captain Leach found his attention drawn to the distant shape of the aged warship far in the distance. The view was magnified on his display, but the ship still looked like some strange apparition, almost ghostly in shape and colour. Her long, sleek form bristling with guns and antenna, and then the mighty engines gleaming blue. As he watched, there was a pulse of light, and the ship began to shrink.

There she goes. And where Hood goes, we will follow.

CHAPTER FIVE

Now under constant attack, and with her shipping lanes blockaded, the Core Worlds of the Commonwealth starved from lack of food, fuel, and war materiel. Still, they fought on, with their fighting spirit sustained by convoys from the neutral territories of the United Colonies of Titania making their perilous journey to keep them in the fight. The Vrokan fleet prepared for the final invasion, with only the ships of the Commonwealth fleet able to stop them.
The Commonwealth's Finest Hour

Commonwealth Heavy Cruiser 'Norfolk', Kamineso Nebula, 9 hours later

The two cruisers moved effortlessly through the nebula, separated by almost three thousand kilometres of light and dust scattered through the frigid void of space. Neither bore external lights of any kind; with their markings and navigational lights deactivated and external thrusters shrouded to disguise their emissions as the vessels adjusted their course. A short burst from the port-side near the bow shifted the ship's heading, followed by a ten-second shunt from the main drive as they moved onto a new course. The ship inched past three massive clusters of rockice and then drifted away from them, leaving little more than a faint ion trail that quickly faded.

"That's it. Take it nice and slow," said Captain Phillips, "Now…deploy the towed sensor array."

"Good," said Admiral Wake-Walker, "They're out there somewhere close. I can smell 'em."

With such a senior officer aboard the ship, the Admiral acted as the effective captain, while Captain Phillips took on the role of his executive officer. The reality was a little different, with the Captain acting much as he would normally, though with the oversight of the Admiral on major tactical decisions. The two men had worked together before and both appeared to work well with the other.

"Agreed. No ship of that size can hide forever. And if they make it to the periphery, we'll pick up their jump drive power-up long before they can leave. We'll find them."

He tried to sound confident about the last part as he looked across to the helmsman whose hands rested on the physical thruster controls.

"Be ready. We don't know how precise their scanners are. If we find them, we need to be able to react, and fast."

"I'm ready, Captain."

The officer's eyes were locked onto his own displays that showed a dozen different videofeeds from various parts of the ship. He had a full three-hundred-and-sixty-degree field of view, leaving nothing to chance. A gentle clunk echoed through the ship, and then a lone cable extended out from a pod fitted towards the rear of the ship. It took almost a minute until finally the object opened up and deployed its full array of sensors. Now freed from the heat, and electromagnetic interference present throughout the heavy cruiser, it could provide much more precise passive data on the area. Almost immediately Alethea's displays lit up with fresh data.

"Good God!" She looked at the information coming back to her, "She's not pretty, but she's one hell of a ship."

She tapped the imagery on her display. "I've never seen anything like it."

The Admiral looked on with interest and smiled.

"Nothing too sudden now. We don't want them looking back. This is what we're here for."

"Comms, narrow band transmission to Hood. Inform them of the target location."

"Aye, Captain."

The main engines cut, and the ship continued to coast forward, with nothing but her antenna arrays moving as they tracked the area of space directly ahead.

"I'm detecting heat blooms at multiple locations along her hull. Her design is…primitive in places, minimal shielding, but by God, the thickness of the armour and bulkheads. If I had…"

She then stopped speaking as the ship began to fade from view.

"Commander. She's doing it again."

He leaned in close and then shook his head.

"That's not just the ship. Look, right in front of them…that's natural. The density of this nebula is surprisingly variable. If I had to guess, I'd say it's been seeded over the last few years and they're adding to it."

Each watched on in silence as the ship turned ghostly grey, and then a pulse of light engulfed her flank. For a second Alethea thought the ship was firing, but then she realised it was the ship's manoeuvring thrusters. The ship altered course, and then vanished into the clouds.

"Encoded narrowband from Hood," said the communications officer, "Rear Admiral Holland wants updated tracking data."

The Captain looked across to his executive officer, who in turn looked to Alethea.

"Can you plot an updated course based on those latest changes?"

Alethea moved her hands over the computer displays as she struggled to plot a series of new paths. It took a few seconds before she was forced to shake her head.

"They've become erratic. They must know we're out here."

"Or they suspect we're out here," said the Commander, "Send me your best guess. We'll operate from there."

He looked to the rest of the crew.

"Nothing has changed. Maintain silent running. We've got them right where we want 'em now."

Alethea strained her eyes as she watched her screens. The ion trail was there, but now it was clouded by the erratic course changes that had left numerous trails heading in multiple directions.

"I don't like this," she muttered, "This is exactly what I would do if…"

Then something flashed in the nebula. It looked like a swirling pattern, and then without warning the bow of the massive battleship appeared, and it was heading right for them.

"Oh…no. Contact!" she yelled, "They're coming right at us!"

The mood inside the ship transformed instantly as the crew of the heavy cruiser went from being the hunters to the hunted in a matter of minutes. The klaxon sounded, and Alethea tugged on her harness as the engines activated.

"Helm, get us into that cloud…fast! Dump countermeasures!"

The engines roared with power, and Alethea struggled to breathe as the vessel pushed forward at ever increasing speed. The videostreams from the external cameras showed clouds and the blurred shape of the ship. Then it was gone as they broke through into thick clouds of white and almost pink coloured gas. On they went for almost a minute until the engines finally cut.

"Where are they?"

"I've lost them, Captain," said Alethea, "They could be heading in any direction by now."

"Dammit! Helm, new course, coordinate with Suffolk. The fleet is depending on us."

He then swallowed nervously before nodding ahead.

"And put me on with the Admiral. We need to talk."

"Captain!" Alethea said excitedly, "Suffolk has spotted them. Two ships moving on victor three-two-three."

She shook her head as she placed the data on her tactical overlay.

"Their captain knows his stuff. They just double backed on us and nearly rammed us. If we'd carried on, we would have missed him."

"Good work. Bring us back into range and get me through to the Admiral. We've done our part. Now it's time for the heavies to get involved."

He visibly relaxed as he ran his hands down along his upper legs.

"Outstanding work everybody. You've earned your pay

today."

* * *

Commonwealth Battleship 'Prince of Wales'
The war room remained silent, as the officers looked at the projected map of the border of occupied Torugan space and the vast clouds of the nebula. A separate bank of displays showed the view outside the ship, each display mimicking the look of a window fitted to the exterior of the ship. Battlecruiser Hood was close, with a long blue ion stream following her as she continued to push forward through the wisps of blue and purple of the periphery of the nebula.

Only two were physically present, both Captain Leach and Commander Percy, while the others were represented by their imagery shown on curved displays, each fitted to gimbal mounts, much like the seats on the command deck. Admiral Holland, commander of the taskforce was there, along with Rear Admiral Wake-Walker, commander of the heavy cruisers, as well as the leader of the destroyer flotilla.

"Well, gentleman, the fox has been spotted, and today he's gone to ground," said Rear Admiral Holland, "I've been in contact with the Admiralty and with Admiral Tovey himself. He's reiterated the importance of stopping these ships. They cannot be allowed to strike our convoys. No ship is to be held back. They must be stopped, no matter the cost."

That changed the mood significantly as each of the officers nodded in agreement. Admiral Holland waited for a moment, then continued.

"So, tell me, gentlemen. What do we know that we did not

ten hours ago?"

His display shifted as he looked to the imagery of the captains of the cruisers. Each looked at the three-dimensional map of the area with equal interest. They were spread out in two groups, with the two capital ships and their escorts at the assembly point, and the two cruisers still chasing after the enemy ships.

"We know a lot more," said Captain Ellis, commander of the heavy cruiser Suffolk, "The two ships are powerful vessels. The heavy cruiser is more than twice the displacement of our own cruisers, and she's carrying guns that you'd expect to find on some of our older battleships."

"And the beast?"

Rear Admiral Wake-Walker nodded before speaking.

"The beast, as you call it, Admiral, is what I would class as a next generation battleship. Codenamed Bismarck, the ship is bigger and more heavily armoured than anything we've put into space before."

"Size is just a bigger target. Anything else?"

"Bismarck is a mobile arsenal. Best we can tell from long-range imagery and her electronic signature is that she's an armoured gunnery platform, designed to take on multiple opponents with overwhelming heavy gunnery. There's nothing subtle about her design. It's all thick plating, and a secondary battery of a level we've never seen before."

He then pointed to the course the ships had been taking.

"But…my cruisers have been tracking them for a long time now, and there's no signs we've been spotted. My engineers are confident they lack the more advanced tracking systems fitted to our newer ships."

"Or they could be bluffing."

"Also a possibility."

Rear Admiral Wake-Walker pointed to a cylindrical marker in space.

"We've managed to pin them down to this area, but we're having difficulty in tracking them without using active sensors."

The tactical map pulled back and showed a vast swathe of space.

"That's not good enough," said the Admiral, "There's a hundred ways they could break through. And once we've committed to a course, it will take much too long to change."

"And there's no jump drives in the nebula," said Captain Phillips of Norfolk, "But we'll find them again soon. We've got ion trace elements to trail. It's a matter of time."

The Admiral rubbed his chin and then shook his head.

"I don't like it. I don't like it at all. We've got the numerical advantage here, but only if we can concentrate our forces."

He remained silent for some time as he examined the data, and so Captain Leach spoke up. He tapped the tactical map and rotated it around to show their own position.

"The priority is to match our heavies to theirs, correct?"

Vice Admiral Holland nodded.

"Yes. Our destroyers are scouts, and a screen to keep in front of our heavies. But have we seen any sign of escorts or fighters?"

"No," said Rear Admiral Wake-Walker, "Not since my cruisers have been hunting them."

"Then it is for our cruisers and battleships to settle this one," said Captain Leach, "And the sooner the better. I suggest we split off the destroyers so they can cover more ground. And move the cruisers closer to their last known position."

"Closer?" Captain Phillips sounded startled; "The odds of us finding them without being spotted are almost zero. And based on the data we've collected; we will not be able to repel their fire for long if engaged."

"Yes, but if you can keep on them, we can come to your aid in a matter of hours. We need data on their location, course, and speed."

His superior, Rear Admiral Wake-Walker nodded in agreement.

"Captain Leach is correct. Our cruisers are here for just this purpose. We have the speed and the armour to hold them off. If we're lucky, we might even get a few hits on them and distract them long enough for the cavalry to arrive."

"Then it is settled," said Vice Admiral Holland, "Our destroyers will break off and move into the nebula. Admiral, you will send in your cruisers as close as you dare. Find out what they're doing and give me an attack vector as soon as you can. God willing, we can muster most, if not all our forces around them and end this…today."

There appeared to be a moment of hesitation, perhaps even doubt among some of the officers.

"Agreed?"

"Yes, Admiral," they replied in chorus.

"Then to it, gentlemen. No solution is the perfect solution on this day. All we can do is the best we can with the information to hand. It is war, and we have ships to find, and a battle to fight. I will contact the Admiralty and inform them of our intentions. Good hunting to all of you."

One by one the images of the officers vanished until the

two men were left alone in the war room.

"It's happening, then. We're going after them."

"We are, Percy, we really are. This will be one hell of a shakedown cruise for the Prince of Wales."

"It's time these new guns were finally put to the test," said Commander Percy enthusiastically, "If they're half as good as the contractors say, we should have slight problem blasting holes in that ship."

"I have no doubt," said Captain Leach, "Number One…I want you to check each station personally. Make sure they have whatever they need. I don't want to go into this fight half-cocked."

"We'll be ready."

The two men saluted, and Commander Percy quickly left. Captain Leach looked back to the projection of the battlefield they were entering. It was a lifeless region of space, with the bright colours of the nebula extending out millions of kilometres in all directions. Markers showed the known locations of hazards, though the odds of running into rock ice, comets, or ship debris were extremely unlikely. Long elliptical markers showed the recorded positions of the enemy ships, with much smaller and constantly shifting curves showing the course taken by the cruisers. His attention shifted to the last known location of the pair of enemy ships, and he tapped it to see the optical recording of the last time they were seen. The images were blurred, confirming intelligence reports of a cloaking fog system of sorts.

"There you are."

His eyes narrowed as he looked to the thick, bulky armour and her massive turrets. It was a ship built to turn warships to molten slag, and he felt a chill through his bones as he imagined what the battle might be like. The ship was an unknown, but just from the exterior he could tell it would not be easy. Just behind the ship was the heavy cruiser, an equally impressive ship, though still quite small compared to the monstrosity of the battleship.

When did they find the time to build them?

Then he caught sight of the Mighty Hood on one of the displays. He looked to her and smiled at seeing her beautiful lines and long main guns. There were none that looked at her and could ever say anything less than positive. While ships of today were built to strict budgets and requirements, Hood was a remnant of a time when aesthetics were considered as important as effectiveness. He imagined the battle with the four heavy ships circling their prey and hammering them with their powerful guns. His confidence quickly soared. He knew the guns, and he knew the commanders.

"Today will be a day long remembered through the Commonwealth."

* * *

Commonwealth Heavy Cruiser 'Norfolk'
2 hours later

Alethea took a sip from the tube hanging down next to her station, all while keeping her eyes glued to the screen to her left. There were four different live feeds showing on the one screen, with even more on the other two. Gas clouds, ion trails, and even some of the many empty pockets of space that appeared to contain little of anything.

"I still see nothing," she said quietly.

"Helm," called out Captain Phillips, "It's time to enter the next waypoint. It's gonna be a real peasouper, so everybody keep your eyes open."

"Ready when you are, Captain," said the officer.

Captain Phillips looked across to Rear Admiral Wake-Walker who merely gave him a nod. This was the fifth cluster they'd investigated now, with nothing to show for their efforts than much greater fatigue in the crew.

"Take us in…and by God be ready if we find them."

"Aye, Sir. All ahead full on the main drive."

Alethea tensed as the engines pulsed with power. Unlike the jump drive that took significant time to charge, the main ion engines were instant, and took power from the main power core to power the ion thrusters.

"That's quick." She grunted as they passed two times planetary normal, and still it increased. She could see Suffolk on the right side of the screen via one of the starboard side camera mounts. A long blue trail extended backwards as both vessels moved.

"Engine slow down commencing. Full cut-off in five…four…"

Alethea exhaled as the engines began to shut down, and the painful forces released the pressure on her body. She looked at her central display that showed the view ahead. The colourful clouds looked thin and scattered, but she could see from the scanner that visibility was down to mere tens of thousands of kilometres.

"Lieutenant," said Commander Lewis, "It's time for you to…"

"Wait!" Alethea said excitedly, "Trace elements, there's something out there."

Her eyes moved to the second screen and her throat turned dry.

"Oh, no."

Alarms sounded, followed by passive targeting sensors.

"We've been pinged," she said loudly, "They've got us!"

"Then go active. Lock her down."

"Yes, Captain."

Alethea activated the main scanners, using a combination of Lidar and Radar to send out a series of radio waves and light to try and more precisely track the distant shape.

"I can't get a lock, but Lidar confirms the rough shape. It's the Bismarck alright."

She looked across to the senior officers, but as she was about to speak, she noticed a flurry of gas puffs along its flank.

"Uh…hold on, they're changing course."

"Helm!" said the Captain, "Be ready to slide."

The warning alarm sounded inside the hull, a constant reminder to stay strapped in.

"Gunfire! Arrival in seven seconds."

The helmsman acted instantly without waiting for orders. At once, the starboard side thrusters, as well as a number of dorsal thrusters activated, each sending narrow bursts into space and shifting the ship to the side, even as it continued forward.

"Now…bring us about thirty degrees, and retro thrust, we need to slow our approach."

"Captain."

Alethea gasped uncomfortably as her gimbal mount turned around so that she was facing in the opposite direction, followed by the retro engines fitted along the bow of the ship activated. They started slowly and then increased to increase deceleration as quickly as was possible.

Here it comes.

Alethea tensed as the streaks of light raced past the ship. She tried to lean away, but the thrusters were already busily moving her in the same direction. She ran her eyes on the screens of data, smiling as she spotted the hull of the massive enemy battleship. Her scanners were still unable to properly lock, but she was able to plot a manual targeting solution, and quickly slaved the guns to her position.

"Guns are tracked and ready."

"You have control. Rotational lock is slaved to your station."

"Aye, Captain."

For the first time in her life, she activated the gunnery stations, sending orders to the gun crews manning the batteries located along the flanks of the ship. Though she retained control over the targeting and range finding equipment, the gun crews handled the actual management of the gun batteries, making sure they were loaded and operating correctly. At the same time, the ship began to roll, moving so that as many guns on each flank could draw a line of sight to the target. Four turrets fitted on each side swung around to point at the battleship, each fitted with a pair of 420mm Mark VIII Linear Accelerator Cannons.

"Hurt them, Lieutenant," said the Admiral, as he watched with interest, "And keep hurting them."

"Yes, Admiral."

She made one final check and confirmed that of the eight dual turrets, seven had a clear line of sight. Only then did she send the final command. Less than two seconds after giving the order, the guns opened fire.

"On the way!"

The fourteen linear accelerator cannons unleashed their solid armoured-piercing slugs towards the distant ship. It took slightly longer for the shells to reach their target than Bismarck's fire due to the reduced velocity, and Alethea found her eyes drawn to the dotted line on her tactical display. It was moving quickly, and then disappeared in the cloud.

"Did we make contact?"

"Unknown," she said disappointedly, "The cloud is making it difficult to see."

"Unless they know something we don't, they're still liable to be constrained by Newton's the laws of motion."

"The First Law of motion…" said Alethea as though reciting some holy text, "Is that an object remains in the same state of motion unless a resultant force acts on it. If they're moving on a course then they will remain on it, and at a constant velocity unless something else changes."

"So, lead them, Lieutenant, and fast. Put a few volleys into them."

The ship shook again as the powerful linear accelerator cannons went to work. One volley, and then another as the shots ripped through the clouds. Each shot left its mark, like a bullet travelling through water.

"No confirmed hits. I will keep…"

She stopped as the bow of another ship burst out from directly below them.

"New contact! Heavy cruiser, coming right for us."

"Keep firing, Lieutenant," said the Captain, "And Helm,

get us out of here!"

"Captain."

The ship rolled so that its underside faced off against the approaching ship, while all eight turrets aimed down at it with their combined sixteen guns. One fired after another, with many of the solid slugs hammering into the heavy ship's prow.

"I see good hits," said Alethea.

Then came a single pulse of light, followed by emergency alerts.

"We've been hit!" called out an officer, possibly the lieutenant monitoring the engineering station, "One turret is gone, and we've got a hole running right through our hull."

Alethea glanced at the status screen and almost cried out. The outline of the ship showed the impact mark in red, along with fifteen compartments that had been breached.

"Make sure all internal bulkhead doors are secured," said Captain Phillips, "Helm, take evasive action."

He then looked to Alethea who was busy firing away with her remaining main guns.

"Cease fire. We need to skedaddle and fast. Everybody hold on."

Warnings sounded again as the ship rotated about so that it was pointing almost directly at the approaching ship. The main drive then activated without warning, and they boosted away from their previous trajectory. Unlike atmospheric flight, they still continued forward, albeit with the curve now shifted.

"Missiles coming right at us," said Alethea as calmly as she could manage, "Activating close-range defence pattern."

She glanced across to the Captain, but he was busily calling out orders to the others. The ship continued to rotate along its axis as it moved away to a denser segment of cloud in the nebula. Tracking alarms sounded loudly, and Alethea knew they had seconds left to react. Without looking for advice or support, she turned over all ship's defensive arsenal to automatic control. Now each segment or zone on the ship would track and defend themselves as best as they could manage. There were twelve point-defence mounts fitted all around the ship to provide complete coverage.

"How much longer till we are out of their sights?" Captain Phillips asked.

"Three minutes," said the helmsman, "Sooner if I increase output to…"

Something slammed hard into the ship, and as the view from her screens shifted, she knew they'd been knocked off axis. The main engines shut for a moment, though the ship continued on the same course as before.

"Jump drive has been hit. We've got leaks on three decks," said the Chief Engineer over the internal communications system. His face shook on the live feed as explosions wracked the stern of the ship, "They scored one hell of a lucky hit. I need to divert crews to repair stations."

"No," snapped Captain Phillips, "Stay at their posts. Flood the compartments with nitrogen and vent them."

His attention turned to his helmsman and the other officers on the command deck.

"Comms, contact Suffolk. They need to get to safety as well. Helm, it's on you now. Get us to safety."

"Aye, Captain."

Then he looked across to Alethea.

"Lieutenant, go weapons hot. We're sitting ducks right

now."

Finally.

Alethea fought against the unending series of blasts from the thrusters and main drive, as the helmsman did his best to move them to safety, all while sliding and rolling to avoid the worst of the approaching heavy cruiser's gunfire. She targeted its gun batteries and fired again and again, unleashing a powerful bombardment of fire from the main linear accelerator cannons.

"Good hits!" she cried out as five projectiles struck the enemy vessel's superstructure, punched though the weaker armour, and then exploded.

"Well done, Lieutenant, well done," said Captain Phillips.

Another impact shook the ship, and the helmsman cried out in pain. Alethea looked across to see three small holes in his body. She spotted several more wounded, with three displays destroyed, and a small fire burning near the rear part of the command deck. Alethea glanced over the internal schematic and almost gasped as she spotted the impact point.

"Citadel breached," she said in astonishment, "We've got fragments throughout the forward levels."

And then the power cut out completely. Displays went dark, and even the interior lighting faded. Alethea could feel a slight tug on her body as the ship careered out of control, spinning slowly away and towards the clouds of colourful fog. She reached for her displays, but there was nothing, not a glimmer of light; save for the flickering lights now showing from the communicator wristbands each of them wore.

"Report," said Captain Phillips.

Alethea licked her lips and then spoke as calmly as she was able to.

"Captain, we took a hit right to the citadel. It's breached the forward decks."

"Understood. The Chief will get us power soon. The rest of you check on the wounded and be ready for what comes next."

Alethea could hear the moans and groans from the wounded, but even worse was the sound of metal on metal as heavy slugs punched through the hull. Norfolk was a tough vessel, with thick armour and powerful guns, but she was not designed to stand up to battleships and the like. Her roles were to hunt down cruisers and to scout ahead of the fleet. Not to do this.

"Comms are coming back," said a voice.

Alethea looked over her shoulder to the light coming from just one display. More and more systems activated, though all showed significant damage. She looked to her own, but it showed nothing but connection failures to the main computers or any of the combat stations on the ship. As she waited, a crackle of sound from a speaker filled the space. It was mostly noise, but then cleared for a second, and came a voice she hadn't expected to hear. There were the sounds of explosions in the background, little different to those that she'd heard only so recently aboard her own vessel.

"This is Captain Ellis. We've drawn the enemy heavies away from you. Get to cover fog safely, my friends. Hood is on the way. We've done our part. We will…"

A long crackle drowned him out, and then the transmission failed. Thankfully, more systems powered up, including the internal lights. Alethea didn't dare look to check on the damage, and instead watched as three live camera streams appeared. She could make out the enemy heavy cruiser, and not so far away the massive battleship. And then right between them was a single vessel surrounded by gunfire.

"Suffolk!"

She watched in admiration as the single ship streamed between the two Vrokan warships with her weapons blazing. Both Vrokan ships fired back, though not with their main guns, probably for fear of striking each other.

"Go get them, Suffolk," she said proudly.

The ship was difficult to make out as it ran the impossible gauntlet of smoke and fire. All around the ship were dotted lines as her secondary batteries and point-defence guns went to work. It was almost impossible to miss at her range, and hundreds of tiny flashes marked the impact before the cruiser then disappeared into the mist and fog that the Vrokan ships had left behind, vanishing from view as quickly as she'd arrived.

"God bless her," said Admiral Wake-Walker, "That was one of the finest displays of bravery I've ever seen."

Captain Phillips moved his focus back to the tactical station, all his attention now on what they could do to help.

"Tactical, tell me you have something operational?"

"Negative, Captain," said Alethea angrily, "I've got passive sensors and some cameras. All batteries are offline."

"Engines are partially operational," said the helmsman.

"Very well. Divert all available power to the main drive and take us in."

There was no warning as the main ion drive activated once more. This time it increased to maximum and then continued onwards, pushing into overdrive. Alarms continued their song, warning each of them of the imminent danger they all now faced.

"Ignore the computer," said the Captain through clenched teeth.

The g-forces were now so strong that he was now struggling to breathe. Alethea spotted two of the officers slump back as they lost consciousness.

"Dump all we have to the engines. Thirty-second burn!!"

He spotted Alethea looking to him.

"Let's hope the fog will do what our weapons cannot and save us from destruction. It's in the hands of the heavies now."

She nodded and tried to speak. But her vision was already fading, and she could barely make him out. All she could detect was the whining of the alarms and shouting from further back along the deck. Alethea tried to move, but the g-forces kept her pinned down. Time slowed, and she had no idea if seconds, minutes, or hours had passed, but finally her hearing began to return, followed by blurred vision. Her head pounded, and as she inhaled, she gasped in surprise.

"We're alive."

She looked to the command deck and sighed in relief at seeing the others doing the same. The red lighting was still on, but so were most of the displays. Captain Phillips was somehow still conscious and calling out to them.

"New course. Rendezvous with Suffolk."

The ship's navigator made the calculations, and a series of new vectors appeared on his display. They also showed the current and estimated position for the other three ships in the area, as well as the distant shapes of the Commonwealth's two heavies.

"Captain, that will put us nearly an hour behind the enemy

warships."

"Then that is how it shall be. Stay as close as you can…"

He glanced across to Alethea.

"And for the love of all that is holy, make sure you've got a good tracking signature. Go active on the radar, just make sure Admiral Holland knows what to expect."

"Yes, Captain, activating now."

The pulses lanced off into the fog of the nebula, and seconds later came back a rough patch of noise. The computer struggled to identify it, but she could already identify key areas that were markers left by the ships.

"I've got them."

"Excellent. Now it's time for the main event."

CHAPTER SIX

What happened to the Gallian Hegemony so early in the war? Even as the landing ships and battle barges were moved into position it was assumed her vast armies would make short work of inexperienced Vrokans. Instead, the fighting was over in just six months, with the mighty Gallian Army broken and her fleets scattered as they fled under the Vrokan assault. The Commonwealth might have fallen that day had it not been for brave rear-guard actions fought by the few Gallian divisions still in action. With them buying time desperately needed, an evacuation by military and civilian ships drafted by the Commonwealth was able to withdraw almost the entire Commonwealth contingents, as well as her allies before the end.

History of the Void Wars

Commonwealth Battleship 'Prince of Wales', Kamineso Nebula, 9 hours later

The pair of massive warships surged forward through the nebula, their turrets at the ready, and moved into position to provide maximum forward coverage. Long beams of blue light extended behind them as if each ship was leaving a marker to make the path for others to follow. From inside the armoured confines of the battleship, Captain Leach looked at vast clouds of the nebula with endless fascination. The colours were a bizarre array of blacks, blues, and purple, and as he looked at them, they appeared to shift ever so slightly. It was an impressive sight, as well as a peculiar phenomenon.

"This nebula is a major problem. It's high time we expanded the mine laying programme."

Commander Percy shrugged.

"The distances are just too big for any reliable return. Mining the shipping lanes near their space ports is more consistent."

"True. But so is getting blasted apart by their defence squadrons. I don't know about you but taking a mine layer to Vrokan territory sounds like a recipe for a trip to the scrapyard."

"True. Losing Torugan Space has given the Vrokan more naval bases and access to our territory. We should never have lost that ground."

"The Torugan campaign cost us an aircraft carrier, two cruisers, seven destroyers, and more than a hundred starfighters. We couldn't keep that fight up forever. It was a bleeding wound in our side."

"And hunting down heavy raiders like Bismarck isn't?"

Captain Leach nodded.

"You're not wrong, Number One. You're not wrong at all."

Commander Percy sighed at the enlarged two areas of space directly ahead.

"They can't be far now," he said optimistically, "Data from Admiral Wake-Walker says we should be almost on top of them."

The Captain nodded.

"Then is it time, my friend. Give the order."

"Aye, Captain."

Commander Percy reached for the intercom that was strangely still attached to the computer console via an elasticated cable. It was a holdover to the old days of naval warfare, but also had its benefits. A hardwired connection was more difficult to intercept or modify, and it also tied the command position to a physical location on the ship. He held it to his face and then spoke slowly and calmly.

"We are minutes away from battle. Check your stations, secure all bulkhead doors, and ready your flash gear."

As he gave the orders, those on the command deck responded the same as the other members of the crew. The flash gear was carried by all of them. It consisted of a thin fire-resistant hood that hung around their necks as part of their duty uniform. It could be pulled up the moment the ship entered battle. They also pulled on their fire-resistant gloves, all to ensure they were protected against flash fires and blasts in combat. As if on cue, an alert sounded for an incoming message.

"Contact from Hood," said Lieutenant Beeson, the ships communications officer, "It's Admiral Holland."

"Put him on."

His image appeared on his screen, and just seeing him there filled him with confidence. The Admiral was a veteran commander in space, with years of service aboard cruisers and battleships. He was also the foremost gunnery expert in the Commonwealth. There was probably nobody else in the fleet better suited to the coming fight. He looked to the Admiral and nodded.

"Admiral, is it time?"

Vice Admiral Holland lifted a warm beverage and drank from the one-way valve fitted to the top. He swallowed and then nodded.

"It is indeed."

The Admiral was strapped into his seat, just the same as the others. He grimaced a little as the engines adjusted their power output as both ships continued towards the enemy.

"Captain…The enemy is minutes away. I'm sending you the latest data sent from Admiral Wake-Walker. He remains in the chase and beating them towards the periphery of the nebula."

"You think they believe they can escape the nebula?"

"Perhaps. It's clear their goal is to avoid open battle if possible. If they wanted to, both could turn on a sixpence and bring their guns to bear. Our cruisers could never stand up to them in a two-on-two fight. But fighting isn't on their mind."

"The convoys," said Captain Leach.

"Yes. No matter how powerful, we still outnumber their fleet close to ten to one. They want our transports, and they would be wise to do so. Starve us into defeat. It's cowardly, but it would work."

His expression softened as he looked into Captain Leach's eyes.

"In any case, it does not matter to us. We are going right at them just as we've trained. We have the ships, and we have the firepower, and soon enough we will intercept them."

"Understood, Admiral."

"The Admiralty wants this ended…today. Our forces are moving in from two sides."

Trajectory data appeared on the Captain's screen, causing him to pull one of the displays closer.

"Scans show we're almost parallel. Hood can't stand up to

a prolonged fight. So we're changing course and angling to meet them at thirty degrees and moving in close. We will intercept them and strike their flanks with every gun we can bring to bear. The closer we can get, the better chance we have of inflicting heavy damage."

"Understood, Admiral. Prince of Wales is ready to do her part."

"I have no doubt. Hood will take lead, and you will follow off our starboard stern. Stay close, and coordinate fire with my gunnery teams. What we fire at, you will fire at. If we can slow or halt their acceleration, our heavy cruisers will be able to enter the fray."

"Yes, Admiral."

The man then looked away, and his expression quickly changed. It was clear he'd spotted something new. Captain Leach looked to the view from his own ship, and there, far off in the distance were the outlines of the ships projected onto the forward view. They were still obscure, but the estimated position told them exactly where they needed to head to.

"There is the last barrier between us and them," said Admiral Holland, "The inner clouds of the nebula. Once we break through, the two ships will be exactly where they should be, twenty-four thousand kilometres away. Put me on with your crew."

Captain Leach gave the nod to his communications officer, who quickly opened up the internal system to the transmission.

"We are advancing into battle, Commonwealth pennants flying, and guns at the ready. Remember your training, and fight to the best of your ability. All eyes of the Commonwealth are on us today. Good hunting!"

"And to you, and the Mighty Hood," said Captain Leach.

He moved his head, and then watched as the long blue streak behind Hood began to decrease. He could easily make out her long, raking lines, and flat turrets, each bristling with brutally powerful main guns. The ship vanished as they smashed into the denser area of the nebula, the final barrier between them and the enemy.

"Now is the hour," said the Admiral, "Let's burn them down."

His image vanished, and Captain Leach focussed his attention on the men and women around him. He could sense the nerves and the tension. Each was apprehensive, and they had every right to be. The rumours and stories of the Vrokan super dreadnought were enough to send the average citizen fleeing in terror. But not them. They knew the danger, and more importantly, they knew they had the skills and the weaponry to do the job.

"Helm…Reduce forward velocity. Tactical, bring our main guns online."

"Yes, Captain," said Lieutenant Coleridge.

"And get our interceptor drones launched. If they return fire, we'll need the cover."

"Captain."

A gentle hum filled the command deck, as power siphoned away from the main reactors onboard and shifted to each of the main batteries. The guns would draw upon the energy reserves to fire, each turret absorbing vast amounts of power.

"Captain, tactical networking request from Hood.

They're requesting we target the lead vessel. Target indicators show it's the Bismarck. Shouldn't we slave to our systems? We have the more advanced targeting platform."

"We're on the battlefield, and God help you, Lieutenant. There's nothing so terrible as a general or admiral on the battlefield. If he wants gunnery command, let him send over the data. You have full override authority, however. Take the requests as guidelines."

"Yes, Captain."

"Now…After all this time, what is the status of our guns?"

"All batteries are charging. They will be ready in…now!"

The Lieutenant's brow then creased in confusion. He made some additional adjustments and then exhaled slowly. It was clear something was wrong, and as Captain Leach looked at him, his mind filled with a hundred different possibilities.

"What is it?"

"Sir. Two of the forward barbettes appear to be malformed. Sensors show anomalous readings along the lower…"

"Spare me the details. How does it affect the guns?"

"It's interfering with the turret rotation. The issue only arises under acceleration. I think it's because of an inconsistency in…"

"Will they fire? That's all I need to know right now."

"For now, yes, Captain. But for how long, I cannot say."

As he looked back, he spotted a crackle of light from the bow of Hood. It might as easily have been a glint of starlight or a reflection from a ship's engines. But then he spotted more flashes near her forward turrets.

"She's firing, Sir," said Lieutenant Coleridge, "All of her

four forward turrets."

She watched with interest as the shells scattered into the clouds. The view vanished for a moment as the Commonwealth warships burst through a thick layer of dark purple, and it hung over them like a fog. By the time they emerged, the enemy ships had moved some distance.

"I see them. Hood targeting control wants us to hit the lead ship."

Captain Leach looked to them with a mixture of fascination and dread. The Bismarck was a monster, and though he was certain his ship could match her under normal circumstances, he was acutely aware he was going into battle with one hand tied behind his back.

"The Admiral was quite clear. He wants Bismarck out of the fight as quickly as possible. Her guns are estimated to be somewhere in the 700mm to 900mm calibre, though we have no idea of the velocity or payload. Those are the kind of shots we need to avoid. The heavy cruiser can be dealt with afterwards."

"I'll target the lead ship."

"Good. And inform Hood of our targeting solution. Maybe we can provide better plotting than her old systems.

"Aye, Captain."

Captain Leach watched as the turrets moved ever so slightly as they continued to follow the movement of the ships. The massive guns were capable of blasting through all known armour types, but until the guns fired, they would have no real idea of the kind of damage they could cause.

"All turrets have good angles. Armour-piercing shells loaded and ready. Fuses set for timed detonation."

"Good work. You may fire when you're ready."

Lieutenant Coleridge nodded, and then moved his hands over the controls. Right now, he was in charge of enough firepower to level an entire city, and just one slip of the hand could send massive heavy ordnance in the wrong direction. Never before had he felt such a sense of raw power and responsibly. He looked to the hazed shapes far off in the distance, each partially hidden as they moved through the thin fog.

"It's like watching whales moving through waves."

He checked the tracking and lead indicators, and then tapped the controls.

"Firing."

A ripple shook the vessel as each of the main turrets opened fire. Due to the angle of approach, Hood was only able to fire half of her sixteen main guns. Prince of Wales was able only able to focus fire from her four forward turrets, with their combined total of twelve guns at the enemy formation. The remaining two turrets to the rear found their view temporary blocked, leaving their combined eight guns out of the fight for now. It still meant she could put out fifty percent more shells per volley than the older ship. The massive volley drowned the ship in streaks of plasma that erupted from the muzzles of the colossal 720mm Linear pulse cannons. Before the clouds of light faded, the autoloaders went to work loading in the next batch of super-heavy projectiles.

"Gun failure," said Lieutenant Coleridge almost immediately, "Forward turret."

Captain Leach gulped nervously as his XO brought up the data on his own display. He'd assumed they would run into difficulties, but not quite so soon. Red marks on one of the forward turrets showed gun failures in the large, armoured housings.

"Two guns out of action?"

"Yes, Sir. Contractors are heading there now to join our repair teams."

"Contractors? No. Keep them back for now. Leave our people to work on them for now. That still leaves us with eighteen guns. Keep firing. The last thing we need is civilians in the fighting compartments. They can get back to work when this fight is over."

"Yes, Captain."

The Captain turned from the fighting for a moment and checked the position of the ships on the tactical display. The four capital ships continued forward, though neither Vrokan ship returned fire, allowing the two Commonwealth ships to launch three more volleys at them.

"That's a hit!" Lieutenant Coleridge yelled excitedly, "Direct hit to their upper superstructure. I see fire!"

"Excellent work," said Captain Leach with relief, "So they're not so invincible after all, are they? Keep shooting."

His eyes moved back to the monstrous battlecruiser to his flank. He'd seen her firing doing drills and demonstrations before, but never seen her in action. Seconds turned to minutes, as the powerful warship unleashed her massive linear bombardment cannons, a variant of the earlier railgun technology. They accelerated massive 800mm diameter armour-piercing projectiles across space at incredible speeds. Once they made contact with armour, a contact sensor would be activated to detonate the demolition charge buried towards the rear of the shell.

"Hood has scored multiple hits on the lead ship. We have explosions along her belt."

"Penetrations?"

"Impossible to tell. They're still moving through the fog banks."

"Very good. But why are the Vrokan ships not returning fire?"

He looked to his XO who barely even noticed him as he concentrated on the streams of footage coming to him.

"Wait. The lead ship isn't the battleship. That's the heavy cruiser."

"You're sure?"

"I concur," said Lieutenant Coleridge, "Our scanners and gunnery radar is significantly more advanced than Hood's. Even with their smokescreen and the clouds of nebula, I can still track components of their hulls. The superstructure is similar, but the gun layout is less pronounced, and the mass is much lower in the lead ship. Lidar is building up a more detailed picture, but the tracking computer puts it at eighty-nine percent certainty."

"Dammit," said Captain Leach, "This wasn't the plan. Tactical…change targeting to the second ship, we need that battleship brought low, and fast."

"Yes, Sir, recalculating now."

"Good. Comms, pass on the updated targeting data to Hood."

Moments later the guns fired again, and the broadside proved so powerful the thrusters on the opposite side of the ship could barely cope with keeping the ship on the same course. The shell came close to the battleship, but still managed to miss.

"She's activated retro thrusters…her velocity has dropped

significantly," said Lieutenant Coleridge, "Gun are aligned, the next…"

A cry went out on the bridge, and Commander Percy pointed to flashing lights on his main display. Captain Leach checked his and spotted the fires burning along the bow of Hood.

"Hood is hit," said the Commander, "Reports from Admiral Holland say it's superficial."

All attention shifted to the grand old lady of the fleet. Imagery on the Captain's display enlarged the view, and he looked on as bright colours flickered and flashed along her upper deck.

"I can still see fires along her forward hull," said Captain Leach.

"I believe it's nothing but superficial, Sir. The fires are burning in the forward superstructure only, not near the main armour belt."

"Still, that is too close. Their guns are powerful, very powerful. Naval intelligence suggested they would be dangerous. That was an understatement."

"Damage data shows they're firing similar calibre shells as Hood, Captain. And they're hitting hard."

"Not surprising. Hood's guns can smash anything they hit. The same must be true of theirs."

"Good luck," said Lieutenant Coleridge, "Targeting Bismarck…Firing."

The remaining forward guns opened fire, and each of them watched nervously as the streaks of light headed towards their target. Though slightly smaller calibre than Hood; what the guns lacked in diameter they more they made up for with speed.

The energy of the impact would be even greater than Hood's, as long as they could breach the armour. Tiny flashes from secondary turrets sprayed around the ships as they tried to cut down the incoming warheads. Several were obliterated, and some missed, but one landed towards the bow of the three-kilometre-long battleship.

"Direct hit!" Lieutenant Coleridge said, "Right into her bow!"

In that instant, the fog cleared enough for a clear view of almost half of the ship. A cloud of fine particles spread away from the vessel, a clear sign that one of the heavy calibre projectiles had smashed through the ship's armour.

"Enlarge that feed," said Commander Percy, "Is she damaged?"

The videostream flickered, and then it focussed the bow, followed immediately by a great cheer. Lieutenant Coleridge leaned in closer and tapped the area around the impact point. At the same time, the ship's main guns fired again, sending yet another powerful volley towards the enemy. Moments later, the image stabilised, and the Lieutenant clenched his fist and almost punched the air. It showed significant external damaged, as well as three smaller penetrations where fragments had ripped away from the shell.

"It went right through. We've got an entry hole of nearly two metres and now internal explosions."

"The shell didn't detonate?"

"Their armoured belt and citadel must only protect the centre of the battleship," he said calmly, "But we've holed them, and passive scans show venting. I think we've breached a number of compartments, and the shattered remnants of the shell will have left a massive exit wound on the other side. It's a good hit, Sir."

"Good work," said Commander Percy, "Damned good work. Keep it up."

The guns continued to fire, as did the Vrokan ships, as both sides poured heavy shots into each other. Prince of Wales shuddered as solid metal slugs struck her armour, but no alerts sounded to mark breaches or serious damage. Commander Percy glanced across to Captain Leach and inhaled nervously.

"So far so good. Interceptor drones are bearing the brunt. They're putting most of their fire against Hood."

"New course data from Admiral Holland," said the communications officer, "We're to adjust our heading to match theirs. Admiral Holland wants all guns brought to bear."

"You heard the man," said Commander Percy, "Helm, make the changes."

The manoeuvring thrusters went to work, and the change became quite obvious as the ships angled themselves so that all of their turrets were cleared. As a consequence, the ships now presented much more of their armoured flanks to the enemy, while still continuing to close.

"Guns cleared," said Lieutenant Coleridge, "I've clear targets ahead."

"You know what to do. Keep firing and hurt them."

The guns roared, this time in a rapid sequence. One turret would fire, and then as it began to reload, the next fired, allowing the ship to put a constant barrage of fire against the enemy.

"Multiple impacts on their armour belt. Light damage."

He then leaned forward and hit the controls.

"Incoming fire! Switching secondary weapons to

interception. Drones are ready."

Captain Leach watched while tensing his body but felt a moment of relief as the gunfire from both enemy ships straddled Hood, with most of the shots missing. Streaks from her secondary batteries clawed out into space, as the automated turrets did their best to hit and destroy or deflect the incoming fire.

"One made it through and has hit Hood, must have gone through her rear."

Captain Leach wiped his brow and could feel the perspiration at his moist forehead. The stress of command was one thing but seeing these monstrous ships hurling so much metal at each other was a true sight to be seen. Both Commonwealth ships made use of their point-defence guns to slow down the attacks, as well as clouds of small, fully automated interceptor mines each little larger than his head that would accelerate at the incoming fire to explode them.

"She looks okay."

Lieutenant Coleridge called out as alarms sounded inside the command deck.

"More problems?"

"Turrets. We've got rotational jams reported from rear turret mechanisms. Crews are…"

He stopped speaking as his attention turned to the massive white light engulfing the middle of Hood. The light expanded, and then blocked off their displays as the camera feeds were drowned in the powerful burst.

"What just happened?" Captain Leach demanded, "Get the feeds back."

There was a deathly silence, save for the pings and alerts

sounds from the computers.

"Cameras are coming back now," said Commander Percy, "I think Hood just took another…"

He stopped and gasped, finding it impossible to find the words as he looked to the monstrous fireball at the heart of the Commonwealth's greatest warship. The hull had split in two, with the entire middle missing, and in its place a cloud of debris that scattered away from the wreck at high-speed.

"Hood." Captain Leach slowly shook his head.

"It's impossible," said Commander Percy, "Utterly impossible. Nothing can bring down Hood."

"No," said Captain Leach, "She's gone."

"We're going to be hit!" said the navigator, "We need to move away, and fast."

"Change course," said Commander Percy, "Hurry, man, hurry!"

The helmsman activated the thrusters, and the bow of the ship moved away from the devastated ship. Moments later, the main engines fired, followed by a barrage from the forward guns against the enemy capital ships. The course change was not enough, however, and in a matter of seconds the ship passed through the debris field.

"Brace for impact!" Commander Percy pulled against his harness, "Incoming!"

The clouds of fragments slammed into the ship with the force of light calibre guns. Many bounced off the thick armour, but other pieces jammed into the metalwork like sharpened spearheads. More and more crashed into the Prince of Wales, followed shortly afterwards by some of the larger sections that hit the superstructure. One narrowly missed the forward rangefinders and tore open a deep wound in the upper armour belt. Three more struck the port-side, hitting so hard they forced the ship off course. Gunfire from the enemy ships clawed out at them, but the debris field followed by the unexpected course changes meant most of the shells missed; just two glanced off the dorsal armour belt, causing little but deep lacerations to the metal plates.

"We're off course," said the helmsman, "Bringing us back is going to put us fully broadside to their ships."

"One problem at a time," said Captain Leach.

He looked away from the helm station and to Commander Percy.

"Getting out of this isn't going to be easy."

The ship continued to take hits from the debris, but the Captain could only look on in horror as the last remnants of the Mighty Hood detonated, turning it into no more than shattered chunks of metal as it disintegrated and scattered off into space. He'd never seen a ship fully destroyed before, and never once had he thought the greatest ship in the fleet would be destroyed so quickly.

"Six minutes." Commander Percy checked the display. Captain Leach looked confused. "I can't believe it. Six minutes."

"What?"

"The fight. It lasted just six minutes. I can't believe it."

"It's not over yet, my friend. We're still here."

He then looked at his own screens and checked the position of Hood.

"Get me active scans of the debris field. Did any part of the ship survive?"

Commander Percy brought up imagery of the area while

constantly shaking his head. Dozens of red frames showed the position of the largest sections. Most now spun away, one narrowly missing the bow of Prince of Wales. He looked to Captain Leach and placed his forehead in his hands.

"Nothing could have survived that, Captain. Scans show utter obliteration from a catastrophic explosion deep inside her hull."

"What about her crew?"

"Nothing. Just nothing."

They continued to look, all while Prince of Wales tried escape the devastation. Captain Leach found it impossible to speak, so choked up at the loss of such a fine ship. He'd known her admiral, captain, and scores of her officers for years. It was a ship filled with friends and colleagues. And now it was nothing, just dust and ash. He closed his eyes, inhaled, and then pulled on his tunic.

When his eyes opened, he'd transformed. Gone was the emotion, and in its place the look of a man on a mission, one to do whatever it took to save his ship and his crew. He focussed on the footage of the distant warships and ran his eyes along their array of heavy guns.

"Okay, gentlemen. We're now outnumbered two to one, and with systems still failing throughout the ship. We need to change the terms of this engagement, and fast."

Though he knew the battle still needed to be fought, he found it almost impossible to draw his eyes away from the field of debris that were still pushing through. The ship had manoeuvred away, but forward momentum kept them on the periphery where they could still crash into pieces of armour and the broken sections drifting away from the mighty vessel.

"How far out are our cruisers?" he asked himself while adjusting the display. He was forced to expand the area significantly until the two heavy cruisers appeared, "Damn…too far back."

Commander Percy and several of the other officers looked to him.

"What are your orders, Captain?"

That was the instant where everything changed for him. Gone was the simple act of commanding his ship as part of a force moving into battle. Now he was the man in charge. His decision would decide the fate of his ship, comrades, the taskforce, and perhaps even the war. His gut told him to dump power to the guns and charge right at them, but looking ahead, all he could see was destruction.

Do that, and we all die.

His head told him to do the opposite, and even thinking it left a sinking feeling deep inside his stomach. It felt cowardly to give the idea any credence, but as he watched the enemy turrets training onto his ship, he knew it was the only option left to him.

"We withdraw."

The words stunned the crew. Every one of them had expected a tough fight, but the idea that a Commonwealth battleship, the newest off the shipyards would retreat after such a short engagement was an anathema to them.

"Helm, take evasive action, and get us out of here."

Commander Percy looked stunned as heard the order. He shook his head, and for a second it seemed like there might even be a mutiny aboard the mighty battleship.

"Captain. Our orders are to fight until the battle is decided. We just need to hold them back long enough for our cruisers to join the fray. If those ships make it out into open space, they will annihilate our convoys. Catching them today is our only chance."

"Energy bloom…" said Lieutenant Coleridge, "Bismarck is about to fire."

"Divert drones to our starboard side. Maximum coverage!" Commander Percy said, "Get everything we have on our flank!"

Tiny dots flickered about as the small swarm of robots clustered around the side of the ship. They were barely visible, yet for all their tiny proportions they were an invaluable part of the ship's defensive systems.

"Incoming fire!" said the Captain, "Brace for impact!"

Commander Percy pointed to his display as the streaks from the pair of ships came right at them. Scores of bright flashes marked impacts on the interceptor drones as they accelerated towards the shells like bees rushing to protect their hive. For each shell intercepted, one still smashed its way through, and many of them struck the battleship's thick armour belt.

"Good God." Captain Leach gripped onto his harness so tightly his knuckles turned white, "Return fire!"

The vessel visibly shook from the combination of its own gunfire, as well as the numerous shell impacts. They looked to the external feeds as huge sections of the outer armour belt were shattered by the blasts. An entire section of the forward superstructure on the starboard side was missing, and multiple fires burned bright blue not far from the bow.

"Good impact on Bismarck's superstructure," said Lieutenant Coleridge, "Switching to high-explosive plasma fire."

More gunfire raked Prince of Wales, and then long streaks of blue extended out as the plasma fire reached the enemy ships, saturating them in the super-heated payload.

"Goddammit! Captain…another turret is down. We're having major electrical problems," said Lieutenant Coleridge, "Each time I fire, we seem to lose another system. We're outgunned, and it's getting worse."

Captain Leach shook his head as he looked to his second-in-command.

"I want to keep fighting, but do you think we can hold them? And even if we can…can a weakened battleship and two cruisers guarantee a victory?"

Commander Percy hesitated, and then winced as more shells hammered into the battleship's hull. Alarms sounded continually, along with numerous fire alerts as the warheads detonated inside the ship.

"If we can't stop them now, who will?"

Captain Leach gulped, knowing his number one was correct. If they abandoned the fight, the enemy ships would have an easy time making it out of the nebula, and then vanishing out into deep space. They might not be seen again for a year, and by then the war could be over.

"Captain, our course diversion around the wreckage has brought us closer to the enemy ships," said Commander Percy, "This is uncomfortably close."

"They're firing their secondary guns at us now," said Lieutenant Coleridge, "Our drones can't cover us for much longer."

Seconds later, the first shots hit. The impact was much lighter, but also continuous as both Vrokan ships focussed scores of guns on the single ship, striking it from bow to stern. Occasionally, a heavier thud would mark the impact of the larger guns, even as the Prince of Wales's helmsman made constant positional changes with the thrusters to throw off their aim.

"We disengage and live to fight another day," said Captain Leach, "Losing Hood is one thing…losing her and a battleship would be an even greater disaster. Prince of Wales will be back…but for now we need to regroup."

Commander Percy reluctantly agreed and called out to the communications station.

"Make contact with Rear Admiral Wake-Walker aboard Norfolk."

Something heavy smashed into the hull, causing the ship to shake, though nowhere as great as the previous impacts. Several of the officers muttered in relief, only for a massive, thunderous roar to echo through the ship. This time the impact was so great it felt as though Captain Leach's teeth were going to shatter.

"What the hell was that?"

"Part of Hood's stern," said Commander Percy, "There's a lot of wreckage out there."

Captain Leach snarled to himself and gripped his harness as the ship struggled to maintain its course. Thrusters fired, as did the main engines, though it still took time to move back.

"No contact from Norfolk," said Lieutenant Beeson, "Either they're running silent, or the Vrokan ships are jamming their transmissions. Wait…there's something. Norfolk is there and confirms they are moving in closer."

"No," said the Captain, "Confirm the destruction of Hood, and that we are falling back from battle. We're too badly damaged, and with systems down. We can't win this fight...not today."

"Yes, Captain."

"Helm. It's all on you. Get us around this debris and clear of their guns as fast as you can."

"Sir."

CHAPTER SEVEN

Drone warfare remained a controversial tactic, even after the first skirmishes of the war. None would dare place warships, or even fully-fledged bombers under the control of a computer, but there was so much more to robotic machines than the mere piloting of a ship. It was the Gallian Hegemony that had pioneered the use of utility drones to service and repair ships at sea, but the Commonwealth were the first to suggest a more militaristic use for them. Small craft, unconcerned with the rigours of movement in space were perfectly suited for use as close-range weapons, or as sacrificial armour to use against incoming ordnance. Expensive and extravagant it might well be, but as the war progressed, the use of drones increased exponentially.

Naval Weapons and Tactics, 5th Edition

Commonwealth Battleship 'Prince of Wales'
Kamineso Nebula

Captain Leach watched on with growing frustration as the massive battleship struggled to disengage from the fight. No vessel, from a starfighter to a dreadnought could simply change course, and Prince of Wales was a massive warship. The forward momentum of the ship, coupled with their erratic manoeuvring, had left them in a dangerous position. Even with the thrusters and main engines working as hard as they could, the ship could still only manage a modest change to her original course as they struggled to turn away. For almost an entire minute their underside was completely vulnerable, and the Vrokan heavy ships took advantage of the opportunity to hit the ship with all they had.

"Tactical. Are our defences even operational?"

"Point-defence systems are functional, Sir, they're just not able to stop their main guns. The shells are smashing right through interceptor streams."

"What about our drone shield?"

"Captain. We're launching more, but we're losing a lot. We need some in reserve in case they…"

"Do what you can and keep firing back."

"Captain. We're losing systems across the…"

"I don't care. Work the problem and keep shooting. Don't give them an easy ride."

More gunfire hit the hull, and numerous small fires broke out, triggering a series of alarms throughout the ship that showed up on the diagnostic monitors.

"Captain. They're using their secondary batteries now."

A constant rumble shook the ship to its core as it came under a continuous and unrelenting assault from both Vrokan ships. Though smaller calibre, the secondary guns were much more numerous and capable of firing more rapidly.

"Let the interceptor fire take care of them."

"We're too close, Captain. They can't keep up," said Commandeer Percy, "We're moving away…now!"

"Interceptor drones are at half capacity," said Lieutenant Coleridge, "I'm moving the shield to provide a screen for our engines. Now, if…"

Lieutenant Coleridge stopped speaking for a second, and then glanced back.

"Active radar tracking systems. I think they're preparing a spread of torpedoes."

"No," said Captain Leach, "We're not being burned to the keel like this. Dump all countermeasures, smoke, the works. And helm, get me to safety, fast!"

The ship groaned as the hull found itself under an array of competing forces. Lateral thrusters turned it about, all while a combination of retro thrusters and the main drive pulse flashed to assist in the course change. Great clouds of powdery smoke spread around the ship, making it look as though it had sustained a series of explosions.

"Torpedoes incoming!"

The shrill of threat indicators howled, and each watched for the spread of deadly warheads to come their way. And then without warning, the Prince of Wales crashed through the fog of colour like some old metal steamer forcing its way through thin ice. Captain Leach gulped as the flash hood automatically deployed around his face without any input from himself. His view was partially impaired for just a second.

"Brace! Brace! Brace!"

No sooner had it moved into position than an explosion on the bridge shattered several displays, showering the officers in debris. Bright light filled the deck, and he heard several of the crew cry out. He then reached for the hood and pulled it down to below his eyes.

"Report?"

"We're okay," said Commander Percy, "Light damage, but

we've got fires on multiple decks."

"One of the torps got through?"

"No," said Lieutenant Coleridge, "A single shot from the Bismarck came after us in the nebula. It hit us amidship and then penetrated three decks inside. It nearly made it right here."

"Here?" asked the Captain, "That could have been awkward."

That drew a mutter from several of the men and women. The escape from the Vrokan ships was perhaps the most terrifying few minutes any of them had faced, including their Captain's. Every thirty seconds or so they would come under fire yet again, with so many shells hammering into his beloved ship's armour he expected the vessel to explode at any moment. But with that last blast there were no more, just the whine of internal alarms, groans from the wounded, and the constant sound of voices as the men and women of Prince of Wales did all they could to keep the ship operational.

"We did it," said Commander Percy, "We're clear. I don't know how…but we made it."

Some on the bridge cheered, but as he looked back, he could tell there was little to cheer about. He looked to Captain Leach who looked equally relieved.

"Good work. Damned good work. That was a close-run thing. I thought we were done for there."

He wiped his lips with the back of his right hand and then tapped his displays to check the external videostreams. There was nothing but the wisps of coloured fog around them.

"All stations report in. I need full damage reports. Leave nothing out."

His attention shifted to the side.

"Comms. Contact Admiral Wake-Walker, and fast. We need to get this under control."

"He's already here," said Lieutenant Beeson, "He wants an update."

"On my display."

He turned to his left, and as soon as the two men looked at each other, the Admiral kept shaking his head.

"I simply cannot believe it's true. We've just arrived at the scene of the battle. There's nothing but rubble here. Is it true? Hood is truly gone?"

"It's true, Admiral. She's gone...and we've detected no lifeboats."

"How? She's the most powerful ship in the fleet. If she can't stand up to Bismarck, who can?"

"It was a single hit from the enemy flagship. We believe a super-heavy armour-piercing round burst through a gap in her dorsal armour. One minute there was no problem, and then it happened without warning."

"Tell me."

"A single massive gout of flame from her middle, like a blow torch blasting out from the ship. Half as second later, she tore apart and scattered."

"Blow torch? That sounds like a hit to an ammunition store or the main reactor cores. I would never have believed it. I...our mission still remains."

"Mission?" Captain Leach was stunned, "You want to continue the attack?"

"Yes. What's your status?"

Captain Leach looked to the status screen next to the view of the Admiral and raised his gaze along the numerous parts of the ship flagged in red.

"I have multiple penetrations, several main guns offline, and numerous casualties."

"But you can fight. Fall in with Suffolk and make what repairs you can. We've detected venting plasma into the nebula. It's faint but can be followed. Did Hood manage to damage one of them?"

"Not Hood. But we managed to put a shot right through her bow. A single solid penetration that tore her bow open."

"Then you may have done more damage than you thought. Venting plasma suggests you damaged her energy transfer system, and that might slow her down a little. And even if it doesn't, she will not be able to use her jump drive for risk of triggering internal detonations."

"Then we've ended her mission before it can begin."

"No. A few days at the nearest space dock, and they'll be heading out into space. They may even have a repair vessel on its way. We need to stay on her heels and end this."

"I've lost partial gunnery tracking and nearly a third of my main guns to system failures. But we can fight."

The Admiral smiled begrudgingly.

"Good. Fall into formation. We should be in range in the next…six hours or so."

"Understood. It will be done."

Admiral Wake-Walker began to walk away when Captain Leach spoke again.

"What about survivors from Hood?"

"We've already deployed Walrus search and rescue craft to the area. If there's anybody out there, they'll find them."

"Very well. Then the hunt continues."

***

Wreckage Site, Kamineso Nebula
The two small Walrus search and rescue spacecraft moved forward as quickly as they dared through the debris field. They were rather short and bulky, with much of their space given over to a larger round crew section to the front and two sets of retractable wings fitted with thrusters at the tips to aid in rapid manoeuvring. They rolled past one massive piece of debris, and then retracted the wings and boosted the engines to escape from a shower of metal fragments that narrowly avoided cutting the craft apart.

"That was close," said Lieutenant Mathew Darius, the Walrus' experienced pilot as he pulled on the controls, "Hold on!"

The Walrus pulled up and then corkscrewed about before settling near three large pieces of hull.

"I can't believe it. There's nothing but rubble here."

Lieutenant Darius looked directly ahead and ran his eyes over every chunk of ship and every piece of wreckage.

"Anything?"

Two more crew sat further behind watched their displays carefully. They moved through multiple vision modes but neither spotted a thing.

"Not yet," said the nearest of the pair, Lieutenant Hodgkinson, a swarthy red-haired man with a sweatband around his forehead. He kept shaking his head as he checked the data over and over, "Switching to thermal imaging."

The display blinked, and then the colours transformed as

the pieces of wreckage became brighter if they were warmer than the frigid void of space.

"I've got sections of turret, and there's even part of the hull still burning inside out."

The view panned slowly to the right, with the crew and the computers working overtime to try and isolate any signs of potential survivors.

"There," said Lieutenant Hodgkinson, "Look…two of the lifeboats, or what's left of them. They're both still attached to the wreckage."

"Poor sods," said Richardson, the second data analyst onboard, "In that case nobody made it off in time. The ship must have been torn apart in an instant."

A second Walrus moved past and away from the smaller chunks of debris, making its way to a large three-hundred-metre-long part of the hull. The Walrus' powerful external lamps moved constantly as its crew peered off into the darkness. The wisps and clouds of colour from the nebula mixed with the fine mists of debris from the ruined carcass of the Mighty Hood.

"Darius," said Lieutenant Hodgkinson, "I'm picking up something faint at this location."

It took a moment before the pilot nodded.

"Next to the engines?"

"Yes. It may just be heat retention on one of the panels, but it might be worth a shot."

"Agreed. I'm taking us around for a pass near that engine," he said calmly, "Hold on."

The winglet thrusters activated, and the spacecraft spiralled away. Curved trails from the wing tips followed their progress as they worked their way through the field.

"The wreckage out here is incredible."

"It's not just Hood," said Lieutenant Hodgkinson, "Some of this is from the Vrokan ships. It looks like we caused some damage at least."

The spacecraft turned around and all the forward searchlights activated at once. The long beams were easy to see as they reflected against the micro fragments from the exploded ordnance and shattered armour and bulkheads from the recent battle. It was like headlights peering into a cold fog at night.

"Mother of God…I can't believe it," said Lieutenant Hodgkinson.

"What?"

"I've got something…No, three lifesigns."

Lieutenant Darius looked stunned.

"You're kidding? Somebody actually survived this thing?"

He activated his comms while repeatedly shaking his head.

"All SAR in the area. We've got survivors. Moving in now."

He boosted the engines just a little and the spacecraft moved in closer. They were now entering the debris field, and small fragments of metal bumped against the armoured dome built around the pilot's position. One in particular rubbed along the dome, leaving a long scratch in the metalwork that began to widen.

"Not good. Reversing thrust."

Puffs of white from the winglet thrusters pushed out to the front, and the Walrus came to a halt, with part of the front now blocked with metal fragments.

"Time to deploy our little friend."

"On it," said Lieutenant Hodgkinson, "Deploying now."

They watched their displays as the small crab-like craft exited the Walrus and began moving away. It was an ugly contraption and connected to the Walrus via an umbilical cable that provided primary power and motive control.

"Watch for the metal shards. Some of them are really sharp," said Lieutenant Darius.

"Yeah, I know," said Hodgkinson, "There's a lot of junk here."

The small robot moved between several metal beams, and then on to what look like a breached boiler door. Thick cabling hung down and blocked access, but some careful manoeuvring brought the robot through without sustaining damage. Once clear, it turned on the spot and shone its powerful lights at the wreckage, and there next to it, and partially entangled in broken cabling were three crew. They were sealed in environmental suits and clinging to the metal housing as small chunks of metal floated around them.

"I see three individuals, all with positive life signs. Moving in closer."

The drone pushed on and bumped against a metal beam, dropped down, and continued downward.

"Beginning communications protocol."

The lights on the front of the craft flashed a series of colours, and then one of the crew lifted a hand and waved two fingers in a v shape.

"How rude!" Lieutenant Hodgkinson laughed, "They're alive and kicking."

"Outstanding," said Darius, "Bring them aboard. Three is a lot better than none."

They watched nervously as the Lieutenant used the limbs

on the robot to attach to the first of the crew, and then pulled him free of the wreckage. At once, they could see burn marks along his clothing where he must have been struck by the blast. It took time, and the other two waited patiently as their comrade was moved to the side of the Walrus. The outer door slid open, and the machine gently pushed him into the open space. It then moved away to get the others, all while the door shut and the airlock began to pressurize and introduce warm air slowly. Darius rotated his seat around for a better look and watched as the seconds slowly ticked on by. Finally, the airlock was ready and opened to reveal the man floating in the doorway.

"Get him inside."

Lieutenant Richardson pulled him inside. The crewman struggled at his neck and then removed his helmet.

"God bless you," he said through his dried-out throat, "We thought we were goners."

"No chance. We never leave people behind. Did you see anybody else?"

"Hundreds." The man shook his head, "None alive, though, if that's what you mean."

Richardson handed him a hydration pack, and he sucked on the tube to empty the contents into his body. He sighed with relief as he handed it back, and then looked to the domed front of the Walrus. From there he could see the wreckage.

"We went in with flags flying and guns blazing. None of us saw this coming."

"Sorry. We've got the next one coming to the airlock now."

Richardson nodded, and then looked back to the exhausted man.

"How did you survive?"

"No idea," he said with a sigh, "One minute I was working below, and the next I was spinning about in space. I was working in engineering, so all of us were wearing our environmental suits. Otherwise, I'd have been dead in seconds."

"What about Hood? What happened?"

That made him gulp.

"We took a hit; I know that for sure. The internal alarms were going at my ears like hammers, and then half the ship disappeared around me. I saw things you never want to see. Bodies ripped up and the hull gutted like a fish."

He reached out and grabbed a nearby rail to stop him from drifting about. He then needed to take several breaths to try and calm himself, all while the airlock warning sounded as it pressurised for the next crewman. It took time, but finally, the man was able to float in and immediately approached his comrade. They embraced for many seconds before finally separating. The new arrival looked to the crew on the Walrus and then snarled.

"Tell me we're going after that bastard."

"We will," said Darius, "Hood must be avenged."

"Amen to that. Which ship are you from?"

"Norfolk."

"Ah...you lads tracked them to begin with, right?"

"You could say that. We ran into them once and nearly lost our ship in the process. But we're not stopping the hunt."

"Good. Then take me back there. I want to be there when that leviathan is turned to slag."

"Just one more." Richardson sent the robot back out into space.

"Did you find anybody else out here?" asked the new arrival.

"You're it. I'm sorry."

"Three men from a crew of thousands. I can't believe it."

"None of us can," said Darius from his position at the front of the craft, "It should never have happened. But trust me…before this is finished, Bismarck will burn."

STAR DREADNOUGHT BISMARCK

CHAPTER EIGHT

This nation, which is no stranger to bad tidings, received grim news today that the Mighty Hood, the largest warship in the Commonwealth fleet and pride of the Commonwealth navy, has been destroyed by a Vrokan Empire Star Dreadnought, codenamed Bismarck. From the Hood's compliment of almost three thousand men and women, there were but three survivors.

Reports from the front lines

Commonwealth Fleet Carrier 'Victorious', Deep Space
Lieutenant-Commander Eugene Esmonde waited on the elevator platform as it moved downwards and past numerous hangar decks. It looked as though he was travelling way down a massive tower-like construction, rather than actually moving towards the rear of the ship. He could see more of the decks contained a small number of spacecraft, the majority still attached to the clamps on the deck floor and ceiling. Most were covered in elasticated plastic covers that functioned as shrouds. Then came the next floor and the elevator began to slow. Before the warning light had turned green, he was off and walking along the hangar deck.

"Lieutenant-Commander," said the deck chief as he

watched him arrive, "I thought you got lost aboard your own ship."

"Well, she's been pretty empty these last few months. It's not hard to lose yourself here. What's the problem?"

"We're in quite the pickle. I've been waiting for you."

"Pickle, huh? Things are that bad? I understood we were being sent fresh squadrons to bring us up to full strength."

"Full strength?" laughed the chief, "The last time Victorious had a full complement of fighters was in the simulator. And now we're on our way to join the fleet on some urgent operation."

"So I've heard. Two hours ago, we were still flagged for training, and now this. Something big must be going on." He gave that some thought, and then smiled, "Don't tell me…somebody forgot our bombers?"

The man moved closer, and then stopped and shook his head.

"Oh…the birds are fine, nothing to worry about there. We've been sent across two full strike squadrons."

"Two? What's that…Thirty-two bombers in total?"

"Aye, but don't get too excited. Most are going to find this operation a little testing to say the least."

Esmonde shook his head in annoyance.

"Most? Do you mean the pilots or the birds?"

That put a smile on the old veteran's face.

"The bomber squadrons. Ahem…well, they're still going through their carrier conversion course."

"Conversion course? What were they flying before?"

"Like I said…we're in quite the pickle. You've got sixteen F25A Valkyries onboard, plus a few recon birds, all with pilots waiting for a chance to shoot down some fighters."

"What about my bombers? I've been waiting for them since I was put in command of the strike element over a month ago."

"You've got your strike element, as promised, but you're not going to like it."

"The crews or the bombers?"

"Come with me."

The two walked along the deck, but it didn't take long to reach the row of antiquated spacecraft hanging from the ceiling like bats. They were rather odd compared to the sleek and power fighters he was used to flying. They were a little larger, with two sets of swept back wings and a long sealed canopy that shielded space for three crew onboard."

"Uh…is this a joke? I was promised two squadrons of Barracudas. Instead, I've got…"

"They're old, but they've got it where it counts, Sir."

"This isn't a joke?"

"It's no joke. The new bombers have gone to frontline carriers. Victorious is supposed to be a training ship. Two squadrons of Swordfish are all that can be spared at short notice." He shook his head and whistled, "They're solid craft, and what they lack in engines and firepower they make up for in toughness. I've heard they can take a hundred hits and keep flying."

"That's because there's nothing important behind the armour, Chief. They're lumps of metal held together with string."

"Well, if you don't like the birds, you're definitely not going to be happy about your crews. I've never seen pilots so wet behind the ears."

"The price of war. Where are they?"

The deck chief nodded off into the distance and to a small group who were involved in a heated debate.

"Good luck, Lieutenant-Commander. Whip them into shape."

The deck chief then turned back and returned to his work, leaving Esmonde to continue on alone. He moved quickly along the metal deck, enjoying the feeling of gravity once more as he walked. With the engines active, they were able to take advantage of the gravitational forces allowing them to move about as though on land. He took a sip from the warm flask and let the tea drift down his throat. He closed his eyes and enjoyed the moment for a few seconds, a luxury that zero-gravity rarely offered him. A rookie pilot might think the mighty ship was stationary perhaps, apart from the engine-induced gravity, but he knew better. There was a subtle rumble and whine from the ship that let him know they were using the jump drive to travel at incredible speeds through open space.

"Lieutenant-Commander!"

He turned and looked to the three crewmen and the group of pilots waiting near one of the antiquated fighters. As they looked back at him, he could tell there was a problem. The pilots looked as though they'd just stepped off their shuttle, and next to them were several bags, all still packed from their journey.

"What is it?"

The pilots glanced to the deck crew and then back to him.

"Sir. We've just arrived for deck training, and we're being told that we're joining the duty squadron. And our fighters aren't even here. Instead, we've got these old buckets of bolts."

Lieutenant-Commander Esmonde nodded towards one of the nearest Swordfish. The spacecraft looked old and worn, and yet it had been retained and serviced to keep it in excellent condition. The panels had been hammered back straight, and parts upgraded or replaced over the years.

"These are the same fighter-bombers that knocked out half the Novan Republic's fleet while still in port. The same birds that struck the Gallian warships at Mers-el-Kébir and crippled the capital ships before they could fall into the Vrokan's hands to be turned against us. No, they're not some fancy new high-speed bombers, but these old buckets of bolts."

"Our Gallian allies were at Mers-el-Kébir. They said they would never let the Vrokan navy take control of the ships," said a man with a thick accent. He was quite tall, with a rakish moustache and the air and confidence of a man used to command privilege, "We shouldn't have been…"

"You'd have left four Gallian Hegemony battleships, five destroyers, and a fighter tender for the enemy to seize? The Vrokan is strong on land, but in space we command the shipping lanes, but only while we have the numbers. The Hegemony are nothing but their puppets now. Either they fight with us, stand back and leave us be, or we will attack them. There's nothing more we…"

He was about to say more when he realised, he was being drawn into a debate with his own pilots. He was the commanding officer on the deck, and he knew this wasn't why he was here.

"There is a time and place for this kind of discussion, and it isn't now. What you do need to know is that Victorious is being declared operational."

"But, Sir, we're never done this before," said the pilot, "We've practiced back at home, on the ground and from the naval station. It's all backwards here, and we've had no chance to practice. We're not ready for deployment."

"Let me guess, the verticality of the ship? And the changes in momentum?"

Both men nodded.

"We've never operated from a ship before, Sir."

The second of the two pilots shook his head and placed a hand on his comrade's shoulder.

"Not just a ship, we've never operated away from a naval base, Sir. We were supposed be training for the next three months."

Esmonde could have cried out in frustration, but that would only make things worse. The fact they were aboard the ship meant they were all skilled and well-trained pilots. What they lacked could be taught, in time.

"Victorious is a big ship, but inside she's nothing like the bases you've operated from. She's loaded up with hundreds of decks, all stacked from front to back. The hangar decks are narrow, but they're tough, well armoured, and with launch access on the flanks. Plus we have topside landing zones for rapid refuelling and rearming."

"But manual launch is almost..."

"Don't worry about launches," he said with a smile, "Victorious is fitted with autoloaders. Your work starts once you're outside. Trust me, the days of landing manually inside a carrier are long gone. Just get your bird topside, and the loaders do the rest."

He continued speaking but stopped abruptly as an urgent

flashcom appeared on his wrist communicator. He tapped it to get the specifics as the Captain's voice sounded through the ship. The deck crew and other pilots stopped what they were doing as they listened.

"This is the Captain. A few short hours ago a battlegroup led by Hood and the Prince of Wales met with and engaged a Vrokan force. Listed in this enemy flotilla was their brand-new star dreadnought, codenamed Bismarck. This is by far the largest and most powerful vessel we have encountered."

The mention of the vessel's name caught the attention of the pilots.

"I regret to inform you that in the engagement, Hood suffered a catastrophic hit that destroyed her. We are joining additional forces to envelop the enemy and to stop Bismarck's escape."

"What?" said one of the pilots, "Did he just say destroyed? My brother is aboard the Hood."

His nearest companion reached out and placed an arm around his shoulders.

"Harry, I'm sure he made it off her. Hood wouldn't just vanish like that."

Esmonde ignored them for the moment and instead looked to the data on his device. As Lieutenant-Commander, he was privy to information they were not, and as he looked at the report, he could feel the blood draining from his face.

"No," he said a little louder than he intended.

One pilot stepped closer.

"Sir?"

"We're the closest reinforcements."

"Closest? What about Ark Royal and the others at The

Rock?"

"No. We're going into action first."

His device flashed again, and this time it was a summons.

"We're needed in the briefing room."

He turned to move away, but when he glanced over his shoulder, the pilots were still there, unmoving and watching him. And so, he turned back and moved to the middle of the group.

"That includes you. Leave your gear and follow me."

"Sir? What about our conversion course?"

"I'm afraid you're going to have to learn on the job."

The man with the moustache and attitude shook his head, and then spoke right at him in a tone that sent the hairs along the back of his neck upright.

"Lieutenant-Commander. We have neither the skills nor experience. Sending us into action like this is a gross…"

"Enough," snapped Esmonde, "What's your name?"

"Lieutenant Edward Howard-Carter, Sir."

He said the name proudly, as though it carried some weight and authority. Esmonde knew only too well who the Howard-Carters were, and at that moment he had little sympathy for the man.

"Well, Lieutenant Howard-Carter. You volunteered to serve the Commonwealth, did you not?"

"All of my family have…"

"I'm not interested in your brothers, your father, or the angel that birthed you. Answer the question, man!"

For the first time since he'd seen the man, he looked visibly shaken.

"Uh…yes, Sir. I volunteered six months ago."

"Well, then. The day you signed the dotted line you

handed over your life to the Commonwealth, as did the two thousand, six hundred and fifty men and women aboard Hood. They went into action as they were ordered, and now they're gone."

"Gone?" Harry Middleton said, the man whose brother had been aboard the ship. He was a little shorter than the others, with a roundish face and flushed cheeks.

"I'm sorry," said Esmonde, "Reports from battle indicate there were very few survivors."

He grimaced as he looked at the face of the near broken young man.

"SAR assets are in the area. If anybody made it clear of the debris field, they will be found."

He moved one step closer and looked to each of them.

"There's nothing, and I mean nothing we can do about what has happened. The Commonwealth stands alone, while the rest of the galaxy either cows down to the Vrokan or turns their backs on the rest of us. We are the last chance any of us has, and the fleet is the backbone of that struggle."

He stopped and looked directly towards Harry.

"And now we have a chance to hit them back, to show them that it is us, not the Vrokan that controls the high seas. They can win every land battle for the next ten years, but while our fleet stays strong, we remain safe and in the fight."

He then ground his right fist into his left hand.

"So, we find the ship that did this, and we can show them what happens to those that hunt our family and friends. And when I say we will find them, I mean we will personally put a spread of torpedoes into their flanks and gut them like a fish."

Still there was nothing from them, but Esmonde persisted.

"Hood is gone, and there's nothing we can do about it. Nearly three thousand crew lost in a single broadside. Prince of Wales, our newest and best battleship is burning, and yet she's still there, in pursuit and refusing to back down."

He tapped his chest and nodded.

"And we're being rushed into action to join a taskforce under the command of Admiral Tovey. We're the cavalry and we have to step up."

"Tovey?" Lieutenant Howard-Carter asked, "He's entering the fight?"

Esmonde fought hard not to snap at the pilot. He suspected the Admiral was probably a family friend of his parents, and that maddened him. He'd fought hard to get where he was, but without family connections it was difficult, sometimes impossible. And here was this young man, possibly part of the junior aristocracy, and he could waltz in without a care in the world. But then to his surprise, the expression on the pilot's face changed, and with it his impression of the man.

"I've followed his career for some time. He's a good commander, and he looks after his crew. He won't let Bismarck get away with this."

Esmonde smiled at that part.

"No, he won't. And he's not going in alone. Tovey is meeting us aboard the fast battleship King George V, and right behind him is Battlecruiser Repulse."

Lieutenant Howard-Carter gave a low whistle.

"So, it's not just us going into the fight?"

"Us? The Admiralty is sending in everything they can muster. But we…we are the spear tip. I need to know if you're with me for this?"

"If it means putting holes in Bismarck, then we're with you, Lieutenant-Commander," said Harry Middleton, "My brother demands payback."

"Too right he does. Now…get your gear stowed and meet me in the pilot's briefing room in sixty minutes. We've not got a lot of time to plan this operation, and I want your input."

"Our input?" asked a surprised Edward, "For the mission?"

"Of course. Only a fool plans an operation without the input of others. What I can think of, so can our enemy. I need input."

Edward looked to his friend, and several of them bumped their fists together, causing Esmonde to shake his head repeatedly.

"Now…I didn't say you'd have anything useful to say. Trust me, when I tell you that the idea of there being no bad ideas has been repeatedly proven incorrect. There're always bad ideas."

And to their surprise he then smiled at them. It wasn't forced or faked, but a genuine smile, that put some of them completely off guard.

"But even those ideas might lead to something better. Let's go!"

Several of them chuckled, with even Edward appearing amused by his new commanding officer as he moved away as quickly as he'd arrived. The small group of pilots clustered around Edward who seemed almost transformed by the experience.

"I don't know," he said quietly to the others, "Maybe he's not as bad as we thought."

"You're joking, right?" Margaret Lipton asked. Until now she had been completely silent, "Haven't you seen his record? He's a hero in the fleet."

"What?"

"He was one of the pilots that attacked Mers-el-Kébir. I heard his flight were laying mines when they were attacked by Gallian fighters."

"What happened?"

"There's a rumour he was shot down, and the only survivor."

"Dammit," said Edward, "No wonder he was pissed at me, Marge. Maybe you could have warned me before I brought it up."

Margaret chuckled at his irritation.

"Why would I spare myself the pleasure of watching you squirm, Eddie. Consider it a thank you for last week."

Try as he might, Edward simply couldn't hide the smile on his lips.

"You're such an arse, Marge."

She leaned in and mock kissed him on the cheek before turning away.

"And don't you ever forget it!"

He watched her go, knowing too well she knew he was watching, as were most of them. She was as fit and active as any in the fleet and walked with a speed and grace that demanded attention. He was sure she stepped in such a way that her hips twisted more than they needed. And then to his surprise, she looked back over her shoulder towards him and smiled. He couldn't tell if it was a look of amusement or a smile directed towards him, but then he found the others looking right back at him.

"What?"

It was Artur Wachowski, his old sparring partner and rival in the group. They were tied on the simulator scores, and in flight training they were always pushing to surpass the other, often to the annoyance of the other members of the squadron.

"You think she likes you?"

"Maybe."

Artur shook his head, laughed, and moved away.

"Edward…She plays with your head. Trust me…I've been there. She's all about the job."

"Job? Aren't we all?"

His eyes then met those of Harry, the poor soul whose brother was now missing. Neither said a word for a few seconds before Edward finally broke the ice.

"If anybody got off Hood, it will be your brother."

Harry closed his eyes and exhaled several times. Edward moved closer and grasped his comrade's forearm.

"Trust me." Harry opened his eyes and nodded ever so slowly. "We didn't start this war," he said angrily, "but we're damned well going to finish it."

The two grasped their hands and shook on it.

"They'll never know what hit 'em, Harry."

* * *

Commonwealth Heavy Cruiser 'Norfolk', Kamineso Nebula, Six hours later

Alethea felt her eyes burning as she looked at the displays for the hundredth time. She'd served aboard Norfolk longer than most of the crew, but never had she spent so long at her post. She knew it was time to take some rest, but just knowing the great predatory monster was still out there forced her to remain. She heard movement nearby and looked back as two technicians removed one of the gimbals. The seat nearby was gone, along with the blood and bodies. As she looked across, she spotted the blond-haired navigator, Lieutenant Richards looking back at her. He gave her a nod that said more than a hundred words, and then turned back to his station.

Stay focussed and concentrate on your job.

Alethea turned back to her bank of displays; to her left the best images recorded by the Commonwealth ships of the Bismarck so far, and on the right a series of charts plotting their course and known movements. The central display housed her weapon controls and tactical targeting data.

"There's the trail...so where are the ships?"

She reached forward and ran a finger over the central display. There were the two cruisers, as well as Prince of Wales limping behind them. She showed signs of heavy damage, and yet remained following the others as she looked for a chance to settle the score. For a few seconds Alethea found her eyes drawn to brutal battle damage the warship has sustained. It was a testament to her design and to her crew that she remained in action, even after such a sustained attack. There were long black scorch marks along the hull, as well as several deep penetrations where large calibre rail gun projectiles had smashed their way inside. Alethea shook her head, and then moved the imagery aside and turned it back to the previous logs.

She could follow the course of Prince of Wales as she struggled to evade the wreckage from Hood, and then absorbed a punishing barrage as she tried to manoeuvre clear of the Vrokan ships, both of whom concentrated their fire on her. She then jumped forward, and to the incomplete plots of the enemy ships.

"Hold on…What's this?"

Alethea moved an overlay onto the data paths and checked them with the same logs from well before the battle. There were similarities, but also two big changes, each of which became more pronounced over time.

"You sneaky buggers."

Alethea moved the data back and watched with interest as the two ships corkscrewed together, creating confusion in their wake in the nebula. They then split apart at three separate points before joining back together later on.

"Captain," she said a little louder than she intended as she looked over her shoulder, "Captain Phillips."

"Yes, Lieutenant?"

"I think I've worked out the method to their madness."

"I'm all ears, Lieutenant. Explain."

"Well, if you watch their tracks, they're clearly trying to throw us off. But twice so far, this one trail has been drowned out with noise. There's no reason for this…unless they are trying something to get our attention."

"They want to be found?"

"I think Bismarck is trying to draw us in every few hours. But then they disappear just as fast."

"They know we're weakened, and they want to pull us in for a fight. That makes no sense, though. Why not just drop speed and wait for us? We're right on their tail already."

"That I don't know. But there's a good reason for…" She

stopped, and her eyes opened wide in surprise, "No…that's not possible."

She gulped, and then brought up data on the passive scans, continually shaking her head.

"Fresh contacts on long-range sensors. I think we've spotted them again."

"Excellent work, Lieutenant Madeline. Show me."

She tapped her screens, and Captain Phillip's rubbed his short cut beard as he looked to the new information.

"That's Bismarck's trail, alright. Prince of Wales definitely did a number on her."

He reached for his intercom and pulled it to his mouth.

"Admiral, we have them."

There was a short pause before the Admiral replied.

"Good work, Captain. Admiral Tovey is approaching fast. Notify him of their course. Perhaps he can find a way to intercept them."

"Captain…not good," said Alethea, "Bismarck is rotating and firing her retro thrusters. She's slowing down."

Captain Phillips responded in an instant.

"Warn Suffolk, and break contact…now!"

Once more the deafening sound of sirens filled the ship, giving them just seconds to strap in as thrusters activated. Metal bulkheads groaned in pain as the ship struggled to change course, all while they moved closer and closer to the target. As she watched, she spotted the unmistakable flashes of light from guns. To her relief, the shots were not aimed at them, but towards the dark, shadowy shape of Prince of Wales as the battleship moved up and away from the fight. Both vessels put two broadsides into each other, with Prince of Wales sustaining further damage before disappearing.

"How much longer until we're clear?" Captain Phillips sounded nervous.

"Not long," said the helmsman, "Just a few more seconds."

Alethea shook her head. "It's too late. She's firing."

Captain Phillips snorted in anger.

"Interceptors to maximum, dump smoke, and helm…Stop dawdling and get us out of here!"

The battleship's guns unleashed sixteen shells at them, and at this range it was all but impossible to avoid them. Wisps of lights reached out as the interceptors stabbed out into the blackness. Flash after flash marked detonations, and then came the impacts. Alethea's vision blurred as the ship shook violently.

"Damage report!" said the Captain.

Alethea's eyes ran over the displays, and she focussed on three points where they'd been hit.

"Three penetrations, all punched through without exploding. It looks like they underestimated our velocity."

"Thank God. Maybe their tracking systems and rangefinders aren't so good after all."

Tell that to the Hood. Alethea thought, though she dared not say it.

"Tactical, drop a spread of torpedoes as we enter the fog. It might be enough to shake them off our tail."

Alethea nodded and activated the starboard side torpedo battery as heavy guns fired once more. Passive scans showed the shots were not coming for Norfolk, and she could only assume Prince of Wales was bearing the brunt as she also fled the fight.

"Firing."

The torpedo launcher fired in sequence and sent off a spread of guided warheads in the direction of the closing enemy ship. They vanished from view, as they turned into their own smoke and countermeasure cloud, and back into the fog of the nebula.

"Any hits?"

"Unknown, Captain. We're being jammed, and I've no visuals on the ship."

As she looked at the display, something else occurred to her that sent a shiver running down her back. Two pages of data scrolled past, and she overlaid the known positions of the ships for the last twelve hours.

"Wait. The cruiser."

"What about it?"

Alethea ran her hand over the screen and moved away the tracking. She then put the Bismarck back, along with its own tracking data, and projected forward. But then tracking alarms sounded, and she watched as the flank of the battleship loomed out of the fog.

"All power to thrusters…evasive manoeuvres!" Captain Phillips ordered.

Alethea already had the main guns trained on the ship and managed to unleash fire from the stern batteries. Multiple small flashes marked impacts, but there was no sign of significant damage. Norfolk continued to power away, the heavy cruiser shaking violently as it rotated about, firing its thrusters in an evasion pattern. All of it appeared for nought as the battleship was moving so fast it zoomed past without firing a shot and back onto its previous course.

"Lieutenant? What's going on?"

"Sir. I think Bismarck was just wasting our time."

"Go on."

"The cruiser has escaped."

"You're sure?"

"Yes, Captain. Her trail has gone cold. I think they were using Bismarck to mask her long enough to hide her. She might have slipped away hours ago."

Captain Phillips thought on that as Admiral Wake-Walker return to his station and slipped into the gimbal-mounted seat. He pulled on his harness and then adjusted the displays in front of him.

"Forget her. The cruiser is not a priority. Let it go. I have orders from Admiralty. We're to stick with the heavy until this is done. Bismarck is damaged, and if she breaks into open space, we'll have her well before her jump engines can activate."

"Yes, Sir. I don't think they intend on fleeing."

She tapped her display, and all three looked to the tracking data.

"Heading back to port?" asked the Admiral, "Prince of Wales must have holed her worse than we thought. Good for her. The problem is…if she makes it within range of Vrokan territory, we'll have their bombers to contend with, and that's a problem so far from our own bases."

He looked towards Captain Phillips.

"Stay with Suffolk, and on her tail. I need to confer with Admiral Tovey."

"Yes, Admiral."

"Comms, put me on with Prince of Wales."

"Admiral."

The image of the interior of Prince of Wales appeared, and

some of those on the command deck gasped at seeing such destruction. Part of the inner bulkheads had gone, and there were several bodies floating away.

"Captain Leach, what's your status?"

"Admiral. Engines are functional, but my main guns are in trouble. We're down to half capacity, as well as damage to the bridge, command deck, and targeting array. We've also sustained damage to our armour belt, and my engineers tell me we have multiple unexploded ordnance still onboard."

"As I suspected. It's clear you've slowed Bismarck down. You've laid the groundwork for the rest of the fleet. I've just received word from the Admiralty. They are in a rage over Hood. Ships are arriving from our bases, including The Rock, as well as ships detached from convoy duty. Everything is being sent here to make sure they don't escape."

"Can it be done?"

"It won't be easy. But God willing, we'll bring her down."

He licked his lips before saying the next part, knowing full well the pain he was about to cause.

"The Admiralty is concerned at the damage you've sustained in the fighting. Prince of Wales is ordered to return home immediately."

"Admiral, we're still in the fight."

"I know, but it's too risky. One more hit, and you could join Hood's fate. Get back to base and get Prince of Wales back in shape. Something tells me we're going to need you back in the fray much earlier than we ever anticipated. This war isn't going anyway fast."

"We would have been with you to the end, Admiral."

"I know you would and trust me. When our heavies run

into that old bastard, they'll send her a message she won't easily forget."

"Hood will be avenged."

"You're damned right she'll be avenged. We shall meet again soon."

"Admiral."

The feed cut, but not before he could see the curious mixture of relief and disappointment on the face of his friend aboard Prince of Wales. He knew Captain Leach would want to be there, but he also knew the battleship was heavily damaged and a significant number of her main guns non-functional. One more full engagement with the Bismarck could be her last, and he had absolutely no intention of losing any more ships.

"He's not going to be happy about that," said Captain Phillips.

"No, he is not. But there's some good news. Look."

He tapped on the tactical map of the jagged border the Kamineso Nebula. Their own position was around a day from the border, but far off to the right, and where the clouds of gas and light were thinner, was the blinking indicator of a second formation.

"Victorious battlegroup has arrived and is moving to intercept. Admiral Tovey wants us to continue trailing Bismarck, while he moves in with Repulse from above. He's called in ships from The Rock as a reserve and to block the routes towards Vrokan territory. Bombers will launch within the hour to move in on Bismarck."

"Bombers against Bismarck? Is that wise?"

"We can leave nothing to chance on this one. Whatever assets we have are being thrown in her path. Bismarck cannot be allowed into open space, and there's no chance in hell she's returning to port."

CHAPTER NINE

Why was it that the Commonwealth Fleet relied upon an outdated, slow, and poorly armoured fighter-bomber so long into the war? Others had already moved to much faster spacecraft, but there were few that would argue against the strengths of that old design. Known affectionately as the Stringbag for her ability to carry and use almost any weapon, payload, or equipment, they were the right spacecraft at the right time. While the Vrokan's allies scorned the slow-moving Swordfish, they soon came to respect them after the stunning success at the Battle of Taranto, where half of the Novan Republic's fleet was knocked out in a single engagement.

Masimov's Guide to Fighting Ships

Commonwealth Fleet Carrier 'Victorious'

Lieutenant-Commander Esmonde looked at the young men and women assembled in the briefing room, and then began to pace. There were twenty-four of them in total, enough crew for just eight fighter-bombers, plus his own, giving them a grand total of nine. Like him, they all wore Navy issue flight suits, a futuristic piece of clothing designed to combine a fully sealed environmental survival outfit, combined with the aesthetic of a military uniform. Esmonde also wore as cap bearing the insignia of the Commonwealth Navy that was styled in the same colour scheme as the uniform.

"So…as you can see, Battlegroup Victorious is closing off this escape route for Bismarck, but there are other directions the enemy can travel in. And if he's able to locate clear regions in the nebula, he may even risk short-range jumps to get ahead of us."

The room was shaped as a sphere, with gimbal-mounted seating all around. Each seat faced towards the centre where a massive projection showed the local map of the nebula, along with the positions of the various ships moving in on the enemy.

"We're approaching from here…"

He pointed towards the upper right of the mapping display.

"And here are our cruisers and Prince of Wales in pursuit. Fresh intelligence from the cruisers under the command of Admiral Wake-Walker confirms the Vrokan cruiser has escaped the area."

That drew groans from some of those present.

"But that should not concern us for now. The cruiser is a problem, but our convoy escorts can handle her with planning and quick reactions. No…all our efforts are to be focussed on Bismarck. Any questions so far?"

Artur Wachowski raised a hand immediately.

"Sir, why don't we just all head right for them? I don't get why we're spreading out."

"There are tactical considerations to take into account here." The imagery changed to show the enemy flagship leapfrogging from place to place by skip-jumping, "And that means the Bismarck has a habit of avoiding contact, and in areas clear of the nebula she's able to make short jumps to skip ahead. If that happens again, she could slip right by and make it back to a Vrokan naval facility. So we spread out, and fighter squadrons will go on the hunt."

He lowered his hand, and the others remained silent.

"We have a chance here, and it is imperative that we cast the net out wide. That's why we have a series of waypoints to search before returning to Victorious, each calculated by tacticians on Admiral Wake-Walker's cruiser. We will be carrying external tanks for the mission to increase our duration and loiter time, as well as a single heavy-weight ship-killer torpedo."

The imagery shifted and changed to show the model of the Bismarck. It was still incomplete, but more than enough for them to make out its vast size.

"The ship is big, heavily armoured, and bristling with defensive weaponry. If we get the chance, we will close fast and attempt to overwhelm their defences with an attack from four directions at once."

He waited a moment, and then continued to the part he knew they would find uncomfortable.

"You will get within ten thousand metres before launching, not a metre further away."

He let that sink in for a second, knowing full well the concern it would cause.

"Bismarck is a modern battleship, and initial assessments show she is well protected with large and medium calibre artillery. Her arsenal will shred anything further away. We need to cut their reaction and tracking time down to a few seconds at the most. And that means attacking at point-blank range."

He could see the look on Lieutenant Lipton's face as she imagined the attack, and as he looked to the others, he could see the worry and the nerves clearly showing on their faces.

"This will not be easy. But we have one thing in our favour."

Many of the pilots leaned forward, expecting some great secret to be revealed.

"Until now, no capital ship has been lost while in space against fighters, only while stationary and in port, often with a partial crew and unprepared for battle."

That drew murmurs from those present. One even called out what many must have been thinking.

"That doesn't sound like an advantage, Sir."

"Perhaps not. But Intelligence suspects that out in deep space they consider an attack by fighters to be unlikely. With our short legs and Bismarck's speed we should be of little threat. Instead, they are prepared for an attack by cruisers and battlecruisers, the only capital ships we have that are able to catch her in most circumstances. If we're lucky, that may help buy us time to close in on her. If we are lucky."

He adjusted the display until it showed his own small battlegroup.

"Very well, then to the specifics. We will launch within the hour, and as soon as we come out of jump space. There will be a change in procedure today. You will stay together in the nebula. Visibility ranged for a hundred thousand kilometres to under a thousand depending on the density and regional conditions. I cannot afford to have any of you getting lost out there."

"Sir?" Edward Howard-Carter asked, "All nine of us are staying together. Isn't that inefficient? In simulation we've always split into pairs for SAR and lone pack hunting."

"Yes. All nine. And normally you would be correct, but

this is different. We will stay together, no matter what we run into. This entire region of space is more treacherous and difficult to navigate than anywhere you've been before. So we stay together until we reach the target."

Howard-Carter nodded along as he listened.

"But our attacks will be launched by sub-flight."

Various points along the enemy battleship flashed brightly.

"Each of our three sub-flights will be allocated a series of priority targets, engines, power cores, and the primary armour belts. The last thing we need is superficial damage to parts of the superstructure."

Again Howard-Carter lifted a hand.

"Go on."

"Sir. Simulations show that hits to the superstructure can be more effective than hitting the primary hull. Perhaps we could split off a few of the…"

"No. Though it's a good observation. The problem is one of time. Vrokan battleship Bismarck is moving fast. We need to slow her down and let the rest of the fleet move in. So if we find her, we're going to hit her with everything we have."

Esmonde looked to the model of the enemy ship one last time, and then gave them a nod.

"The ship schematics, assault vectors, and tactical information have been sent to each of you. Access to the rest of the ship is now blocked. You may travel to your attached quarters and the hangar only for the duration of this mission."

That seemed to surprise some of them.

"You have a short while before launch. Do what you must, file messages to loved ones, or grab some tea. But when lights flash red, I expect you to be waiting on the launch deck. Understood?"

"Yes, Sir!"

"Excellent. Then you are dismissed."

* * *

Commonwealth Heavy Cruiser 'Norfolk'

Rear Admiral Wake-Walker strained his eyes as he looked ahead at his displays. The rest of the command deck was almost silent as each looked for their illusive prey. There was a tension aboard the ship, one made worse by each passing hour.

"Where is she?"

Captain Phillips was positioned at the next station along and shook his head. He looked positively exhausted, having been on station now ever since the first sighting of the Vrokan ships. Stubble was just about visible at his cheeks, and yet he refused to leave.

"She was there three minutes ago, but right on the edge of our scanner range."

"Then take us in closer."

"That's the problem, Admiral. Each time we lose her, she makes course changes. If we push too close, we risk moving right past her and never finding her again."

"Then it is time to split up."

"Sir?"

"If Suffolk separates, we can cover two locations at once."

"And if she turns back to fight?"

"Then we flee. We're the bloodhounds now. It's for the heavies to end this fight."

"That might be our only chance, then. This nebula is almost impossible to scan thoroughly at this range. And each time we overload the sensors, we let them know where we are, and where to avoid."

The Admiral did not look impressed. He rubbed his forehead and then looked back to his displays.

"The Vrokan are no fools. But they're not slipping away this time. We need them tracked until all our assets are in place. We've got Ark Royal coming directly from The Rock, as well as other ships being dragged in from wherever we can find them. Rodney and a flotilla of destroyers are on approach at maximum burn. The net is closing, but all of them are reliant upon us."

Captain Phillips glanced across to the tactical station, and then to helm. He could have chased them, but they knew the importance of their mission as much as he did. The last thing any of his crew needed was having him on their backs.

"Captain," said the comms officer, "I'm detecting a faint transmission."

"From the enemy?"

The officer listened again and then shook his head.

"I can't tell. But it's coming closer, and it's coming fast."

"Tactical, anything?"

"Nothing on passive sensors, Sir."

"Then go active. I don't care if Bismarck knows we're here. We need a positive match."

"Yes, Sir."

A moment later a series of flagged shapes and objects appeared. With each additional ping the picture became clearer. There were three inert objects, either scattered asteroids, or even the remnants of long lost or destroyed ships.

"This place is a graveyard," said Captain Phillips, "Vessels have been lost and abandoned out here for centuries."

"Still nothing," said Alethea, "Overloading wide band transmitters."

A warning flashed up on her display, and she swiped it away without bothering to read it. She already knew that by doing this she risked damage to delicate instruments installed on the cruiser, as well as increasing the chances they would be detected by the enemy first. Then two more patterns appeared, and she knew she'd found something.

"Two readings, faint, but there's definitely something there."

* * *

Lieutenant-Commander Esmonde looked to his right and for a brief moment thought he was in fact looking at fresh Vrokan ships. But then he spotted flickering lights from the monstrous, oversized hull Victorious that was already several hundred kilometres away. Gone were the flush lines of the battleships and cruisers, and in their place something more akin to the design of heavy transport ships, albeit armed to the teeth and bristling with fighters. A few seconds later, the ship vanished, leaving just two ships in this part of open space.

"Look!" Lieutenant Lipton said, "They're leaving now."

"King George V…and Repulse…" added Edward, "Off they go."

"Cut the chatter," he replied sternly, "But yes, they're leaving, and that's our cue to enter the nebula. And from now on, remember your code names, call signs and codes only.

Anybody uses a ship name again, and you'll be making your way home under normal power."

Every single one of them was familiar with the two ships, especially the King George V battleship. She was the first of her line, and the start of the Commonwealth's fleet rebuilding programme. Every soul in the fleet knew her lines by heart. Bright light engulfed them, and then they were also gone, leaving the massed formation of spacecraft alone and in space.

"To the first waypoint."

Esmonde looked over his shoulder to Sub Lieutenant Jenkins, his navigator. The man was busily making subtle changes to his heading before giving him the nod.

"It's all ready."

"Good work."

He then checked around his Swordfish to check on the others. The fighters were arranged in three groups of three, each spaced apart and with a sub-flight leader in front.

"Boost in five...four..."

Warning lights blinked as his main engines drew power from the main core, and then as the indicator hit green, he activated the boosters. The power from the engines forced him back into his seat, but that didn't stop. The fighter moved faster and faster, with the other fighters doing the same. He tried to turn his neck, but his muscles couldn't force past the g-forces compressing him into his seat. Instead, he looked forward and checked the videostreams from the plethora of cameras fitted throughout the fighter.

There they are.

The fighters were all within fifty kilometres of his position, allowing him to see their engines trails are they burst through into the great clouds of the nebula.

"Stay close together. It's easy to get lost out here. And there's no jump drives out here for rescue ships, not unless you want to risk them being torn apart by hidden debris."

There was no reply from the others, and that drew a smile to his face.

Good. They understand.

He looked to the view ahead and shook his head. The clouds whooshed on past, and there were entire areas devoid of anything but blackness. But just as the area seemed clear and safe, they would burst right into another sea of colour, rendering half their sensors useless and leaving them temporarily blind.

This is going to be a long flight.

"Cut thrust and adjust course by four degrees."

Esmonde settled back into the seat as the pressure on his body reduced to something a little more comfortable. It was still a far cry from the zero-gravity normally experienced as he coasted through space, but it at least let him breathe relatively comfortably. Seconds turned to minutes, and before he realised it, they'd been travelling through the nebula for more than an hour. An indicator flickered on his display, with the ident code of Victorious showing. He tapped the device and a familiar voice spoke.

"Theta Leader. Your status?"

"Good to hear your voice. We're on course and proceeding to Waypoint Bravo."

"Understood, Theta Leader. You're making good time. We've received fresh intelligence on the target. Updated tracking data uploading now."

Esmonde looked down to the smaller display and watched

with interest as the target tracks changed to show the original path of the enemy ship and its pursuers, compared to the new updated course.

"Is this confirmed?"

"As best we can tell. The target has managed to evade once more, but she's still venting, and we're able to obtain a close track of her course. Combined with the fastest and most direct route back for them, we have a good idea of where she is and where she will be. Even so…there is a margin for error of almost ninety thousand kilometres over the next nine minutes."

"Ninety thousand? That's a lot of space to search. Visibility out here is getting worse by the minute."

His eyebrows rose as the updated tracks completed and showed where the Bismarck's course was expected to intersect his own.

"Interesting…according to my tracks, that puts them less the fifteen minutes from Waypoint Beta and almost dead on our approach vector."

"That is correct."

"Do I have permission to utilise active tracking?"

"You…"

The audio transmission crackled, and then broke apart completely to leave little more than noise. Esmonde changed to the back-up channel and boosted the transmission output to its overload position and tried again, but still there was nothing but static. He exhaled slowly in frustration and then opened the squadron channel.

"It looks like we've entered jamming range."

"Confirmed," said Theta Two, "My reception range just dropped to less than a thousand kilometres."

"Then it looks like we're on our own. Check your weapon status, and close up."

One by one each of the other two sub-flight commanders reported in, confirming the status of each fighter and their weapons.

"Good. Now...it is paramount that we stay as..."

"Contact!" Lieutenant Wachowski said, "Capital ship in the blue clouds, range nine zero zero kilometres."

Esmonde's eyes flashed back to the view from his cockpit, but all he could make out were the wisps of colour. He looked down and used the long-range cameras for a better view. The fog of colour changed to a large grey shape pushing its way through the mist.

"Good eyes, Lieutenant. Bloody good eyes. Is that a confirmed sighting?"

"It's a ship. I can't confirm anything else."

"It might be one of our cruisers out here sniffing around. Send them our IFF codes, and let's see what we find."

* * *

Commonwealth Heavy Cruiser 'Norfolk'

One moment the ship's crew were busily working at the stations, and then next came the warning each of them dreaded. It wasn't the ship alert warning, or even a call-to-action stations, but something much worse.

"Torpedo detected!" Lieutenant Madeline yelled.

"You're kidding?" asked a nearby science officer, "I see nothing."

"It's coming in fast." Lieutenant Madeline looked into her

comrade's eyes. Then she looked back to her bank of displays and called out without looking away, "Impact in twelve seconds."

Captain Phillips shook his head angrily, not to his crew, but to the situation that forced him to risk all their lives. By reaching out further and further with their radar scans and tracking, they were essentially a bright beacon to the enemy. While Bismarck kept slipping away, they were announcing their presence to every soul in the region.

"Helm, evasive action. Do whatever you can to shake it off."

"Already on it, Captain," said Lieutenant Richards, "Hold on, this is going to get rough. Really rough."

"Tactical."

"Countermeasures active, Captain. Deploying smoke."

Multiple vents along the ship dumped the mixture of metal filament and a complicated concoction designed to obscure their position and signature, even for just a few seconds. The thrusters fired again, and Lieutenant Madeline gasped in discomfort. She could barely breathe as the opposing forces pushed and pulled her about.

"Guns!" said the Captain, "Put down fire."

"Not yet," said Lieutenant Madeline, "Letting them get a solid tone first."

She tapped the controls, simultaneously grunting as the thrusters fired again in sequence, rolling the ship about while also using a combination of the main drive and the retro engines to move them off course by almost fifteen degrees.

"They've got a lock, heading for our stern. Defence turrets going live with a focussed stream."

Alarms sounded, followed seconds later by the clatter and rattle of gunfire that could be felt through the innards of the ship of numerous point-defence turrets activating. The officers watched impotently as the ship defended itself without their input. The small turrets moved, tracked, and fired far quicker than any human could. And thanks to Lieutenant Madeline's careful timing, they were granted a relatively easy plot to follow.

"There it is," she said happily.

She tapped the tracking point and watched open-mouthed as the warhead came right for the rear of the ship, exposing itself to numerous turrets. It was moving fast and made it to within fifty kilometres when the guns managed to hit it. A trail of sparks marked the impact point, and then a full two seconds later it exploded in a bright white fireball. Those watching cheered, though it was much more muted than might be expected.

"Good work everybody," said the Captain.

"Sir…I've got something else. Sixteen more targets, moving fast and ranging far ahead of us."

"More torpedoes? Or ships?"

"Too small to be warships."

Then she gulped, realising what was happening.

"Fighters! Ours. And they're moving in hot."

"Bloody hell!" Captain Phillips snapped, "They're tracking the wrong ship."

"They need to be warned," said Admiral Wake-Walker, "Else we might end up facing a wave of torpedoes ourselves. I think I speak for all of us when I say I'd rather that did not happen."

"It's okay," said Alethea excitedly, "It's Theta Flight, from Victorious. They've adjusted their course and continuing towards the target. They're moving in on Bismarck."

"Excellent. Tactical, increase the range of our scans and network our data with Theta Flight. What we see, they see."

"Yes, Captain."

Expanding rings flickered on the main displays as the complex array of scanners reached out to hunt for the enemy ship. And then without warning, the radar system picked up a shape at the extreme periphery of its range. Lieutenant Madeline would have leapt for joy, had she not been strapped into her gimbal-mounted seat.

"Yes. I've got them. It has to be Bismarck, and she's changed course again. She's moving away fast. We can't catch her."

Admiral Wake-Walker crossed his arms and nodded.

"That's okay. Keep on her tail and keep hitting her with the radar tracking. It's up to Theta Flight now. With luck, they may be able to slow her down."

* * *

Lieutenant-Commander Esmonde kept shaking his head as he checked his scanners, and then to the new plots passed on from Norfolk. The dotted lines showed the previous plotted course and then fresh markers their new waypoints.

"Understood. We're adjusting our course now. Thanks for the update."

So...she skip-jumped at least twice. They're taking risks.

Something glinted in the corner of his eye, and as he looked across, he could make out the clouds of blue and purple with interest as his squadron of fighter-bombers continued forward. The Swordfish were a curious design, and he found his eye drawn to them as their wingtip thrusters left long white trails through the dust clouds. It was like watching a formation flying demonstration back home, except this time there was no audience. The mission wasn't to entertain, but to hunt down a great steel beast.

"All flights, report in."

Each of the other three groups did as asked, and a quick check on the status display showed they were all where they should be, though he could also see that they were reaching the limits of their external tanks. Each had been fully charged before launch and more than doubled their endurance in space.

"Theta Nine, I'm seeing ordnance warnings on your rack. What's the problem?"

"Unknown, Theta Leader. Diagnostics show potential locking failure on the torpedo. I'm still trying to route repair nodes to the brackets."

"Understood. Keep me appraised."

"Sir."

The more he thought about it, the more the problematic warhead concerned him. In theory, it meant they might be one torpedo down, but the worst case could be a premature detonation at the worst possible moment.

"Theta Nine. Change position and let your flight leader perform a visual. Let's leave nothing to chance."

The fighters began a slow sequence of rotations followed shifts on a flat plane to change their position in the flight, while continuing forward on their present course.

"The latest data puts the enemy directly in our path. It looks like she'd been skip-jumping."

Lieutenant Wachowski gave a low murmur over the channel.

"That's a risky move, Sir. Especially out here. You have no idea where you'll arrive."

"Exactly. But if she keeps doing it, she has a chance to escape to safety. So keep your eyes peeled. According to the new data, she could be out here right now."

"Active scanners?" Lieutenant Lipton asked.

"Negative, Theta Three. We stay silent until we can confirm that…"

At that exact moment Lieutenant-Commander Esmonde spotted something in the clouds ahead. His eyes narrowed as he looked to the telltale wake markers where a ship had passed through just minutes earlier.

Finally. This is more like it.

Data continued to arrive from Norfolk, though on narrow band only. It was sporadic due to the tight line of sight required, but at least it could not be easily jammed. It only showed where the ship had been eleven minutes ago, rather than where it was, or perhaps more importantly, where it would be. He checked it, and then looked to the wake markers.

This has to be her.

"Sir…I've definitely got something ahead," said Theta Two.

"Passive scanners only. We don't want to let them know we're coming. Narrowband back to Norfolk. I think this is it…Get your birds ready. This will happen faster than you can possibly imagine."

One by one each of the other pilots released the safeties on their weapons and activated the primers. Then without warning, a series of explosions ripped through the formation. For a second Esmonde thought Theta Nine had experienced a catastrophic failure, but then he spotted the white lines marking their path from the clouds towards them. The fighter to his right commanded by Lieutenant Edward Howard-Carter wagged its wings; the old-fashioned way of confirming an enemy had been spotted.

Bloody hell. We're down a bird already!

"Target spotted and tagged," said Theta Four, piloted by Lieutenant Harry Middleton, "It's her. I'm sure of it."

Esmonde looked into the clouds but could only make out part of the ship's spectral form. With each shot fired, he could make out more and more of its superstructure. The ship must have loosed off hundreds of shots as its stern appeared, and then half of the ship materialized from the fog.

"Good God," said Theta Four, "That thing is monstrous."

"There she is!" Esmonde muttered, "Bismarck is trying to escape."

He knew this was it and immediately activated the squadron-wide channel. The direct line of sight communications channel was designed so that each fighter then cross-linked to any nearby craft, thus creating an ad hoc network even if some of the fighters could not track a direct line of sight to Theta Leader. As long as each member of the squadron could track another in the formation, the network remained active and live. Before he could speak, a fighter directly above him split on half, and a moment later the fuselage exploded, scattering wreckage throughout the flight.

"No!"

Esmonde glanced down and winced as the status indicator

for the fighter turned red, marking is destruction in the battle. Two other fighters showed similar markers, though the amber colour indicated damage rather than destruction, confirmation that they'd been damaged in the blast. It was enough to call off the mission, but he was too close, and he knew the gravity of the situation. The Vrokan battleship might have been hurt, but she was still making significant speed away from the ships heading for her.

"Bismarck sighted. You know the drill. Break formation and attack. Withdraw to the rally waypoint after launching your torps. Good hunting!"

The fighters pulled away with three remaining with him, and he focussed on his target.

"Stay in formation. We're moving topside."

The fighters circled away as best they could and then once correctly aligned activated their boosters. The fighters accelerated away at ever greater speed, with streaks of light chasing them as they moved like missiles to the target.

"Ninety kilometres away and closing," he said over the intercom, "Remember to slip, and do what you can to avoid incoming fire. Get in quick and get out even quicker! We'll be there in seconds."

The fighter to his left flank jinked rapidly towards him and came so close he was almost forced to change his own position. But at the last moment, its thrusters activated, and the fighter settled back onto the correct path.

"Okay, open up the formation, it's time to split. It's getting tight in here."

The four fighters split apart like a flower opening, all while continuing to increase speed forward. Each moved away onto what looked like four completely different approach vectors.

"I'm taking fire!" Theta Three said, "It's too…"

The fighter lost a wing tip, and the other winglets forced it into a spin as they continued to fire.

"Use the computer stabilisation," said Theta Four, "It can fix it."

Esmonde wanted to say something, but the enemy battleship was now in almost full view on the computer displays, with the clouds of colour just behind it. It was the best view yet, and the thing looked even more monstrous than he'd expected. He looked up to the cockpit view and was surprised how small it was at this distance. Her secondary turrets were already firing as heavy guns struggled to pluck out of the darkness, but from here all he could see was a constant flicker.

"Forty kilometres."

Esmonde gripped the controls and did his best to block out the others from his mind as he concentrated on the target. A quick look to the tracking data showed they were well within launch range, but he knew they needed to wait. The range dropped to thirty kilometres, and now the defensive fire became a torrent. One burst cut over his fighter, and he felt the impact as solid slugs punched through the thin hull.

"I'm hit," he muttered.

A quick glance to the right confirmed two penetrations to the upper starboard wing. Then another shot struck the hull, but there were no warnings, just a slight rattle from behind.

"Their shots are going right through us!"

He double-checked the range and gasped at seeing they were now within fifteen kilometres.

"Hold your course. Jink for all your worth, and fire on my

mark."

The defensive fire transformed as the lighter turrets opened fire. Streaks of lights and long lines of white dots reached out towards them. Flashes from the left showed the third flight moving in. Esmonde could see the four Swordfish as they pushed on through the hellish firestorm and nearly cried out, as two were cut apart.

"I'm hit again!" Theta Three said, "Cockpit penetration…"

Her voice became muffled, and then she cried out.

"I'm bleeding. My suit is…"

She never said another word as fire converged from a dozen turrets on her fighter. The Swordfish ripped apart, leaving the rest to move on without her. The incoming flak was now so great it was almost impossible to make out the superstructure or the gun mounts that covered the warship. Esmonde pulled on his controls and slid his fighter upwards and slightly above his intended line of attack. He spotted two more fighters explode, and still none of their warheads had been unleashed.

"Ten thousand metres," said Theta Four.

"That's it," said Esmonde, "Fire at will!"

Each of them activated their weapons, and one by one unleashed their heavyweight 533mm Mk XII torpedoes. Streaks of light extended from their rear-mounted pump turbine thrusters. In just two seconds they were well away and a short distance from the warship.

"Break formation and regroup!"

Esmonde pulled on his controls and boost his winglet thrusters. The craft rotated away, but it took significant thrust from the main engine to have any discernible effect on his course. The battleship was visible immediately from below, and so that he could get a better view, he rolled the fighter into an inverted position. He looked upwards and towards the top of the Bismarck as his fighter screamed overhead. Gunfire reached out in all directions, with lances of light punching towards the fighters. At the same time, the short trails from the torpedoes marked their approach as they zigzagged their way ahead. Less than a dozen had been fired, and he almost cried out as one by one they were knocked out. Just four more remained, with the first one detonating in a blue flash.

"Come on! Get through!"

The defenders' fire became erratic and wild as they struggled against the weaving torpedoes.

Those turrets are being manually controlled. Either they lack automated defences, or they've been forced to take over.

That last part put a smile on his face, just as one managed to make it through. It slammed into the starboard side of the upper armour, just behind one of the massive gun batteries. The torpedo vanished in a fireball that extended out into space as its warhead detonated inside the ship's plating.

"That's a hit!" Theta Four shouted, "Right on the armour belt."

Two more crashed into the battleship, one into a secondary turret and another that hit the superstructure towards the aft of the ship.

"Beautiful," said Esmonde, "Absolutely beautiful."

His fighter continued to circle away even as it came under further turret fire. He was forced to jink multiple times with some of the shots still managing to pierce his fighter's thin armour. As he pulled away, he glanced down at the status display and almost choked.

"Seven down," he said sadly.

With a short movement of one hand, he ejected a tracking buoy and rolled to the left to avoid more fire. The other fighters coalesced back together, though staying a reasonable distance apart to avoid making an easy target for the enemy. They were already twenty kilometres away from the battleship, and with the distance increasing by the second.

"Lieutenant-Commander!" Theta Two yelled, "I'm detecting a massive internal overload inside the ship. Maybe we hit something."

"The Bismarck?"

"Yes, Sir."

He tapped his left display and brought up the schematic of the mighty ship, as well as the locations where they'd scored hits.

"No…that's no damage overload; that's coming from their core. They must be preparing to skip-jump again."

He checked the display again and almost cried out in disappointment.

"Has anybody got any torpedoes left? One hit just as she jumps could detonate her jump drive. If we're lucky, it could tear her jump drive apart, maybe even the ship."

"Just me," said Theta Nine as the fighter came right through the formation and blasted its way towards the battleship. The others scattered as it moved in the opposite direction, leaving a blue streak of colour in its wake.

"Negative, Theta Nine. Your systems have failed. It's time to withdraw."

"Negative. I'm not letting her escape."

The pilots kept on accelerating away from the battleship, all while watching the single heroic pilot racing towards the Bismarck. Most of the guns had stopped firing, save for the smaller calibre weapons that were being manually controlled. Fire started towards the bow of the ship, and then scores of turrets poured fire into the lone Swordfish. Projectiles hit her, sending pieces of metal off into space, and then it crashed into the ship's hull.

"Good God," said Esmonde as light pulsed from behind the ship. At first, it looked like the ship had exploded, but them it surged forward into the nebula, leaving the broken metal and debris of the battle behind, including what remained of the destroyed fighters.

Lieutenant-Commander Esmonde shook his head bitterly as he changed course and circled back, with the surviving seven fighters staying in formation with him.

"Did we get Bismarck?" asked one of the pilots.

"Negative," said Esmonde, "We hurt her, but not enough to stop her from escaping."

We failed.

STAR DREADNOUGHT BISMARCK

CHAPTER TEN

As the rising economic power of its time, why did the United Colonies of Titania stay away from the fighting? Some argued it was a war not of their making or choosing, and that to involve them would be to invite catastrophe. As evidence of the Vrokan brutality and lust for power grew, so did the demand for intervention. It started with neutral convoys of ships providing humanitarian aid and supplies. But would there ever come a time when the Union would unsheathe its swords, and join battle alongside its old allies?
History of the Void Wars

Commonwealth Fleet Carrier 'Victorious', Deep Space

Lieutenant-Commander Esmonde stepped out of his cockpit and worked his way down to the deck. He was only halfway down when he noticed the scars and lacerations along the flank of his fighter. The wings had suffered significant damage, but the holes punched through the fuselage caused him to raise an eyebrow.

"It looks like they turned your ship into Swiss cheese," said the deck chief while waving to his crew. Some were detaching parts from the fighters, while a small group surrounded one of the craft with fire suppressors as smoke drifted from its power core.

"Thanks," said Esmonde as he moved to the bottom of the ladder, "Luckily, they missed anything important."

"Including you," chuckled the Chief.

On any other day that would have drawn a smile from Esmonde, but not today. As his feet hit the deck, he felt a pang of pain through his heels and up through his ankles. It was nothing more than plantar fasciitis, but it hit him at just the wrong time. It was a condition he'd avoided for the last few years, except on a rapid change from zero-gravity to the gravitational change once aboard a ship. There waiting for him were five of the remaining seven pilots of Theta Flight. Two were on floating gurneys and being taken off to the nearest attached medical bay. There were also several deck officers, including the ship's CAG, Major Matilda Sykes. The Chief waited next to her as she ran off a list on her tablet. He saluted and then turned away, but not before giving Esmonde one final nod.

"Good to have you back, Sir."

Major Sykes reached forward to help him as he winced for the first few steps.

"Lieutenant-Commander," she said in a grim tone, "Injured?"

"Just the old foot pains, give it a few seconds." He rolled his right foot back and forth on the deck, and then sighed, "Better."

He then saluted the Major and slowly shook his head.

"Have you reviewed our gun cams? Tell me we hit something more important than plate?"

The Major nodded, and right away he knew the news wasn't good.

"She got away, though you put some excellent hits on her before she could flee. Our spotters confirm two deep armour penetrations and a turret detonation. They may have fled, but they're hurting."

"A turret? We hit that ship with everything we had, and we did what, killed a turret?"

"I know you've been through the wringer, Lieutenant-Commander. But the Admiralty isn't going to let this rest. We're moving back into a pursuit course in case she doubles back. Ark Royal is coming up along with half the assets in this region."

She then tried to smile, or at least give him a comforting glance. Something to try and soften the blow Theta Flight had suffered.

"Delta Squadron is taking over for the next twelve hours. I suggest we get your debriefing out of the way now, and then your people get some rest. We have spare birds in storage, and some crews who're itching to get you some payback."

"Can't the debriefing wait?"

"I'm sorry, Lieutenant-Commander. It has to be done, and fast. I've got another assignment for you."

"Against the Bismarck? I can't do much good stuck behind her."

"Oh...unless she turns back there's not a lot we can do now. But Admiral Tovey aboard King George V wants your full tactical analysis within the hour."

"Why? I can't tell him anything that will help his warships."

"Maybe...maybe not, but right now all we know is that Prince of Wales holed her bow, and you punched through her armour and knocked out a turret. We need to build a picture of what it is exactly we're facing."

One of the gurneys moved past and both stopped, watching as the wounded pilot moved away. The young man had dressings along his thigh, shoulder, and neck. His face was covered with a mask, but he still managed a messy salute as he was taken away.

"I'll tell you what we're facing," said Esmonde, "A battleship that is too fast to catch, has guns that blasted Hood of out space, and armour enough to save it from at least four direct torpedo strikes. If you ask me, this is best left to a port assault. Send in the carriers and swamp their base with bombers."

"Then you know what you have to say to him."

"How long do I have?"

She looked to her wristwatch; an antique mechanical device rarely seen in the Navy anymore.

"Fifty-seven minutes…and trust me, Admiral Tovey doesn't like to be made to wait."

"Well, Theta Flight doesn't like getting butchered either."

"Lieutenant-Commander, Eugene. We're all disheartened by each and every loss. But don't forget the Mighty Hood, nearly three thousand dead, and the flagship of the fleet gone. The Admiralty, nay, the entire Commonwealth feels broken. We need this win. If we don't, this war may already be over."

* * *

Commonwealth Heavy Cruiser 'Norfolk'
Kamineso Nebula

Lieutenant Alethea Madeline pulled the straps around her to

hold her against the bunk plate, grunting as they pinned her in place. There was still relatively heavy artificial gravity aboard the ship, a consequence of their unending pursuit of the enemy battleship. The straps were not to stop her from falling out of the bunk, but to keep her there as the various opposing forces changed during space travel. If the engines were cut, she might easily float about inside the ship, only to slam into exposed surfaces once the engines restarted.

"Madeline," said a man, as he slipped out of his bunk and reached for his clothes. He looked just as exhausted as she did, with a thin growth of fresh stubble at his cheeks.

"Jonesy. You going back on duty?"

"Yeah. And I didn't sleep for more than ten minutes. It's impossible."

Alethea nodded in agreement.

"It's not easy."

And with that, he was gone. Alethea rubbed her forehead and pulled the cover over her half naked body. Once hidden from the rest of the crew, she allowed her eyes to close. It was a strange feeling being there, knowing too well that more than half of the crew were at their stations while the rest tried to sleep. She'd been on duty for so long it had become hard to concentrate, but now that she was in bed her mind was racing.

Calm down. Forget about the Bismarck...and get some rest.

She moved her hand down to her side and thought back to home, and to the city. She imagined the trams and the tall buildings. But just as she began to slow her breathing, she was greeted with the great bulk of Bismarck once again. In her mind she saw the ship vanish, and then appear in a different location surrounded by fog.

Wait. What if she does it again?

This time she activated her comms and pulled back the cover. There were two other crew in the quarters, both of whom were settling into their bunks.

"Captain."

"What is it, Lieutenant? Aren't you off duty?"

"Yes, Sir. But there's something about Bismarck, something I don't like."

"Go on."

"Her course. Her helmsman steers in a pattern. Each time he's performed a double partial rotation, he's skip-jumped."

"Yes, we know. It's how he's staying ahead of us."

"But, Sir...On the third, he changes course."

"You think he'll try it again."

"I do, Sir. I think he may already have."

"Interesting. They're close enough to home now that a course change could take them to more than three ports. We can't cover them all." He hesitated, and then continued, "Then we may be racing away from her, instead of towards her."

"It's a possibility, Sir."

"Well...there's nothing we can do about it right now. I'll pass that on to the Admirals. Maybe they can make use of it. Now...get that rest. You deserve it. If we find her, you'll have your chance to take another shot."

"Yes, Captain."

The channel cut, and Alethea remained there, utterly still. But now, instead of thinking of home, her mind ran wild with the thought of the enemy battleship as it slipped away into the fog of the nebula and raced home. The last thing she wanted was for it to escape, and for the Hood, and those killed about

Norfolk, to remain unavenged.

We have to find her. No matter what, we have to.

* * *

Commonwealth Battleship 'King George V'
1 hour later

Vice Admiral Tovey remained alone in the war room, looking to the three-dimensional model of Hood. The beautiful vessel slowly rotated so that he could see it from every angle. Red markers showed impact points, overlayed with videostream stills from the actual battle.

Hood…how did they do this to you?

He stepped closer, moved his hand through the model, and then pulled it apart to see inside. One marker was not far from a series of bulkheads, each fitted with heavy doors. A shaft ran from one of the main turret batteries and down to the armoured magazine.

Did a fluke round punch through to the ammunition store?

He spun the model about, and then let time track forward to the detonation. One frame showed a fire burning near the rear turrets, and the next frame was nothing but white light.

"Admiral," said a voice to his right.

Tovey turned and nodded towards the rotating display showing the face of an officer.

"Wake-Walker. You look like a man that could do with some rest."

"You're not wrong, old friend. It's been a long few days."

More images appeared, with Captain Leach of the Prince of Wales, Captain Ellis of the Suffolk, as well as Vice Admiral

James Somerville of Renown, who led the ships of Force H from The Rock.

"Gentlemen," said Admiral Tovey, "Our hunt for the Bismarck is stretching our resources thin and fuel is running low. Bismarck has taken us on a merry-go-round. Prince of Wales is already falling back due to heavy battle damage."

The floating image of the Hood vanished and instead showed the tracked course of the enemy battleship, as well as the numerous ships moving on its position.

"Victorious and Repulse arrived with only a partial fuel load. They will have to do the same over the next few hours. And in any case, they're too far away now to do much more."

"Can we not re-task tankers to the periphery of the nebula?" Admiral Wake-Walker asked, "It would buy us a few more hours out here."

"It's much too dangerous. Vrokan Jaeger ships are already taking advantage of our position. Each vessel we pull from convoy escort duty is one less ship to protect our transports. Since this hunt began, I've seen another fifteen transports lost with all hands. We cannot risk sending fuel transports out this far unprotected."

He continued to shake his head.

"You will escort Prince of Wales home, rearm, refuel, and get back into action as quickly as you can."

Captain Ellis spoke up, causing the Admiral to shake his head.

"I'm sorry, but it's the same for us, Admiral. Our scouting operation during the hunt has stretched our fuel expenditure beyond anything we could have anticipated. Suffolk is already running on reserves. We've another three hours loitering time left and then we will have to withdraw."

"Yes," said Admiral Tovey, "I suspected as much. That's why I've brought in fresh warships moving in from three directions."

He waved his hand, and the mapping data flashed to show the positions of the new ships.

"I'm still in pursuit, and right behind Bismarck's expected position, with Rodney moving in as fast as her old engines can take her."

Admiral Tovey's wrist-mounted communicator device blinked, and he raised it to see the message alert.

"Yes?"

"Admiral," said the communications officer, "Apologies for disturbing you, but we've just received a priority message from a Catalina scout ship."

"Go on."

"Admiral, the Bismarck has been spotted. She skip-jumped immediately, but we've a good idea where she's heading based on her jump."

"Where?"

"Brest Star Fortress, in the occupied territories."

"I knew it." The Admiral clenched his right fist, "If we get too close, we'll be swamped with fighters and bombers. Show me her estimated position."

The map in front of the assembled officers shifted to show the area from their own ships, and to the border of Vrokan space. It showed three enemy ports, as well as a long curved line that marked the outer reaches of Vrokan fighters.

"No," exclaimed Admiral Tovey, "Bismarck must have doubled back and changed course. Their commander is crafty.

He turned away from home, moved behind us, and then changed course. There's a good chance he'll get away."

"There's more," said the officer, "The reconnaissance craft identified significant fuel leakage from the Bismarck as she jumped. The jump failed almost immediately and triggered a series of additional blasts in her hull. Wherever she goes, so does the trail."

"So she's unable to skip-jump?"

"That's what the report says, Admiral."

"Thank you, Lieutenant."

The image vanished, and he then looked back to the tele presence devices.

"Good news," said Admiral Wake-Walker, "Perhaps our first break in this hunt. Norfolk is ready to continue the pursuit."

Admiral Tovey rubbed his chin, and then looked across to Vice Admiral Somerville. He looked confident, albeit just as concerned as he'd been before the news had arrived.

"This manoeuvre has thrown us off the scent. We can give chase, but we're a matter of hours behind Bismarck."

He reached forward and tapped the small group of three ships that were moving in from the direction of The Rock. As he tapped it, the imagery enlarged to show the carrier, battlecruiser, and light cruiser.

"No heavies anywhere in range, just you, Admiral Somerville. Force H is going to have to go above and beyond today."

"We're ready," said the commander of the Ark Royal.

"Good. It's all on you and Force H. You need to turn her back or slow her down…or this is over."

Admiral Somerville inhaled and looked away as he spoke

to somebody off camera. It took a moment, but when he looked back, Admiral Tovey could see the strain on the man's face.

"Can it be done?"

"We're moving in fast, but deceleration into combat range will not get us close enough." He thought on that, and then shook his head, "No…there's another way. If we overcharge our engines, we will get one, maybe two chances to intercept with bombers. There won't be time to decelerate in time to come back for a third as we coast on past her.

"Then that is how it must be."

"I will launch my bombers as soon as we're in range."

"Excellent. Are you able to maintain contact with Victorious?"

"For now, yes."

"Good. Then speak with Lieutenant-Commander Eugene Esmonde and get everything you can from him."

"I've seen his after action. My CAG has a lot of questions."

"Then I will leave you to it. Good luck, gentlemen. To the hunt."

One by one the displays cut off until he was left alone in the war room, and with the map still showing their dispositions. A third of his force was on its way home, but he had more than enough capital ships in the area. He leaned in closer and placed a finger on the estimated path taken by the enemy.

"There you are. We have you…but can we catch you?"

* * *

Commonwealth Fleet Carrier 'Ark Royal, Force H

Lieutenant-Commander James Stewart-Moore waited inside the cold briefing room, as the other commanders of Ark Royal's five embarked squadrons looked at their target. There in front of them was the same model so recently examined by the ship captains of the taskforce assembled to hunt down the enemy battleship. Stewart-Moore walked in front of the massive model of the ship and watched with interest as the tracking markers of the attack were played back.

"That was a messy strike," said Lieutenant-Commander Coode, leader of 818 Squadron. They put out nine Swordfish in three flights and managed to only hit a turret with gunfire and her belt armour with a single torpedo. That's not going to stop a battleship."

"They took almost fifty percent casualties in that attack. I don't quite see what they could do differently."

"If this is going to work, we need to land better hits," said Coode, "I'd suggest getting closer, to within three thousand metres, and launching the torpedoes at point-blank range. Anything more, and her guns are just going to shred everything."

"I agree," said a voice from further back.

Both men looked to Lieutenant-Commander Mervyn Johnstone, commander of 810 Squadron. The man stepped forward and pointed to the ship.

"We need to saturate that ship's defences to have any chance."

"Anybody else?" Stewart-Moore asked.

"How far away is the target?"

"Just out of radar range. Sub Lieutenant Hartley is leading scouts to find her, but this nebula is becoming more treacherous by the hour. Visibility is dropping, and we're running into some heavy electrical storms."

"The fighter defences. Are they as tough as they look?" Johnstone asked.

"I have Lieutenant-Commander Esmonde on narrowband from Victorious, perhaps we should ask him."

All attention moved to the flashing markers on the slowly rotating model of the enemy ship. A ghostly shape appeared alongside the model as Esmonde showed what had happened in the battle. He moved his hand, and dotted lines showed the approach angles from each torpedo; most then vanishing well before they made contact with the ship.

"As you can see…we scored good hits on the Bismarck's armour, and we paid the price for it."

"Tell us more about the ship's defences," Johnstone asked.

"The ship's defences are substantial. Her primary weapons played no part in the fighting, but her secondary batteries are powerful and accurate. We were able to evade the worst with heavy manoeuvring, but that threw us off for the final attack. That's where the last line of defence comes in."

Instead of dozens, nearly a hundred small flashes of light lit up the model.

"She's equipped with a vast and powerful defence array, but it had trouble tracking us at close-range."

"How so?"

"Halfway through the fight, it became obvious they'd switched to manual gunnery. Either they sustained damage to their automated gunnery control, or more likely they were not prepared to engage small bombers. The fire was heavy, but survivable for a short time."

Stewart-Moore walked towards the flank of the massive ship and pointed to the large superstructure that bristled with smaller turrets. He remained there for a moment as he looked to the angles of approach and the lines of fire from the ship's batteries out into space.

"Best I can tell, her only weakness is from behind."

"I agree," said Esmonde, "Though there are four secondary batteries fitted at the stern to cover the approaches."

"Thank you," said Stewart-Moore, "Your attack did more than damage the beast. You brought back data that we critically need to strike back."

"That's something. Now…"

The image crackled, and then froze. A moment later it vanished, leaving the briefing room in silence.

"What happened?" Johnstone asked.

"Victorious must be out of range now," said Stewart-Moore, "It's all on us now…so let's plan this to perfection. Nothing can be left to chance with this one. Each and every one of us needs a good, clean launch at the battleship."

The others moved around the model, each giving various parts of the ship significant attention. Stewart-Moore spotted movement, looked to his wrist, and then smiled.

"They've done it. I can't believe it."

"Done what?"

"Hartley's scouts have found the trails, and they're moving in to confirm. Get to the hangars and make your final checks. We're going into action."

"Yes!" Johnstone said, "It's payback time."

STAR DREADNOUGHT BISMARCK

STAR DREADNOUGHT BISMARCK

CHAPTER ELEVEN

Jaeger ships were some of the most celebrated and reviled ships to have ever been constructed. Rather than engage in honourable warfare with fleets of ships massed against each other, the Jaegers would use their stealth and heavy torpedoes weaponry to appear from nowhere, strike without waiting and then slip away into the void. The Jaeger ships had the chance to bring the Commonwealth to its knees, not by berating its fleet or invading its worlds, but simply by capturing or destroying its merchant ships, the very lifeblood the Commonwealth's worlds depended on. It was economic warfare at its most ruthless.

Masimov's Guide to Fighting Ships

Lieutenant-Commander Stewart-Moore grunted as his Swordfish fighter-bomber burst free from the launch bay built into the flank of the ship. As his craft moved, he could see the others doing the same as they accelerated away from the rapidly moving carrier. As he cleared the ship, he looked down and checked on the status of each craft. There were fourteen Swordfish in total, each armed with the brand-new heavyweight 533mm Mk XIII torpedoes, an upgraded version of the weapons carried by Victorious' Swordfish.

"Form up into flights and follow me in," he said calmly.

"All looking good back here," said Flight Sergeant Mathews as he rotated his turret to check on the other fighters, "We've got a ship to kill."

The fourteen fighter-bombers arced away, vanishing into the coloured clouds. Stewart-Moore looked over his shoulder and watched the carrier and the nearby battlecruiser slowly disappear behind them as they chased after the fighters, while staying a wary distance away from the possible course of the enemy warship. Neither could stand up to its armour and firepower until help arrived. One moment he felt as though the entire Commonwealth fleet was at his back, and then with the ships gone, it was just them in their Stringbags scurrying through the fog towards their target. As he looked back, he spotted a flash of yellow light and then an arc of lightning reached out in front of his fighter-bomber and exploded.

"Bloody hell!"

The light vanished as quickly as it had arrived, and in its places the distant flashes of light as more of the tendrils of energy struck out randomly. Even stranger the flashes of light interacted with the parts of the nebula to create great strobe light effects. Some of the clouds even shifted in hue and colour, creating outlandish patterns before slowly fading back to their original.

"Everybody in one piece?"

He looked to his status screen and breathed a sigh of relief that all the other Swordfish appeared undamaged. And as he did so, he realized they were moving too quickly from their expected course.

"Switching to active tracking. We need a course update, and fast."

It took time as the spacecraft sent out an ever-growing pulse directly ahead to penetrate the fog of the nebula. Seconds passed on by, with little more than noise. And then to his relief, he spotted a shape in the upper left quadrant.

"I've got something. There's nobody else out here but our target. Close up, and follow me in."

The fighter-bombers lifted their noses and made subtle course corrections as they headed towards the tracked target. They were painted in dull grey, with some of the detailing picked out in white. Their winglet thrusters drew long curved lines behind them as they moved through the layers of colour and fog.

"Activate magnetic detonators."

"We're good to go," said Flight Sergeant Mathews from his tactical console, "Torpedoes are ready, and so are our guns."

As if to confirm the latter, he swivelled about in the stern-mounted spherical turret with its pair of light 40mm chain guns that could be moved about to cover almost every direction; save for directly ahead or where the view was blocked by wings or the fuselage.

"Good. Very good."

The other pilots responded as they checked with their own crews, and then waited in silence as they moved through the thick fog and to the still-hidden target. The detonators were upgraded components designed to ensure the warheads activated when in contact with metal armour of a warship, as opposed to the simpler contact detonators normally used. It apparently made them harder to trick with decoys launched by defending ships. Not all of them were from his squadron, but they were all experienced pilots, and used to training and flying together.

"Remember, when we get into position, we'll swarm the target. Overwhelm their defences. Understood?"

He checked again and noted they were just fifty kilometres from the target.

"Sir..." said Stewart-Moore's wingman, "They must have detected us by now. We might be small, but we're not that small!"

"Maybe, but let's not jinx it. Break into pairs and begin your attack runs."

The formation split apart, moving into two large groups. One moved in from above the ship, while the other came in from the port-side bow. Stewart-Moore looked ahead as he looked for the shadows to coalesce into something more tangible. The range continued to decrease until he was within five kilometres.

So close...and still no defensive fire. We've got them on the trot!

"This is it, chaps. Spread out your torpedoes. We want to make sure they can't escape this time. No matter where they turn, they'll be struck. No mercy."

The next two thousand metres felt like an age as he jinked back and forth in case defensive gunfire began, but still there was nothing. He squinted in a desperate attempt to make out much more than the bow and part of the forward guns pushing out through the coloured clouds. And at that moment the rangefinder blinked, confirming the range.

"Mathews...it's all in your hands."

"I know. We're almost there," he said as he concentrated on his targeting array, "Just a little more...Launching!"

The single large torpedo detached and boosted forward,

heading right for the vessel. The fighter-bomber shuddered as the heavy weapon separated from the spacecraft, and a long streak of light extended behind it as it moved ever faster. He then rolled and boosted the engines to move away. Streaks from the others marked the approach of the torpedoes as they accelerated towards the target. One hit near the bow, and another behind the forward turrets, but there were no explosions.

"What's going on?" he demanded, spinning his fighter back around. More and more torpedoes hit, while the second group prepared to fire.

"Good God!" said the flight commander as he ordered his pilots to cancel their attack run. They scattered before hitting the ship and pulled away.

"What's going on?" Stewart-Moore shouted again.

"Sir. That's not the Bismarck…That's one of ours."

Stewart-Moore could scarcely believe what he was hearing. He rolled the fighter back around and boosted his engines to move through the fog. The ship was there, but it was impossible to make out the configuration.

"Stay back," he said firmly, "I'm moving in closer."

He then activated his short-range wide band communications.

"This is Lieutenant-Commander Stewart-Moore from Ark Royal."

The curt answer came right back at him.

"This is Commonwealth Light Cruiser Sheffield. Might you explain why you're attacking us?"

"That's why they didn't shoot back at us," said Flight Sergeant Mathews, "That could have ended badly."

"My apologies," said Stewart-Moore, "Sorry for the Kipper."

"Understood. Get home safely…and next time check your fish. None of them detonated…Thankfully."

Stewart-Moore wagged his wings in acknowledgement and circled back to join the other fighters. His cheeks were flushed, and he struggled to not call out in a bizarre mixture of embarrassment and rage.

What the hell is going on? Why is she out here?

* * *

Commonwealth Heavy Cruiser 'Norfolk', Kamineso Nebula

It wasn't the alarms that woke Lieutenant Alethea Madeline, but the thunderous booming sound as something lashed the hull of the ship. She nearly fell from her bunk as the ship shuddered violently. She tried to move upright, but the shaking proved so intense she was forced to hold onto the harness straps for a full ten seconds.

"What's happening?"

"Hold on," shouted a voice off to her left, "Stay where you are."

And in an instant a myriad of possibilities entered her mind. Not one of them good.

Have we been breached? Are the Vrokan already aboard?

Alethea pulled back the cover and looked with her eyes opened wide as the other in the room were pulling on their protective exposure suits. She spun out her legs and dropped down to the deck. The metal was cool and made her wince as she reached for the storage bin housing her gear. By the time she'd pulled her gear half on the ship shuddered again.

"Action stations. All crew to your posts!" said the Captain over the speakers, "This is not a drill!"

"What the hell are we doing out here?" asked one of the engineering lieutenants. Alethea simply shook her head.

"There are entire regions of the Kamineso Nebula that are off limits to shipping."

"Well…Not anymore."

The man moved away, and Alethea watched him go as the internal lights dimmed slightly before returning to full power. She could feel a change in her weight, as though she'd been standing on an elevator platform that had suddenly begun to descend.

We're slowing down. I need to get to the combat centre.

She made her way through the ship, passing by multiple stations until finally reaching the secured doors to the command centre and bridge. As the door opened, another crewmember arrived.

"Richards?"

"Looks like none of us are getting any rest today."

She smiled as both were let inside. Immediately, she could see the place was a hive of activity as the new arrivals filled out some of the vacant secondary stations. One man was sitting in her place, and she stopped there, looking at the station awkwardly until finally Captain Phillips called out, "Lieutenant Madeline, take his place. Malley, you're relieved."

The man looked back to her, and she gasped at seeing a dressing along his cheek.

"What happened?"

"Electrical storm," he said angrily, "We ran into it at cruising speed and nearly sheared off the bow. We ran right into it."

The ship vibrated violently, and some of the gimbal mounts groaned under the pressure.

"Get to medbay. I've got this."

He unfastened his harness without hesitation, groaning as he moved from his position. Alethea took his place, pulled on the straps, and waited a moment as the security system checked her credentials before allowing her access to the ship's defensive and offensive arsenal.

"Sitrep, Lieutenant," said the Captain.

"Uh…All systems are online, Sir. Turrets partially retreated, and the status indicators are all green."

"Good, very good."

She looked to the left display and almost choked at seeing shapes appearing in the scanner.

"Uh…Captain. We have fresh targets, and they are moving just past us."

Before he could speak, she noticed the short-range IFF transponders activating.

"Sir. It's Rodney and King George V."

"Good. Damned good," said Admiral Wake-Walker, "I thought Tovey had got himself lost again."

"Well, it's about time," said Captain Phillips, "But I'm not liking the odds. Look at their trajectory."

The Admiral snarled as he looked to the dotted line marking the position of Bismarck and the pursuing ships.

"Tovey is just a few hours too late. Unless something changes, we're not going to get to her in time." He looked to

Captain Phillips, "We've got twenty-four hours to stop her, and not even Admiral Tovey can break the rules of physics and reach her in time."

"So what do we do?"

Admiral Wake-Walker looked at the positions of the various ships, and then pointed to the heavies that were pushing ahead.

"We stay right behind them, Captain. Push our engines as hard as you dare."

"We'll be right at their heels, I promise."

Lieutenant Richards was already looking to Captain Phillips, waiting for his orders.

"You heard the Admiral, Lieutenant. Follow the heavies as best you can."

"That will put a heavy strain on the hull, Captain."

"Can she take it?"

The Lieutenant smiled.

"Norfolk has it where it counts. She can handle it. I have no doubts."

"Good. Then you know what to do."

"Aye, Captain. Increasing forward velocity by a twenty percent."

It was a gentle, but perceivable change as the engines increased their output. A low-pitched whine increased in intensity, as the engines struggled to push the heavy cruiser through the fog of the nebula and its erratic electrical storms. The ship vibrated as something slammed into the port-side, causing some of the crew to look to their comrades.

"It's nothing but the waves of space lashing our bow," said Captain Phillips, "We're like cruisers of old forcing their way through heavy seas. Focus on your stations and be ready."

Admiral Wake-Walker crossed his hands in front of him and watched the small shapes moving slowly on his tactical screen.

"It's all in the hands of Ark Royal now."

* * *

Lieutenant-Commander Stewart-Moore opened his visor and wiped the sweat from his brow. It was difficult to focus, and the closer they moved to this part of Vrokan occupied territory the worse the nebula became. One moment he could see more than thousand kilometres directly ahead, and then a second later it would drop to a hundred.

"I've never seen such conditions before. This Nebula is vast."

His eyes moved to the port-side of the canopy and found his gaze drawn to a vast clearing. It gave him an obscure but partial view of the distant stars. Wisps of white moved past at speed, and then the stars vanished as quickly as they had arrived.

"Where is she?"

"IFF shows she's right in front of us," said Flight Sergeant Mathews, sitting right behind him in his ball turret, "I'm tracking the transponder, but can't get any more accurate. The electrical storm is messing with my sensors. I've never seen anything like this before."

He then snapped his head to the right and cried out, "Good God! Take evasive action!"

One Swordfish drifted much too close as lightning flashed nearby and struck its wingtip. Part of the fighter ripped apart, and the craft entered a slow roll. A second fighter moved in from below, and in just seconds the entire formation scattered apart like a shoal of fish ambushed by a large predatory shark.

"Bloody hell!" Stewart-Moore muttered, as he did his best to avoid the confused mass of fighter-bombers swarming all around him. At first, he slid to the right, but the nose of a Swordfish came into view.

"No. Just no."

With nowhere to move, all he could do was boost his engines to try and pull away. Streaks of light extended from his main engine, as well as from the secondary thrusters used to provide rapid direction change to keep the fighter-bomber manoeuvrable in battle.

"All bombers, watch your spacing. I said watch your spacing!"

Two of the Swordfish came so close their wingtips touched. One slid away from the impact, but the pilot of the second craft overreacted and jerked away, narrowly avoiding hitting another, and then vanished off into the clouds.

"Disperse formation. Use my transponder as a rally point."

It took nearly a minute for each of them to return, and as he counted them, he sighed in relief.

"They all made it."

We're almost…"

The flashing lights were the first indication that Ark Royal was ahead, followed by the massive hull and blinking markers on the outer landing deck. The ship looked like a city as it loomed ever larger, and the lights blinked brighter and brighter.

"Get your birds down, and fast!" Stewart-Moore said, "It

looks like the Ark is getting ready to launch more fighters."

He eased back on the power, and then waited as the first pair of Swordfish moved towards the landing deck. Much like aircraft carriers of the distant past, the landing deck was a long open space that made it that much safer for them to land, especially with the differences in velocity. A third Swordfish tried to match speed and slowly moved to the surface, only for arcs of light to crash around it, sending it spinning away with smoke trailing from its engine.

"Get down now!"

This time the fighter-bombers swept in with their landing skids extended out below as they made contact with the metal of the deck. Sparks spread around them as they bumped and jostled along the plating, the mag-locks struggling to hold them down. The first three made it down in one piece, but the fourth broke a skid as it struggled to line up and slid sideways before coming to a halt. The fifth banked to avoid a collision and tore off its left wing before settling down.

"I suggest we pull back and realign," said Flight Sergeant Mathews, "The storms are throwing us about."

"No. We need to get down, and fast."

He adjusted his controls, and then brought in his fighter-bomber low and fast. First, he moved over the secondary turrets, and then towards the landing deck itself. Off to one side was the rubble from one of the Swordfish. The wreckage slowly slid backwards, and he was forced to swerve to avoid being struck by the pieces of metal.

"Hold on. This might be a little rough."

Light crackled and flashed around them, and then without warning the skids hit the deck. Stewart-Moore felt a pain in his neck and back as the impact jarred his body so hard his vision blurred. The fighter-bomber lifted a metre from the metalwork and then settled down onto its skids with such force the skids crumped underneath.

"Reversing thrusters!"

The retro thrusters burned away to slow their advance, but still they continued forward. They moved over a hundred metres along the plates and then partially rotated to the left, and still the Swordfish refused to stop. Metre by metre they moved along the deck until finally slamming into the side of a turret mount fitted along the edge of the deck and spinning to the left. He looked back to the two crewmen sitting behind and groaning from the discomfort of the landing.

"Anybody hurt?"

"Hurt? Maybe a little shaken," said Flight Sergeant Mathews, "Any landing you can walk away from is a good one in my book. Look, our little friends are here."

Both watched as the wheeled machines moved along the surface of the ship. They were small, each little larger than a child, and moved on a series of small wheels. A pad extended out below the body to make contact with the deck to tether them and to stop the small machines from vanishing off into the void. Three of them moved around the damaged fighter-bomber and latched onto it like a group of tiny tugboats. The Swordfish groaned as it was turned about, and then began to move along the deck. They covered less than twenty metres when they stopped and began to sink inside the ship.

"I tell you, one day it will be them flying these birds, not us."

"God help us them," laughed Stewart-Moore as they were

enveloped in darkness, only to reappear attached to the hangar autoloaders and being moved into position, "The day the machines take over is the day we retire to a life of brandy and warm fireplaces. They're welcome to a mission like this one!"

That made his weapons officer chuckle with amusement. The fighter-bomber turned to the left and travelled a short distance to one of the waiting bays. Before they'd even stopped, Stewart-Moore could make out the shapes of the other Swordfish being moved ready for launch. The device clunked as they locked into position, followed shortly by the canopy releasing and allowing the ship's cool air to waft inside. Stewart-Moore didn't wait and swung out even as the pain in his back and shoulder tore through his body, leaving him grunting in pain. He looked off to the right, and to where one of the squadron commanders was giving a last-minute briefing as his Swordfish were moved out onto the main autoloader mounts. There were another six pilots, plus weapons officers, and all bearing the wings of 818 Squadron.

"Coode!"

The officer looked back and gave him a nod.

"Stewart-Moore! You crazy fool, you made it back in one piece."

He made his way from his damaged fighter, doing his best to disguise his slight limp and discomfort in his upper body.

"We thought you got lost out there. CAG said you went for the wrong ship. Bad show, old chap, not what…"

"Coode. Forget that, we were fed bad intel on the raid. But it might be the best thing that ever happened to us."

"What do you mean?"

"We struck Sheffield with at leave seven fish, and none

detonated. It must be the new magnetic detonators."

"I knew it," muttered Coode, "I bloody well told them they needed more testing before we switched over. Typical bureaucrats. Who sends out a carrier into action with untested weapons?"

"The same person that sent us out without warning us we had friendlies in the area."

Coode reached forward and placed a hand on Stewart-Moore's shoulder.

"I know it was rough out there, but it wasn't your fault."

"Yes, but the lads are still sore about it. We've lost our chance to hit back."

"No," said Coode as he whistled to the deck crew moving past.

"Get me the Chief. We're not launching till our torps are changed."

One of the men looked at him in surprise.

"Changed?"

"That wasn't a request. Get to it."

"Sir!"

Coode then looked back to Stewart-Moore and the rest of his pilots as they moved closer. There was tiredness and anger to them, the look that had seen their chances for glory and duty stolen before their eyes.

"You're right," he said as he looked to them, "This screw-up might have saved the entire mission. You could have gone in like Esmonde and his pilots from Victorious, lost half your people. And for what?"

He noticed a pilot muttering to himself and wondered if perhaps something much worse had happened. Perhaps one of the pilots had been killed without him knowing about it.

"What about your people, and your birds? All back home?"

"My crews are beaten up, and we've got some injuries. As for the Swordfish, none of them will be flying anytime today. The electrical storms out there are brutal, and visibility is all over the place. Half of my people came back with damaged fighters, and three of them wiped out on landing. It's grim out there, bloody grim."

"I tell you what. I could do with you assisting the CAG on the command deck. You've been out there, and you know what we can expect."

Before he could reply, more pilots from the other squadrons approached. He could see men and women from 810, 818, and 820 Squadron rushing to their stations. All were dressed in their environmental suits and their helmets under their arms. Stewart-Moore reached forward and grasped Coode's forearm.

"I'll be there watching you all the way."

Coode smiled.

"That's all I can ask. Wish us luck."

"You don't need luck. Just put a hole in that bastard ship big enough to park a frigate."

"We'll do our best."

The two men saluted each other, followed by the other crewmembers from the various squadrons. They then moved away, with Coode taking the lead.

"It's too late for us to get back out there," said Stewart-Moore, shaking his head. His weapons officer was right there and nearly snarling in irritation.

"We lost our chance alright," he said in frustration.

"Yes. Now it's down to Coode and his lads."

He rubbed his chin and then nodded to himself.

"We'll debrief in ten minutes. Grab fluids and get there. After that, I'm needed on the command deck."

The crew of the attack squadrons separated, leading him standing alone and looking at his mangled fighter. He'd managed to bring it back home relatively undamaged, but as he looked more carefully, he could see how it had been burned and shattered both in the storms and during his rough landing.

"And they have more to face than just the elements. They're going up against Bismarck, and this time they'll be ready. God help them out there. They'll need it."

STAR DREADNOUGHT BISMARCK

CHAPTER TWELVE

The torpedo as a weapon of naval warfare faded in and out of use for more than two centuries. Though devastatingly powerful, there were numerous countermeasures capable of stopping or reducing their power on the battlefield. What started as a weapon for use by capital ships to be used against each other soon found itself in the hands of Jaeger ship captains, and even slung under the pylons of fighter-bombers launched from starcarriers. In time, they would become larger, faster, and harder to stop. All while countermeasures become more complex in the unending war against them.
Naval Weapons and Tactics, 5th Edition

Lieutenant-Commander Trevenen Penrose Coode whistled, and then waited as the other flight leaders approached. He placed one hand on the ladder attached to the autoloader gantry leading up to his waiting fighter. Underneath were two technicians making adjustments to the ordnance hanging under the Swordfish's hull.

"Godfrey-Faussett, Keane, Hunter, Owensmith, and Willcocks. For the love of God tell me your lads are ready?"

Lieutenant Godfrey-Faussett nodded slowly as he came to a halt. He was a rakishly thin man, with a smart moustache in the style so favoured by the fighter-bomber pilots of the Commonwealth Navy.

"I've managed to scrape together three birds. 2nd Flight should have been four, but the engines are still waiting to be swapped out."

Coode turned his attention to Lieutenant Keane.

"Tell me you've got me a few more pilots?"

"3rd Flight is looking a little ragged. Just me and Jewell."

Lieutenant Hunter rubbed his hands together as he nodded to the bulkhead doors leading to the next hangar and the remainder of the fighter-bombers being prepped for battle.

"Three for me, Skip."

"And two more for 5th Flight," said Lieutenant Owensmith.

That left just 6th Flight, and as Coode looked to Sub Lieutenant Willcocks, the man lifted his hand and showed two fingers. Coode tried to look confident, but as the numbers came in, he realised he was short by a good margin.

"So, fifteen all up, that's the entire muster from 818, 810, and 820 Squadrons?"

"Aye," said Hunter, "Or give it an hour, and with the repaired fighters, and what's left of Stewart-Moore's lads, we can get that up to twenty, maybe a little higher."

"There's no time. We launch in the next ten minutes, or we might as well not bother. She'll skip-jump so far ahead we'll never catch her. It will just have to be us. Very well."

He put one foot on the ladder, climbed up two steps, and looked back to them.

"We'll take no chances this time. Once we've launched, we will rally near Somerville's flagship. From there, onto

Sheffield. She's already tracking Bismarck as best she can. We will use the nebula and the electrical storms for cover, and to get as close to her as we can."

"Isn't using the clouds a little risky?" Owensmith asked.

"Yes…But it's that, or a ten-minute advance right at her guns in the open."

"Fair enough," laughed Owensmith, "Maybe not this time."

"Then this is it. To your birds. Next time we see each other, it will be after the attack."

They each pushed their hands forward and took turns shaking hands.

"Good luck, gentlemen," said Coode, "The Commonwealth is depending on us. Let's show them what we can do."

The pilots quickly scattered, heading towards their waiting Swordfish and the other pilots and crew of the remaining fighter-bombers. Coode climbed into his own craft, and then looked back to his waiting weapons officer, Lieutenant Edmund Squarey Carver.

"Up for a scrap?"

"Am I ever?" Carver chuckled as he checked the seal on his helmet. He then moved his fingers to the controls and panels around him as the domed turret slowly sealed itself, "5A is as ready as she'll ever be. Fully fuelled, and I've checked the fish as you requested."

"Excellent. Luckily for us Esmonde and his lads were able to test their weapons before the final test."

"Who would have thought such bad luck would be so beneficial?"

"Quite."

The canopy began to close, sealing Coode from the air of the hangar. For now he relied on the air circulating inside the cockpit as he ran his checks.

"Run through your lists," he said, looking to his own, "We can't afford any mistakes today."

"Too right," agreed Carver.

It took several minutes for both men to finish running through the array of checks necessary to launch. By the time Coode looked up from his displays, his fighter was already moving as the autoloader shifted his fighter into position. He could make out three other Swordfish also doing the same and watched with interest as the monstrous mechanical system moved them around like the automated hoists used on the battleships for their main batteries. Eventually, they reached the side of the hangar, the layered blast doors slid open, shutting as they moved through. They were now outside of the hangar and protected from space by a single armoured barrier that remained closed.

"This is the bit that always gives me the willies," said Carver.

Alarms sounded, and then the bright status light built into the exterior door began to flash. The bright red light sent flashes of colour over the nose, cockpit, and wings of the Swordfish. He looked to the right and out across the long, straight wings of the fighter. Most fighters utilised the more modern angular wings to mount their thrusters on, especially those designed to be capable of atmospheric flight. But not the Swordfish. Instead, the wings were completely straight and fitted alongside the pilot at the very front of the craft. This granted more space for the weapons officer behind, as well as to give the ball turret more space to move. The flashes changed in intensity, letting them both know they were getting close to being ready for launch. The fighter shuddered a little, and then everything became silent.

"We're on the rail," said Carver, "Thirty seconds to launch."

Coode nodded but said nothing. He was too busy checking the mapping data and the course positions for Bismarck and the pursuing ships. Any but a fool could see it was all in his hands now, and he could feel the tension and the pressure in his body. Once satisfied with the planned waypoints, he activated his comms.

"Ark Royal, this is 5A. We're ready for launch."

"Affirmative," replied the ship's CAG, "Get out there and hole her for us."

"Roger. We will do everything we can. 5A out."

He looked back to his weapons officer safely ensconced behind him in his turret, as he turned from left to right, checking the tracking. He held up his right hand and showed him the thumbs up.

"Good," said Coode, "This is 5A. All flights prepare to launch on my mark."

The flashing red light finally turned green, but nothing happened to the fighter-bomber. Instead, the outer blast doors slid open to reveal the spacecraft to the void. Coode watched the coloured clouds whoosh by as though they were flying through the skies of a colonised world rather than travelling through space. The fighter pushed out a short distance, and as Coode leaned forward, he made out the noses of three other Swordfish as they joined him in the ready-to-launch position. He reached for the control panel and let his fingers hover over the release panel. With a single movement, he opened the transparent safety cover and revealed the single button that would release the lock on the launch rail, allowing Ark Royal to shunt the launch sled away from the ship.

"All good to go," said Carver.

Coode nodded, and then hit the button. The sled shunted forward at speed, forcing him back into the seat as the fighter was thrown clear of the carrier. As soon as they were far enough away, he activated the main thruster, and then sent the Swordfish into a wide arc to join up with the others. It took almost ten minutes for each of them to clear the ship and move to the first waypoint just fifty kilometres from the still accelerating battlecruiser Renown. Carver swung his turret directly up to look at the majestic warship.

"She's not slowing down," he said with obvious admiration, "Somerville is out for blood."

"Well, he'd better not get too close. If Bismarck could rip Hood apart so quickly, then a smaller, older battlecruiser isn't going to do much better."

"True," said Carver, "Very true."

"All Flights," said Coode, "It's time to move to Sheffield. Watch your spacing and lock onto their transponder. The storms are getting rougher by the minute."

He hit his burners, and the fighter accelerated rapidly away from the warship towards the wisps of fog and cloud. The other fourteen fighters remained in their five small groups, each staying a safe distance away in case of the storm. They travelled through thick banks of colour, and even some large open channels of space, but after almost an hour, there was still no sign of life, save for the regular tracking pulse sent out by Sheffield.

"There!" Carver swung his turret about, "Sheffield. And she's less than twenty klicks away."

Coode looked in the same direction and then sighed.

"No wonder they had such trouble finding a target with the first attack. Sensors are almost useless in this nebula, and visibility is terrible."

He tapped his comms system and shifted to the encoded channel used for fighter to ship communications.

"Sheffield, this is Fighter 5A from Ark Royal. Requesting fresh bearing on our target."

"Hello, 5A. And thank you for not torpedoing us this time."

Carver laughed away to himself in the back of the fighter, but with the internal intercom active it was easy enough to hear him.

"Affirmative," said Coode, keen to avoid a long, and potentially awkward conversation with the captain of the Commonwealth light cruiser, "Do you have course information?"

"We do. We have course, bearing, and current velocity. Bismarck is not far ahead of us. She's well within our radar range now. Their captain is not even trying to hide anymore."

"Understood, Sheffield."

"Good grief," said Carver, "She's close…about twelve minutes away at our current speed."

"Thank you, Sheffield," said Coode, "We will take our leave of you."

"Good luck, and good hunting, 5A. All our prayers are

with you."

He wagged the wings, though it may not have been obvious to the crew of the cruiser so far away. He then checked on the Swordfish nearby and did a quick head count to make sure all fifteen were present.

"All wings, synchronise your target data. Bismarck is just twelve minutes away, and she knows she's being trailed. They must expect an attack, so we'll have to be fast and decisive in our strike."

Each moved away from the light cruiser and off into the fog. Their blinking navigation lights were all that allowed them to make out their shapes as they rocked back and forth in the appalling conditions. Every few minutes a flash of lightning would erupt, scattering into long tendrils all around them before vanishing just as quickly. As Coode looked to his right, he spotted 4th Flight slipping away as they moved to avoid more flashes of energy. A great explosion of light almost tore them apart, but they managed to move away at the very last minute.

"Coode…we're awfully close. I'm detecting traces from her wake. She's still leaking. And they must know we're coming."

"Dammit. How so?"

"Jamming. It started up twenty seconds ago, and it's already blocked off comms with Sheffield. We're on our own now."

Coode continued to shake his head.

"This was supposed to be a carefully coordinated attack with each of our sub-flights moving in simultaneously from multiple angles."

"I know. It's the only way to force Bismarck to split her

fire and divide it against our attacks. And the only way to make it harder for her to evade torpedoes."

"And now we've got a storm that's getting worse by the minute. Whoever heard of clouds and fog in space?"

"This nebula is infamous," said Carver, "Frankly, I'm amazed we've made it this far already."

Coode did his best to laugh, but all he could see was the fighters now missing, their transponders barely detectable due to the interference and the jamming coming from their target.

"Very well," he said angrily, "This may be the last time we're able to communicate. Any closer and Bismarck will drown out our comms."

Carver nodded in agreement as Coode opened up the secure channel to the other flight leaders.

"This is 5A. Jamming and interference are becoming stronger. Descend and try and stay together as best you can. Don't linger. Just get in there and launch your attacks in groups. Then get home as fast as you can. I don't want any of you getting lost in these storms. Understood?"

Godfrey-Faussett, Keane, and Hunter responded in the affirmative, though there was some delay as he waited for Owensmith and Willcocks to follow suit. Only then did he look to his continually updating nav charts and the projected position of the enemy warship.

"This is it, chaps. Good hunting, and all come back safe and sound."

The flights nearest wagged their wings, and then pulses of light from their thrusters marked their subtle changes in course. Seconds later, it was just Coode with Child and Moffatt at his flanks. He checked on both of them for signs of damage or any missing torpedoes, and once satisfied looked directly ahead.

"Let's go, lads."

They accelerated forward, and within a minute came the cry over the intercom from 2nd Sub-flight. Coode tried to lean forward, and suddenly spotted half of the Bismarck as the massive battleship loomed out from the fog. He could see the small group of Swordfish arcing towards the warship's starboard beam, all while scores of turrets clawed at them with gunfire. Flashes of yellow and white marked the impact of the exploded shells, though none detonated as they punched through the fragile fighter-bombers.

"This is 2B, we're hitting heavy flak. Damage to port-side thrusters!"

Coode could see the trail of fire and smoke from the lead Swordfish. Five separate dotted lines tracked towards it, but just as it was about to be hit, the craft dodged away.

"2nd Flight, pull back! You can't survive that kind of fire!" Coode yelled.

They either didn't hear him or chose not to, as both 2B and 2A flown by Pattisson unleashed their torpedoes before being engulfed in flame. The wreckage from both fighters scattered towards the Bismarck as the ship continued to plough ahead. There was so much gunfire it looked as though the ship was surrounded by fire and explosions.

"They've locked onto us," said Carver, "Deploying countermeasures."

Flares and puffs of radar absorbent filament exploded around them as the battleship's guns tracked them.

"Returning fire."

The rear ball turret rotated around so that he could fire

forwards in a depressed position. The dual guns chuntered away as he fired at the closing shape of Bismarck, the other fighters did the same, for all the good it did them.

"Okay, chaps, line up with me. Let's get in there fast and low."

Height meant little, even though he was referring to their position relative to the flanks of the battleship. As he rolled the fighter around, two more sub-flights whooshed in from both above and below, releasing their torpedoes at the same time. One fighter lost a wing but managed to spin away and vanished into the fog and clouds.

"I've lost my lads," said Keane as his fighter raced in from above, and then formed up alongside Coode, boosting his flight up to four Swordfish from the original three.

"That's alright," said Coode, "You stay on my wing. And keep jinking."

He looked back to the predatory warship, now bellowing smoke as it tried to hide from the incoming fighter-bombers. The flight moved into a bank of white, made worse by the bellowing clouds coming from the ship, and were temporarily blinded.

"I'm seeing nothing." Carver stopped firing.

"Just be ready," said Coode, "We'll be there in…"

He gasped as they lurched out from the clouds and into position just fifteen hundred metres away from the ship. The ship was a monster, with its large hull and raised superstructure on the upper and lower sides of the hull. The main batteries were split equally to the front and rear, while alongside the superstructure were multiple medium turret installations, each fitted with guns capable of crippling cruisers and destroyers, as well as knocking down fighters at long-range. But all of them paled to insignificance next to the small point-defence turrets covering every single part of the ship. Coode winced as one concentrated its fire on his fire, with streams of slugs ripping through his port-side wings. Another burst raked the hull; with several slugs slashing through the canopy and leaving cracks all down one side.

"You okay up there?" Carver asked.

"Don't worry about me. Just be ready on that torpedo."

"Already ahead of you. Torpedo is armed, locked, and ready.

"Good show. All Swordfish, fire away!"

Carver acted first and released the torpedo towards the battleship. Just two seconds after it burst free, they took another stream of fire that cut up into the hull. One round punched into the engine cooler, triggering a raging fire to the side of the turret.

"We got a little banged up back here. Let me see what I can do."

A puff of white vapour engulfed the Swordfish, followed by the flames subsiding, and being replaced by a stream of smoke. As Coode struggled to maintain control of his craft, the other three Swordfish released their torpedoes. The weapons rushed ahead, all while the battleship's array of turrets struggled to hit them. One exploded, but the others continued towards the battleship, striking the hull in a series of fiery blasts.

"Good hits. No significant damage, though."

"We can only do what we can do," said Coode, "Back to the rally point and the Ark."

He pulled on his controls, weaving left and right to avoid fire. As he did so, he spotted 5C alone and heading towards the stern of the battleship.

"Scratch that, keeping firing on the Bismarck. Keep her guns off our lads!"

Each spun away and headed towards the mighty battleship. Even Coode gasped as he flew over the superstructure and gazed down at the array of massive guns; the very weapons that had obliterated Hood in a single well-aimed shot.

"Hit 'em!"

Carver swung the turret around the raked the ship. Coode became so close he was forced to weave in and out of the ship's towers as he moved from bow to stern. Looking ahead, he could see the shape of a single Swordfish heading right for the stern of the ship. The spacecraft was already on fire, but the stern was relatively poorly protected with turrets. Coode took aim with his own guns and blasted away, hitting two small turrets as he whooshed on past.

"Launching!" Lieutenant Moffatt said.

The torpedo broke free, and his fighter-bomber pulled away, narrowly avoiding slamming directly into Coode when struggling to clear the ship. He looked back and cried out with joy as the warhead slammed into the stern, right between the main engines and the secondary thrusters. A single flash marked the detonation, followed by a series of secondary fires that wracked the stern.

"Bloody good show!" Coode said.

Another explosion shook the vessel, and then to the cheers of the Swordfish crews, the ship's main engines shut down, and it began to weave uncontrollably.

"I can't believe it," said Carver as he watched the ever-shrinking ship from inside his turret, "I think we've slowed her down."

Coode smiled as he tapped the communication console and waited as his computer struggled to link up with the distant fleet.

"Nothing," he muttered, "Too far away. What about Sheffield?"

He changed channel and tried again. It took a few seconds, and then came back the partially broken voice.

"This is 5A, we've hit the Bismarck. I repeat; we've hit the Bismarck."

"Understood," came back the reply, "We're moving in as fast as we can to confirm. Splendid show, Swordfish, get home safely."

That wiped the smile from Coode's face as he glanced down to the status screen. It showed all the fighters either destroyed or damaged from the fight.

"Understood, Sheffield. Heading home."

CHAPTER THIRTEEN

Why did the Commonwealth keep fighting when the cost had been so high? The cities of the Core Worlds were little more than rubble and her fighter defences torn apart with massive, almost unbearable loses. And with her allies in the Gallian Hegemony Torugan Coalition what chance of victory ever remained? There were many that wanted peace, but many more refused to cow down before the feet of the Vrokan and their reviled leader Luther Maximillian. Buoyed on by the strength of the fleet and the promise of aid from distant allies, they rallied for one final apocalyptical effort, one that could be decided only in blood.

History of the Void Wars

Commonwealth Battleship 'King George V'

Vice Admiral Tovey made his way from his cabin towards the combat centre of the battleship. The constant acceleration provided him with relatively normal gravity, and as he moved forward, he did his best to enjoy the moment. Small portholes one side of the passage showed a simulated view outside. It was almost perfect, though the flat two-dimensional videofeeds were unable to show depth or to shift with his viewing angle. Even so, he could see the appalling conditions outside, as well as the electrical storms that continued to lash them.

"We have him by the tail," he said grimly, "But this storm

could be our undoing."

He turned away from the windows and made his way to the door leading to the combat centre. It didn't take long to move through the narrow room, and then to the more spacious nerve centre of the ship.

"Admiral," said Captain Patterson, the battleship's captain, "We're making good time. We should be in range within the hour."

Admiral Tovey nodded and moved to his seat before saying anything else. He placed his hand on his left display and brought up the tactical mapping data for the area, as well as the meteorological forecasts for the nebula. On the middle screen was the list of Commonwealth ships, along with their fuel and ammunition levels. Many of the vessels were below half their stated capacity, with a few, including Rodney almost at critical levels.

"Rodney, Tartar, and Mashona have joined us, and are moving at maximum speed to the target."

Admiral Tovey nodded.

"Good. I see even Rodney is managing to keep up."

"Captain Dalrymple-Hamilton reports heavy strain on her engines, and significant energy drain."

"Understood. Reduce our velocity by ten percent and coordinate with the taskforce. Conserve what fuel remains and maintain formation."

"Yes, Admiral."

The Captain passed on the orders, and then nodded to the blurred and barely visible imagery being broadcast from Sheffield. The ship remained on a pursuit course, though just out of range of the battleship's effect gunnery range.

"Sheffield reports Bismarck's course is erratic. She's unable to maintain a course to port and is arcing heavily onto this trajectory."

A single white line showed the ship's position as it veered away to the left and began to turn back.

"Bismarck is turning back to fight?"

"No," said Captain Patterson, "Engineering and tactical have assessed her position, course, speed, and damage. We believe she has sustained heavy damage to her propulsion. You can see where she makes course corrections, but every time she activates her main drive, she pulls off course."

"The old Stringbags did it." Tovey smiled, "By Jove they did it."

So thrilled by the news, he banged his fist down onto the display, causing the gimbal mount to shudder for a moment. He looked across to the Captain who was now speaking with the other officers.

"Captain...Update the board with the revised plotting data. I have no intention of attacking within the hour," he said, much to the Captain's surprise, "Postpone the attack for..."

He moved his finger along the map, and then paused as he performed various calculations in his head. Six...No, five hours."

Captain Patterson's eyes opened wide in surprise.

"Five hours?" He sounded stunned by the news and kept shaking his head as he waited for the Admiral to explain his orders, "By then she will be through the storm and closer to the occupied territories."

"Yes...and we will be clear of these storms. I do not want half of my fleet torn asunder as we unleash hell on her. Use the time to close the distance and ready our crews."

Captain Patterson considered arguing, but he could see from the look on Tovey's face there was no room for discussion.

"As you wish, Admiral."

He reached for the intercom and held it to his mouth.

"This is the Captain. We expect to be going into action at seven hundred hours. In the meantime, all hands will remain at action stations."

As he replaced the unit, several of the other officers turned to look at him. Every one of them knew they were engaged in a desperate race against time, and that the race had now turned to a crawl for some imperceivable reason. Tovey could see their confusion, but rather than speak with them, he focussed on Captain Patterson.

"I want every turret, every gun, and every combat station to be ready for the attack. When we go into action, it will be fast, violent, and decisive. There can be no time for mistakes."

"Understood, Admiral. King George V is ready to do her duty."

* * *

Commonwealth Destroyer 'Cossack', 4th Destroyer Flotilla, 2 hours later

The interior of the ship was so dark it looked as though the vessel had lost power. Instead, only the red tint from the internal emergency lighting and the glow from the displays provided any illumination. Everything was small and cramped, with all the ship's bridge officers forced into a space little larger than most ship's captain's quarters. There were just half a dozen men and women, each facing towards their displays and banks of controls. The room was shaped more like a sphere, with the officers facing away from the central area occupied by the senior officers.

"Incoming message from Admiral Tovey," said the communications officer as he looked over his shoulder, "Captain…Our orders are to advance and harass until the heavies are in position."

The entire ship shook violently, rocking them all by the brutal conditions outside.

"Harass? That's what we're here for," said Captain Vian from his position in the centre of the room, "Send me the orders."

There were no computer displays or controls in front of him, just a single small panel attached to the side of his chair. He looked down as the orders appeared, along with the enemy warship's position.

"Very well. Tactical. Liaise with Sikh, Maori, Zulu, and Piorun. I want them to follow us in on these attack vectors."

He tapped his small panel and drew a series of lines that moved back and forth around the enemy ship.

"Yes, Captain," said Lieutenant Hartridge.

"And where is Captain O'Connell and his destroyer flotilla?"

"Coming in right behind us. Three more destroyers, and they're being led by a pair of Town Class light cruisers, Newport and Highbridge."

"Good. I want him to follow us in as a second wave. Those light cruisers could prove useful."

Lieutenant Hartridge nodded while Captain Vian turned

his attention to the view directly ahead. He looked over his helmsman's shoulder as he watched the shifting clouds of white. The newly arrived destroyers were relatively conventional, while the light cruisers were ancient, and of the same vintage as the now lost battlecruiser Hood. At thirteen hundred metres in length, they were larger than many heavy cruisers, and coming close to some of the smaller ships of the line.

"Let's give her crew something to complain about. Advance to flank speed."

He then reached for the intercom.

"This is the Captain. We're going into action. All crew prepare for battle."

The vibrations in the hull increased as bright flames stretched out behind the small vessel. At just six hundred metres-long, she was a tiny minnow compared to the almost three-kilometre-long enemy battleship, even though she was one of the new generation heavy destroyers built for the fleet. With a longer hull, thicker armour, and upgraded weapons, she was built to tackle ships well above her size, though nothing as significant as a battleship. Next to the other four ships in the flotilla she was noticeably larger, with the Piorun even smaller than Cossack. Of the five destroyers, Piorun was remarkable in being the only non-Commonwealth vessel. Though her crew had been forced to flee the occupied territories, they still fought alongside their allies, loyal to the last.

"We'll be in visual range in a matter of minutes," said Lieutenant Hartridge, "Bringing weapons online."

"Good work. This will all happen much faster than you might expect."

"Faster than Altmark?"

That put a smile on the Captain's face.

"At least this time it's a little more cut and dry."

He nodded towards the communications officer.

"Comms, put me on with the others."

"Yes, Captain."

"This is Cossack. We have orders to harass and annoy these devils until the fleet is in position to deliver the coup de grace. You will avoid heavy combat, just keep them busy, and do not let her crew sleep. The Admiral wants them dead on their feet for the final battle."

He then checked his mapping data one last time.

"Spread out and operate individually…but for the love of God keep an eye on the rest of us. The last thing I want to see is my ship with holes in it from you chaps. Any questions?"

The channel remained silent, until the captain of Piorun spoke up. His voice betrayed excitement and his opportunity for revenge.

"We can destroy her?"

For a second, Captain Vian thought the man was joking, but it was obvious from his voice that he was not.

"Just concentrate on the harassment, Piorun. She's a lot of metal to deal with. But…if you think you have a good shot, far be it for me to say no."

"Excellent. We look forward to the hunt."

"Very good. Good luck, and good hunting. It is time."

Captain Vian looked to his small panel and to the view ahead. He could still just see the clouds with streaks of energy flashing back and forth. Under normal circumstances he would never have come this way for fear of damage to his ship, or even becoming lost in the nebula. But today was different. Today there was a purpose that he could not avoid. He closed his eyes and took in long, slow breaths as he waited. His crew were all highly experienced, and there was nothing for him to do just yet. And then came the report he'd so desperately wanted to hear.

"Captain. Bismarck spotted at maximum range. We have her on visual."

"Excellent, show me."

The imagery shifted as the cameras focussed on the ship. This was the first time any of them had seen it with their own eyes, and for some time the crew were utterly silent.

"Good God," said one, "She's a monster."

Captain Vian gulped as he looked to the bulky superstructure and array of turrets at the front and rear, each bristling with what looked like linear bombardment cannons. The weapons were designed to punch through the thick armour of capital ships, and he knew too well that just one could potentially split his ship in half.

"Very well…increase speed. Tactical. Are we ready?"

"Aye, Captain. Guns and torpedoes armed and ready."

The ship rocked again, but this time it was from the starboard side thrusters firing. The ship altered course slightly, and they all looked on in awe at the massive vessel ahead, as her flank revealed itself as the ship moved almost entirely out from the fog.

"There she is," said Captain Vian, "All ripe for the taking."

He watched as the fully exposed ship continued to move in a wide circle. He then pulled the intercom to his mouth and called out to the others ships in the destroyer flotilla.

"Bismarck…Range, seventy kilometres, and closing. Her weapons are coming online."

"All ships…break formation and move into position."

It took time, but after a few minutes, the other destroyers and the single light cruiser quickly vanished, moving off to attack from different directions. The light cruiser left a pair of blue trails behind it, making it hard to hide its course from the enemy battleship. While they moved away, Cossack continued to plough ahead and on course towards the ship's starboard stern, the ship moving away at almost thirty degrees. Alarms sounded, and in an instant, each officer knew they'd been spotted.

"Gunnery radar has a lock on us," said Lieutenant Hartridge, "They'll fire any moment now."

"Good. Now let's keep their attention."

On cue the secondary guns opened fire, with two entire batteries focussing their fire on Cossack. The ship began to slip to the right, but it wasn't enough to stop several projectiles striking the hull and bursting through the armour. Another came close, but the four of quadruple 40mm point-defence turrets managed to break it apart. The shattered fragments still struck the ship, triggering a small fire.

"Two penetrations. No casualties," said Lieutenant Hartridge, "Our armour is useless against that ship. Permission to return fire?"

"We're still fifty kilometres from the target," said the Captain, "Can you hit her from that range?"

Lieutenant Hartridge shrugged.

"That's well within range for our weapons."

"Very well. Focus torpedoes on her stern. Let's see if we can hit her where she's bleeding. Another good hit might see her unable to accelerate."

"Yes, Captain."

The engines fired again, and then the ship began an erratic corkscrew motion as the helmsman did everything he could to try and shake off the worst of the incoming fire. Shots came at them thick and thin, followed moments later by smaller calibre shots designed for knocking down missiles and fighters. They punched scores of holes in the hull of the ship and inside the hull.

"Bring our bow online," said the Captain, "Let's try and shake off at least some of these shots. Then cut speed and activate smoke!"

Lieutenant Hartridge nodded and activated the countermeasures as the ship slowly drifted back around. The heavier calibre shots still punched right through the frontal armour. The next volley of smaller calibre shots struck the angled bow, deflecting off to the sides, much to the cheering officers. Within seconds, a cloud of smoke, much like the fog of the nebula spread out from outlets fitted to the superstructure of the ship. The smoke was a combination of heated gas expended from the coolant system, mixed with countermeasure compounds to create a wall of white that was difficult to penetrate.

"Changing course now," said the helmsman.

Now that the ship was shrouded in smoke, it was the perfect time to change course and to throw off the enemy's targeting systems. More shots crashed around them, but soon the worst of the fire was ripped into the clouds of white, rather than the ship.

"We're getting awfully close, Captain."

"Good, close is what we need."

He looked to his display panel and noted the approach of

each of the ships. They were moving in from three directions and staggered to make it difficult to track or guess their numbers. He opened his mouth to speak as a blast of energy from the lightning storms arced out and struck the battleship. It then scattered and lashed the nearby clouds with tendrils coming towards Cossack. Captain Vian could only watch in horror as the lightning hammered his hull, leaving thick scorch marks on the plating and starting fires.

"Report!"

"Light damage," said Lieutenant Hartridge, "Forward turrets are offline and restarting."

"Damn the guns. Get some torpedoes out there, and fast."

The ship adjusted course again and turned away from the battleship to allow the flank-mounted launchers to have a clear line of sight.

"Ready, Captain."

"Fire a spread, make them wide."

"Firing."

The ship shook repeatedly as the quadruple torpedo launcher sent one warhead after another towards the Bismarck. The torpedoes burst out from the clouds of smoke and towards her stern at ever increasing speed.

"She's turning," said Lieutenant Hartridge, "It's erratic, but she might just make it. Wait...I'm detecting interceptor guns. Our fish are being tracked."

The torpedoes moved closer and closer, and then one by one detonated as the point-defence guns went to work. One torpedo made it through the gunfire, but then missed as the ship's engines roared, pushing it just a few hundred metres ahead of the impact point.

"We need to get a lot closer if we want to get past those defences. There's just too much time to track and focus fire on them."

The ship shook even more violently than before, followed by alerts as numerous systems failed.

"Are we hit?"

"Not from Bismarck. That was the storm. We took a hit to the stern. Three metres further forward and the main storage cells might have been hit."

"Maybe Tovey was right," said the Captain, "A fleet engagement in this firestorm could cripple half our ships."

"Maybe that's Bismarck's plan, Sir. To draw us into the worst of this storm."

"Perhaps. I suspect that by now all her captain wants is to reach a safe harbour. And that cannot be allowed to happen."

He pointed to the enemy ship.

"Don't get too close. Remember, we're here to harass only. Let's not show them any more leg than we need to get their attention."

"Tell that to Piorun, Sir. Look!"

They all watched in astonishment as the vessel moved to a range of less than forty kilometres and opened fire with her guns.

"What are they doing?" asked the helmsman, "Are they mad?"

"Mad, perhaps. But they want revenge. It's not every day you have a chance to settle an old score. Piorun managed to flee the occupation of their lands, and they will not stop until it's theirs once again. I suspect that…"

Dozens of small explosions wracked the hull of Bismarck

as Piorun unleashed all of her weapons against the ship. The destroyer then rolled away, dumping smoke and vanishing into a storm cloud. Moments later tendrils of energy lashed out in all directions, some into the clouds, and others along the hull of the enemy ship. Each impact left deep scars on her hull, as well as lighting numerous small fires.

"Piorun," said the Captain, "You're one slippery fish."

"Sir!" Lieutenant Hartridge said, "Bismarck has reversed thrust, and Captain O'Connell's light cruisers are moving in to strike at point-blank range.

"No," Captain Vian snapped, "That's too close!"

"Captain, he's taking his ships in to attack from the port-side and is preparing torpedoes."

Captain Vian pulled the intercom to call out to the Captain, but it was already too late. Bismarck's change in velocity, combined with the increasing thrust from the pair of light cruisers conspired to bring them alongside each other. The light cruisers looked impressive, with their long, rakish hulls making them look more like grand yachts than warships. In many ways they looked like half size versions of Hood, but unlike that great ship, they lacked the armour and protection that hadn't even saved her in battle.

"Madness," said Captain Vian, "Sheer madness."

His eyes opened wide as one destroyer took hits from Bismarck's secondary guns. The pair of light cruisers was right behind and opened fire with their main guns. For just a few seconds they looked like wooden ships battling it out on the high seas, but then a salvo from Bismarck's four secondary dorsal turrets hit Captain O'Connell's light cruiser. The projectiles hammered into the ship so hard it was visibly pushed away from the star dreadnought. Fires started in numerous locations, followed by an array of explosions that wracked the hull from bow to stern.

"Get back!" Lieutenant Hartridge muttered, "You can't hold off that kind of firepower."

The light cruiser's main battery answered just once as it fought back, only to be hit by another volley that ripped apart the ship as though it were nothing. Though large compared to the destroyers, it was a design from a hundred years earlier, with an emphasis of range, duration, and speed. Bismarck was a floating metal fortress and quickly made short work of the cruiser as Newport split apart. More explosions ripped through the fragments, forcing the nearby Highbridge to turn away and loose a volley of torpedoes as it struggled to flee into its own smoke. Bismarck fired again, its guns reaching into the cloud and managing to start fires aboard the fleeing ships.

"One cruiser gone and one destroyer heavily damaged," said Lieutenant Hartridge.

"That fool. Our orders were simple, to stay well clear and to harass her. And now he's paid the price."

He rubbed at his chin and then pulled the intercom to his lips, all while watching dozens of lifeboats moving away from the wreckage.

"All ships will fall back to rally position. Pop smoke and keep launching torpedoes. Remember, we are here to harass. Leave the ship-to-ship stuff to the heavies. We'll pick up survivors when the fighting is over."

He was about to say more until interrupted by the debris travelling quickly through space. The clouds of broken fragments triggered Cossack's proximity alerts.

"Evasive action!" Captain Vian shouted, "Do not get too close!"

Cossack felt as though she was breaking in half as the tortured metal creaked and groaned under the immense pressures from the numerous engines and thrusters firing. They'd turned nearly thirty degrees when gunfire from Bismarck's stern batteries reached out to them.

"We're taking fire!" Lieutenant Hartridge said, "One of the stacks is gone, and we've taken damage to the stern batteries."

Another volley struck just below the ship, with some of the rounds glancing off the angular plating and creating showers of sparks. A dull booming sound marked the depressurisation of several compartments, and each of them looked to their screens for signs of damage.

"Captain, we have ruptures on the lower armour plating. Outer compartments compromised, but sealed," said Lieutenant Hartridge.

"And no causalities," said the Captain with relief, "Cossack is one tough customer."

His right hand moved to the Lieutenant's screen and pointed to Bismarck.

"Now it's our turn. Fire back!"

"Yes, Sir. Already on it. Main guns are online and targeting her main drive."

The reverberation of the guns filled the bridge with cheer as they fired back. These were no mere light guns, as Cossack was heavily armed for her size. Unlike other destroyers, she was equipped with a combination four main turrets fitted to the forward deck, and another four matched to the rear. Each carried a pair of powerful 180mm linear accelerator guns, the standard secondary armament of battleships and battlecruisers, allowing her to punch way above her weight against other destroyers and even light cruisers.

"Good shooting!" The Captain watched numerous bursts along the stern of Bismarck, "Now…Helm, keep turning, and tactical, get more fish out there. I want them under threat from this direction at all times."

"Sir!"

Four more streaks of light reached out towards the battleship, and now the entire hull lit up as almost every single weapon station activated. The battleship's main battery joined in, its brutal main cannons firing explosive shells that detonated at fixed ranged, showering the area with a multitude of tiny warheads. One destroyer lost half of its superstructure as it spiralled away and managed to escape while trailing smoke. Bismarck's array of secondary guns continued to fire, making it almost impossible to see the ship due to the unending flickering lights.

"Good God," said Captain Vian as he watched the spectacular light show, "She must carry guns on every exposed surface. I've never seen a ship like her."

"She's a monster alright," said Lieutenant Hartridge, "A ship designed through and through for brawling."

Captain Vian winced as more shots hit nearby, but through the skill of his crew they managed to avoid the worst of it and kept weaving away inside the smoke. Two more streaks of energy from the electrical storm hit them, causing the lights to dim with each impact. As he looked to the tactical station, he noticed the main feed cut, and when it reappeared, he spotted the torpedoes heading right for the enemy ship's rear flank. And then came a series of flashes.

"Did we get her?"

"Negative, Captain. None of the torpedoes made it to within ten thousand metres. Bismarck's defences are just too strong. But they have forced her to change course again."

Hartridge shook his head and looked back to the Captain.

"Sir. I think the damage to her stern is worse than we thought. The Swordfish did the impossible and got through her defence screen to inflict a brutal blow on her."

"Explain."

Lieutenant Hartridge brought up imagery of the ship's stern and pointed to the blackened areas right between the main engines.

"I don't know if it was intentional or not, but the torpedo managed to miss the engines and struck the bulkheads between them. One has been knocked out and twisted into the path of the second, forcing it out of alignment.

"Can it be fixed?"

"Sure, in drydock, but out here in this storm, and in the middle of a battle. No chance. But, Sir, there's more. From my data over the last hour, it looks like they can barely hold true when firing their main engines. If you look at my gun cameras, you can see all of the thrusters on the port-side are firing to try and keep their bearing true. They still have to cut the main drive after a few minutes to change heading, else they'll keep turning away from home. Without the main drive, they can manoeuvre freely.

"So each time we launch torpedoes, they're forced to cut their main drive so they can try and move away from the warheads?"

"Exactly. And the damage is too great to risk skip-jumping. Assuming their system is even active now."

"So, if we keep up the attack, we can slow them down further?"

"I think so, Sir. If we time the attacks right, we can hit them just as they start using their main drive again."

"Excellent. Comms, send a flashcom to Admiral Tovey. Tell him we've slowed our prey down and will maintain harassing her until his arrival."

"Yes, Captain."

As his eyes shifted back to the viewscreen next to Lieutenant Hartridge, his lip circled slightly. He could make out the other destroyers circling like hyenas around a wounded animal. Bismarck continued firing at them, with great streaks of fire clawing out to meet them. And every few minutes, long trails from the destroyers marked the course of yet more torpedoes.

"Bring us back around and keep up that damned smoke screen!"

"We're going back in?" Lieutenant Hartridge asked.

"Oh, yes. But stay a good distance away. Now she's angry! It's time to press the attack."

The flank thrusters forced the ship around and the main drive thundered away. Moments later another destroyer moved in close to her flank, and they proceeded forward at a slight angle back towards the star dreadnought.

"Ready the torpedoes and prepare to fire again."

Sirens sounded, and the crew went back to preparing for yet another strike. The sound of heavy motors loading in the torpedoes might not be audible in this part of the ship, but the subtle vibrations could be spotted by those more familiar with the ship.

"Tubes are loaded and ready," said Lieutenant Hartridge.

The Captain lifted a hand and looked to the imagery of the wounded, but incredibly powerful beast. He could see the destroyers circling it like flies, and the gunfire…the unending gunfire that surrounded it.

"Fire!"

Once more came the shudders as the volley of 533mm torpedoes burst free from their launches and accelerated towards the Bismarck.

"Fish away!"

Some of the crew cheered, but further alarms sounded that struck fear into their hearts.

"Bismarck has a radar lock on us. She's launching anti-ship missiles."

Captain Vian visibly gulped at the news.

"I wondered when they'd show up. I want a full countermeasure spread and keep the smoke running. What they can't track, they can't hit."

The ship rolled to port and then pushed downward, causing some of the crew to groan. Captain Vian placed his hands on the rounded metal bracing bar attached to his seat and grimaced as they performed a seventy-degree rotation.

"Impact in ten seconds. It's going to be a close one."

"Keep our scanners offline, boost the main drive!" said the Captain.

The engines activated and increased output to full in less than five seconds. In that time, a terrible whine filled the ship as the coolant turbines were pushed to their limits. Hot gases were vented out into space and mixed with the countermeasure smoke, in a desperate attempt to trick heat and radar tracking warheads away from the ship. The force on the crew was immense, causing some to even pass out from the strain. The thrusters continued to fire for a few more seconds just as the missiles whooshed through the cloud of smoke and detonated.

"Detonation!" Lieutenant Hartridge shouted.

Though there was no shockwave in space due to the lack of atmosphere, the blast was still able to send a cargo of tiny bomblets out in a scattered spray. Some hit the stern of the destroyer and exploded.

"Two turrets offline and breaches to the rear port-side compartments."

Captain Vian nodded along as he ran his finger over his small panel.

"Evacuate the compromised compartments and seal her down." He listened for a second and then shook his head, "I don't care if we lose gunnery control to the stern battery. Get my people out of there and lock it down. That's an order."

As he placed the intercom back in its mount, he could see the nerves and the fear in his ship. They appeared to be fighting an impossible battle, and with each passing minute, the damage and casualties continued to mount.

"Do not fear," he said as confidentially as he could manage, "Our prey is wounded, and she is struggling to escape."

Lieutenant Hartridge looked across to him and was surprised to see him smiling.

"Let's give them the night terrors. By the time Tovey arrives, they'll be barely able to stand. By God let's give them what for."

The Lieutenant nodded in agreement.

"We're through half our torpedo stock, moving to reserves."

"Just keep hitting them, Lieutenant Hartridge. Who knows…you might even get lucky!"

STAR DREADNOUGHT BISMARCK

CHAPTER FOURTEEN

What was it that made the Vrokan soldier so unbeatable in battle? They were men and women, like any other, and yet achieved victories that seemed impossible. Some believe it was a combination of motivation and new battle tactics, while others look to the years of preparation that her rivals strove to ignore to their near ruination. Man for man, was there any city, colony, or world more capable in the art of war?

Fascism, war, and the Rise of the Vrokan Empire

Commonwealth Battleship 'King George V'

The two battleships burst through the lightning storm towards the expected position of Star Dreadnought Bismarck. Leading the charge was powerful King George V, sister ship to the mauled but still operational Prince of Wales. And at her side the strangely shaped Rodney, named for the illustrious sailor that was regarded to have created the tactic of *breaking the line* in battle. At the flanks of these two behemoths were two destroyers, Tartar and Mashona, each of which looked small and almost insignificant next to the bulk of the two ships. Protected inside the armoured confines of the ship was a veritable hive of humanity, with thousands of crew now waiting at their stations.

"This is the Captain speaking." The voice quickly brought the ship to silence. The crew had been waiting hours for this message, and not one spoke as they listened to each and every syllable.

"We will be within firing range in approximately one hour. Our destroyers have worn them down and are now withdrawing to give us the space we need."

Captain Patterson checked over his shoulder and waited until receiving the nod from Admiral Tovey, who remained busily checking the tactical maps of the area from his seat.

"We've trained for this a hundred times since we left home. You know your drills, and you know what this ship is capable of."

He inhaled slowly, letting his words sink in for the crew. Admiral Tovey might be using his ship as his flagship, and in command of the fleet moving in on the enemy star dreadnought, but it was still his ship, and they were his crew.

"Do not let the next hours become a battle in your minds. Take it easy, take is slow, and treat this battle as nothing more than practice. Run through your drills as normal. Remember, less haste, more speed. For our ship to function, we must work as a single machine. Each of you has a part to play."

Admiral Tovey seemed to like the last part and nodded along as he listened. Finally, the Captain lowered the device and called across to him.

"You're on, Admiral."

"Thank you."

He cleared his voice, and then pulled the device closer.

"Sailors of the Commonwealth. Today we fight to protect our convoys, our worlds, and our cities. But we also fight in the name of vengeance. Our fleet rushes forward once more, but today the advantage is with us. Bismarck, the scourge of open space, is wounded and unable to escape. And so, we move in to engage her in a final, decisive engagement. We will finish what others began, and by God, the Mighty Hood will be avenged by our hand."

He then pulled the intercom to his lips.

"Remember the words of Captain Patterson and remember your training and your drills. When times seem pained and difficult, they will provide solace and protection. Listen to your officers, and you will come out of this unscathed."

"Captain…Flashcom from the Admiralty. It's flagged urgent. For the fleet commander's eyes."

"Send it to me," said the Admiral.

In an instant the message and attached mapping data appeared on his screen. He moved them alongside the live feed from his own ship, and then began nodding.

"Comms. Send an acknowledgement."

His gaze then moved to Captain Patterson who instantly assumed something must have gone wrong.

"Problem?"

"Not quite. By they have issued orders that Rodney and King George V are to manoeuvre independently in the coming fight, supported by our escort cruisers and destroyers."

"Interesting. So that we give the Bismarck a further complication by presenting two different targets to think about."

"Yes. And by implication avoiding Admiral Holland's supposed error of maintaining a close formation between Hood and Prince of Wales."

"I fail to see how their formation was at fault for the

disaster."

"Nonetheless, these are the Admiralty's orders, and they are to be followed."

He looked back to his displays and tagged the others ships in the fleet. In a matter of seconds, he sent new data and orders to each of them. It took a few minutes, but eventually, the formation began to separate into two powerful forces, each led by a single battleship. The storm continued to crash behind them, but as they emerged into the sparse periphery of the nebula, they began to increase speed. Long blue streaks ran out behind them as they moved to close the distance. Their turrets all faced forward, with their barrels waiting for the order every single man and woman aboard was waiting for.

"Captain," said Lieutenant Parker, the ship's communications officer, "Contact from Admiral Wake-Walker."

"What does he want?"

"He says he's made contact with the Bismarck."

"Where?"

Icons flashed up on his displays, and a moment later Lieutenant-Commander Perkins, the ship's senior gunnery officer called out.

"There! Range 320 kilometres and closing awfully fast. They misidentified the target and thought it was us. Norfolk is falling back, but still a little over 120 kilometres from the target."

Each of them looked to their screens and strained their eyes. The lightning storms had begun to weaken, though there were still numerous banks of fog to dart in and out of. Although that still made visibility far from perfect, it was a far cry from the brutal storms they'd left behind. Other ships from the fleet were also there, having been able to finally catch up due to Admiral Tovey's strategy.

"Wait…I see something," said Captain Patterson, "Yes, there!"

"Gentlemen," said Admiral Tovey, crossing his hands in front of his body, "May I present to you the Vrokan super dreadnought, Bismarck. Flagship of their fleet, and the greatest calamity of our time."

The bridge officers looked on at the mighty vessel with a mix of horror and awe. And then without warning, it burst out from the fog bank, its bow coming right for their ship.

"Captain, they appear in good heart and keen for the fight. Are you ready?"

Captain Patterson nodded without saying a word.

"Good. Then it is time."

He turned in his seat and looked to each of the officers on the deck.

"We have bought time to bring in every asset we can find. Now it is time to end this."

To the men's surprise, he then crossed himself and whispered quietly to himself.

"My God protect you all."

Captain Patterson rubbed his hands together and then spoke the fateful words, those that would be repeated ever after by those that had heard them.

"Tactical…Report."

"Target has now reduced the range to 240 kilometres. Her guns are moving into position. Her course remains erratic. I think she's having serious steering problems."

"Plot a target vector."

"I have a visual lock, Captain. Radar lock still not achieved; she's dumping heavy countermeasure clouds."

"Visual will have to do."

"Very good, Sir. Range now set at 210 kilometres."

"You may fire when ready."

"Yes, Captain."

The officer looked back to his screen, and then spoke to the other officers sitting nearby. Though he was the senior gunnery officer, it took an entire team to manage the guns crews, technicians, and crew throughout the ship, unlike smaller vessels.

"Forward turrets...fire!"

The four forward turrets made subtle corrections as they aimed their gun directly to the target. The two larger targets carried four brutally powerful 720mm linear pulse cannons, while the two smaller turrets fitted further back and directly in front of the superstructure, carried just two of the cannons. A mighty rumble rattled through the ship as they fired in sequence. One turret after another unleashed their super-heavy armour-piercing shells towards the target.

"Reloading. Shell impact in seven seconds."

The whine of the autoloaders was just about audible even this far inside the two thousand two hundred- and seventy-metre-long battleship. The whining sound was punctuated with heavy clunks, and even hisses from the hydraulic equipment that could function in zero-gravity, as well as under the duress of heavy acceleration and manoeuvring.

"No impacts," said Lieutenant-Commander Perkins, "Adjusting tracking. Firing again."

The tension increased considerably as they watched the

rapidly moving lines on their displays. The powerful cannons could hurl the 800mm diameter shells at incredible speeds allowing them to cover the distance to Bismarck in around seven seconds. Perkins looked across to the Captain and shook his head.

"Close...but still no hits."

"Keep at it. You'll get her range soon enough."

The guns were about to fire again when the man's eyes lit up.

"Captain, our type 284 radar has burned through their countermeasure screen. It's not a perfect match, but it's good enough for a solid lock. I have her range, course, and closing velocity."

"Excellent, you know what to do."

The senior officers watched the forward view from the front of the ship, with Rodney moving off to the port-side, and the usual long blue streaks from her engines marking her course.

"Firing!"

The forward guns unleashed another devastating bombardment, with twelve guns putting a flurry of projectiles towards the enemy warship. Before they could land, the entire front of Rodney disappeared in a cloud of white and blue. Captain Patterson gasped at the sight.

"God...no!"

But then the clouds began to dissipate, and the tactical overlay showed projectiles from both ships heading towards the target.

"Come on!" Lieutenant-Commander Perkins said.

Two more seconds passed, and then a cheer rang out as half of the projectiles slammed into the bow and upper superstructure of the ship.

"Good hits," said Perkins.

But then his expression changed as he zoomed in on the blurred live videostream. They showed the star dreadnought crashing through the shellfire with little to show against her bow armour save for black marks.

"Captain. We didn't get through."

"What about Rodney? She's carrying the heaviest guns in the fleet."

"Nothing on the bow, and one penetration on Bismarck's superstructure."

Admiral Tovey lifted his intercom and then gave a nod to Lieutenant Watkins.

"Put me through to Rodney."

"Admiral."

He licked his lips, and then spoke slowly and calmly so that he wouldn't be misheard.

"Captain. Are you seeing the same problems?"

He waited, and then nodded along as he listened.

"I see. It seems her main armour belt is proof against gunfire at this range."

Admiral Tovey moved one display to his side and pulled the central display closer.

"Very well. We will change our course and turn away to free our stern turrets. That should draw them right at us. I want all interceptor drones launched and brought along our flank. Let's try and reduce the incoming fire as best we can."

The crew appeared confident with his orders, and none heard him whisper to himself as he looked away, "But that isn't going to be enough."

His right hand moved along the mapping imagery and drew lines for each of the ships. He started to speak but stopped as one of the tactical officers removed his headset.

"Incoming!" Lieutenant-Commander Perkins said.

The tension was palpable on the deck as Bismarck loosed off shots from her forward guns. The 800mm shells were the same size as those fired by Hood, but heavier and moved with significantly greater velocity.

"Good God, those are fast," said Tovey as they came in towards King George V.

"Brace, brace, brace!" The Captain held the intercom to his mouth, "We have incoming."

The shells whooshed on past. Though close enough that one detonated as it hit the interceptor drones. It exploded in a fireball and showered the starboard bow with debris.

"Are we hit?"

"Negative, Captain," said Lieutenant-Commander Perkins, "Interceptors stopped it. The impacts were just shell splinters. Should I discharge smoke? They'll be firing again soon."

"That's a negative, Lieutenant-Commander. We need our sights and scanners kept clear. We will just have to take the chance."

The battleship returned fire again, scattering heavy shells against her bow and forward hull. Flashes marked detonations, but still she came on and right at them. Her stern rear turret batteries joined in as she hit out at battleship Rodney moving off past her flank. The two ships unleashed a veritable hell against each other, their gunfire ripping holes into each other and starting numerous fires. Tiny groups of drones moved around the outer hulls of each ship, with some struggling to put out electrical fires or fusing up breached bulkheads. Most were simply expended as ablative armour as they moved in to absorb some of the incoming fire.

"Keep firing," said Captain Patterson, "Don't spare the hoists, just keep our guns hot, and under no circumstances do you stop."

"Yes, Captain."

Admiral Tovey left the management of the ship to the Captain and focussed on the disposition of his forces. His ships were approaching from the sides and behind, at different levels so that the gunfire came in from all possible angles.

"Norfolk, Dorsetshire, follow these vectors and support us. Hit her with everything you have."

The two heavy warships quickly moved into range and opened fire with their batteries of dual 420mm Linear Accelerator Cannons. Though incapable of penetrating Bismarck's main armour, they were more than capable of punching through the superstructure, and even knocking out the smaller turrets.

"That's more like it. If we can't destroy her, we'll burn her from inside out."

"Rodney has moved in to close-range," said Admiral Tovey, "Let's see if her guns fare any better."

Even as he spoke, the mighty battleship unleashed a massed volley from its array of forward mounted turrets. The extra heavy calibre gun hammered into the main superstructures in a series of blinding lights.

"Good hit!" Lieutenant-Commander Perkins yelled, "Their bridge is heavily damaged, and some of the fire control directors have been blasted apart. Rodney is doing her job!"

"Good," said Admiral Tovey, "Now all…"

He then grimaced as two of Bismarck's forward guns fired again, and this time the shells slammed into the lower hull with such force he could feel it in his teeth.

"Penetrations!" said Perkins, "We have breaches on multiple decks, fires under control."

"I want damage control teams in there fast," said Captain Patterson, "Get the fires out before they can spread further."

A single shot struck directly above the command deck, splitting the ceiling and sending smoke out and around the officers. Alarms sounded as respirator tubes automatically extended for them to grab. Admiral Tovey grabbed his, pulled it to his mouth, and inhaled deeply. Only then did he look around to the others. Captain Patterson was already there and busily checking that each of them was unhurt and breathing. His job proved more difficult due to the clouds of fire suppressants spreading through the compartments.

"That was too close," said Admiral Tovey, "We need to end this before it…"

A dozen small holes appeared to the right, and smaller slugs, each little larger than a man's finger, burst through, slamming into the innards of the ship. Tovey tried to move away from the gunfire, but the manoeuvring thrusters, combined with the main drive, made it all but impossible to do anything other than spin around the interior and slam into the other officers. He remained there strapped to his seat, as the injured cried out in pain or the dead sat completely still as globules of blood floated about. He tried to ignore the carnage and focussed on the battle.

"Captain…Are we still in this fight?"

Captain Patterson looked across the smoke-filled room and tried to wave some of the cloud away.

"This isn't over yet, Admiral. We took some hits, but we're in the fight."

"Good. Our heavy cruisers can move in to harass her, but I'm sending in Rodney to point-blank range. Her guns can rip through her armour but not if she's focussed by Bismarck."

"Understood, Admiral. We'll keep as many guns off Rodney as we can."

"Another urgent Comflash from the Admiralty."

"What is it now?" Admiral Tovey asked.

"Fresh reports of Jaeger ships moving into the area, Sir."

The message caught the attention of Captain Patterson who looked across with a look of grim uncertainty about him.

"How long until their arrival?"

"Within the hour, Admiral. And there's one more thing."

"There always is. Go on."

This time the officer's gaze shifted from him to Captain Patterson.

"King George V is to stay in this area until the battle is decided. Even if that means we run out of fuel."

"What? Where does that come from?"

"From the top, Captain."

Admiral Tovey snorted at the very idea.

"Orders or not, we will end this battle come what may. But I promise you now, Captain. We're not staying dead in space with Jaeger ships swarming around us. We lost Hood; we're not losing another."

Captain Patterson barely nodded and turned his attention

to his officers.

"Helm, change of course. Bring us about…Take us thirty degrees off her bow. Clear the stern turrets. Tactical, keep firing! We need to cover Rodney and our cruisers as they move in closer."

Admiral Tovey sent additional orders to the cruisers, as well as calling in the remaining destroyers to spread out and begin searching for the enemy Jaeger ships. There was little more worrying for a battleship commander than the stealthy vessel that could attack without being detected. In his hand was the bloodstained intercom, though by now he had no idea whose blood it was. Once satisfied, he lifted the device to his lips, the channel still open from his last conversation.

"Rodney. I need you to move in close and go broadside to broadside and put shots into her port-side as close as you dare. I mean right down their throats."

He hesitated, knowing full well that the next order was one he never would have asked under the circumstances.

"The bridge has been destroyed, and possibly along with their senior officers. I need you to get inside and wreak havoc. Get their attention from their guns and elsewhere. Do you have enough marines onboard for that? I see…Very well."

He nodded again and then raised his eyebrows.

"I will keep her guns busy and target her main batteries. Get close enough and send all of them at her in breaching landers. I will scrape together lifeboats with reserves to assist you. Send them in with demolition charges. No…this is a destruction operation. There's no time to tow her home. Get inside and wreck the place."

He listened a little longer and then nodded.

"Very well, we will keep the port-side clear for thirty minutes. After that, she's fair game. Time is running out for us."

He then replaced the handset and began to speak before being interrupted. He licked his lips before telling them news few would believe.

"Rodney is the closest and she's sending in marines to board her."

That drew a stunned silence from the others, until finally Captain Patterson said what all of them must have been thinking.

"Rodney is boarding a Vrokan star dreadnought? He'll be outnumbered a hundred to one."

"Yes. Assuming we haven't already killed most of the crew."

He bit his upper lip before asking something he knew the Captain wouldn't like.

"I need every marine you have onboard to the lifeboats. Get them ready to assist Rodney if she calls for aid. If we can't destroy her from the outside, it will have to be from within.

"Admiral?" asked the stunned Captain, "We have no breaching landers onboard."

"I know. It's risky, but much must be risked in war if we are to emerge triumphant. Pray to God that Rodney alone proves sufficient."

Admiral Tovey settled back into his seat and watched as the Captain began issuing orders. He looked frustrated, perhaps even a little angry at the orders. But Admiral Tovey was sure the man understood the gravity of what needed to be done. To fail now after so much had been lost would condemn the sacrifices of those already gone. The ship began the slow, tortuous process of turning away while bringing all her primary and secondary guns to bear. The forward guns fired two more volleys by the time the ship had fully changed course and began a slight roll to unfurl every single turret. Now the vessel's arsenal of twenty accelerator cannons was lined up on the Bismarck.

"Captain. Their course is shifting wildly. Each time they try to move forward they being to rotate off to port. They can barely maintain a true course now."

"Good. Maybe it will throw off her aim."

The guns fired again, and this time all six turrets put down a punishing barrage that exploded along the upper hull of the ship. Return fire slammed into the flank of King George V, sending terrible vibrations through the hull. Admiral Tovey gulped nervously as he looked to his screens.

"Light damage," said Captain Patterson, "Starboard armour belt penetrated, but the citadel remains intact."

Four more shells then came in and hit near the forward turrets. One exploded in a bright fireball, tearing off one of the ship's 180mm Linear Accelerator gun turrets. The damaged battery mounts continued to burn, venting blue and white smoke into the void.

"She doesn't seem that damaged to me," said Captain Patterson, "We're landing shots, but her armour belt and citadel are just too strong."

"Then hit the softer targets," suggested Admiral Tovey, "Casualties will slow her down, wherever they're caused."

"Aye, Admiral."

"Secondary batteries are firing," said Lieutenant-Commander Perkins, "We're hitting them with everything we have. We're turning her upper decks into slag, but for every turret we knock out, there are another two right behind it. She should be a hulk by now."

The infrequent shaking turned to something much more violent as the remaining fifteen turrets began firing. Though much smaller than the main guns, they were still significant weapons, with the turrets equipped with a pair of rapid firing 180mm Linear Accelerator Guns, the same weapons used to equip cruisers and heavy destroyers.

"I don't like this," said Admiral Tovey.

Captain Patterson saw him shaking his head and called across.

"Admiral. Time is running short. I'm reaching the limits of our supplies. Another twenty minutes and we'll be dry."

"It's the same for Rodney. I'll give Bismarck one thing…she is putting up a hell of a fight."

Another series of flashes lit up the enemy warship, and for a second it looked as though she had been destroyed. But as the light quickly faded, the grey behemoth remained, and with most of her guns still firing and hammering the ships around it.

"Okay, that's enough," said Admiral Tovey, "Comms, I want to speak with Ark Royal, and fast."

"Yes, Admiral."

He pulled the intercom close and spoke in a voice that sounded much calmer than it should have been, all while the gunfire raked the ship and opened up the armour plating in a dozen places.

"This is Tovey. I know, I know…but there's one last thing I need you to do before you move out of range."

The battleship shuddered. He looked to the display to his right and watched as King George V unleashed a full salvo from all her guns. Half of the shots hit Bismarck's superstructure in a blast of fire and explosions. But the flames quickly subsided, and there behind the smoke was the still functional, but badly damaged Bismarck. The vessel turned one of its main turret batteries towards them, and then fired again. Each turret bore a pair of guns that narrowly missed the battleship, sending its shells off into the void.

"Admiral," said Captain Patterson, "She's no longer coordinating her fire. I think her primary gunnery command and control has been destroyed."

"Good." Tovey placed a hand over the intercom, "Then we must overwhelm her defences as best we can. The greater the confusion, the safer we will be."

"Agreed."

He tried to move his attention back to Ark Royal, as she sped away from the fighting and prepared to use her jump engines. But the videofeeds of the battle proved utterly memorising. The beams of light that followed the shells' trajectory were now visible at this close-range, and the clouds of point-defence guns arced back and forth, hitting incoming shells as well as the few remaining interceptor drones. All three large capital ships were now wreathed in fire and the crackling of light, as armour plates blasted into space and compartments were ripped apart.

"Yes," he said finally, pulling his eyes away from the carnage, "Whatever you can spare. We're running low on fuel and ammunition, and Bismarck's still float. You have a matter of minutes before it's too late. Send everything you have left my way. If it has engines and can fly, launch it!"

***

Commonwealth Fleet Carrier 'Victorious', Deep Space

Lieutenant-Commander Coode let his eyes close, doing his best to try and calm his body. Even now so long after the strike, he still felt the adrenalin surging through his body. It would take hours to let his body come to rest, but he refused to back down. He took in a long, slow breath and then almost choked as a voice to his left called out.

"Coode. We're being scrambled."

"What?" His eyes opened wide in surprise, "I thought the heavies were doing the job?"

He blinked twice and then noticed it was Lieutenant-Commander Stewart-Moore.

"James...you're sure?"

"Apparently, they've got hunters moving in on them. If they stay in the area too long, they're going to get hit. We're moving away from the fight before the bad guys arrive."

"And the star dreadnought?"

"Bismarck can't escape. Your lads made sure of that."

Coode grinned at the mention of their recent escapades. He'd rewatched the video footage so many times it was now burned into his memory. The clouds of gunfire, and the hundreds of holes punched into his fighters. But what stuck in his mind more than anything else was the single torpedo impact that had struck the beast astern, finally slowing it down. Some said it was luck, but he knew better. It had taken skill and courage to get into place for the attack, and hitting the stern was far from easy. Just thinking of that attack brought him right back to his pilots, and the knowledge that in the battle against

Bismarck they'd already lost many and might soon lose more.

"So what's happening? We can't let her escape."

"That's where you come in. We don't know how, but Bismarck is still crawling away like a wounded beast, and she's still fighting. CAG wants us to put up whatever birds we have left in the next five minutes and get back there and to the fight."

Coode had suspected as much, but he still gasped at the suggestion they could do more than get a few spacecraft into the void in that time.

"We got shot to ribbons out there. I doubt I can muster more than three airframe."

"Either way, Bismarck is still standing and we're running out of time. There're two battleships and two heavy cruisers going at her, and she's fighting back. Last reports said both our heavies are burning."

"Good God. Not another Hood."

Stewart-Moore pulled himself upright, and then rose upwards onto the metal decking. The engines were still firing, though the force was less than before, making him feel less than half his normal weight.

"Let's go, we've got work to do."

They moved towards the hangar, using the grab handles to help them as the ship continued to fire its engines. The internal lighting remained as normal, though the combat lighting was also on, sending a curious mixed message to the men and women aboard. They moved onto the deck to find the crew already moving the fighters into position. Half lacked torpedoes, and most of the others bore signs of damage. Waiting on the metal plating were nine crewmembers, each with their exposure suits already on and their helmets under their arms. Two had already pulled on their helmets.

"We're ready for this," said one of the men, his face hidden behind the helmet, "Are we going to sink her?"

Coode grinned from ear to ear as one of the deck crew handed him a checklist. He passed it to Stewart-Moore who ran a finger down the list. He tapped each entry, and then did his best to look as confident as possible to the men and women waiting on the deck.

"It's not a lot, but there's enough for a single flight. The only question is are you up for another crack at Bismarck?"

The pilots responded with raised fists and stamping of feet. Half of them had already been in action, with two from Stewart-Moore's failed attack. Two more had been in the reserve flight, and so far missed out on all the action and were desperate to get out there and do their part.

"Very well. Get to your birds. You'll be briefed en route."

He then reached forward and each of them shook hands.

"To the hunt!"

CHAPTER FIFTEEN

Bismarck, as she was known to the Commonwealth, was not the only battleship built by the Vrokan. In the years leading to the war, they'd amassed a small force of powerful and fully modernised warships, each more than capable of holding their own against any of their rivals. Commonwealth intelligence believed that more ships were in production, with reports showing that Vrokan designers were planning on constructing a new, larger and more powerful version of the ship known only as the H Class. Even more worrying, reconnaissance flights showed shipyards were being prepared for at least six of them. Was this a deadly new threat, or a ruse by the Vrokan to keep most of the Commonwealth fleet in port and waiting for attack?

Masimov's Guide to Fighting Ships

Commonwealth Battleship 'Rodney'
1,902nd day of the war

Royal Marines Captain Jackie Thompson moved to the large circular hatch at the side of the craft and stopped to look back at her squad. At her side was the short, squat figure of Sergeant Hammond, her right-hand man, and one that none would dare say a word against. What he lacked in height, he made up for in a body built like a tank, strong, muscular, and brimming with confidence. The two had proven inseparable for more than a year, allowing them to hone their marines into an elite and unstoppable force.

"Marines," she said calmly, "out there is the Vrokan Star Dreadnought. It's a battleship bigger and tougher than anything we've seen before. But they've never fought against Royal Marines, have they?"

"No, Sir!" replied the marines.

"We've been given the job that none of the battleships can do. We're to get inside, fight our way to her core, and blow her to kingdom come."

"No second chances, this is the real deal," said Sergeant

Hammond, "Are you ready for this?"

"Yes, Sergeant!" came back the chant.

"Good, because you're in for the toughest fight of your lives. These Vrokan might be cruel, miserable bastards, but they're damned good fighters. Remember your training, and don't get sucked into hand-to-hand. The Vrokan will draw you in and never let you go!"

The hatch clunked fully open, and then each of them moved inside. The craft looked tiny on the inside compared to the outside, with double-layered bulkheads throughout to give it structural strength far beyond a normal spacecraft. There was no crew, just the small passenger compartment. As the marines moved to their allocated positions, he continued speaking.

"When we get inside, you will watch your fire. King George V is preparing lifeboats and a reserve should we need it. If they come aboard, I don't want to see any unfriendly fire. Understood?"

The marines nodded in agreement and waited as he moved along, checking each of them. Captain Thompson moved to her own place and let the metal barrier lock her down into place. Once satisfied they were all secure, he moved to his own place. By then, the outer door had closed, and the internal lighting changed to red.

"There's no gravity on that ship. She's dead in space, with her engines gone. So you'll be freewheeling it or using your gravboots. Remember, use every surface to your advantage. Floor, ceiling, walls…it's all the same in zero-g."

An alarm then sounded that increased in tempo.

"Hold on. This won't take long."

The sound stopped, and then without warning, the small

craft burst free from the battleship and made its way out into space. It travelled so far some of the passengers blacked out for a few seconds until the engines cut, and they coasted along at high-speed. Captain Thompson knew they were under fire well before the alerts sounded. The telltale rattle and shudder as the point-defence guns hit the craft's armour was something she'd experienced twice before. The guns raked the spacecraft as Bismarck's defenders did their best to shake off the swarm of assault landers crossed the killing ground between the Commonwealth battleship and the Vrokan Star Dreadnought.

"Impact in ten seconds. Check your clamps! Brace yourselves."

Thompson looked to the other side where a row of heavily armoured marines waited. There were sixteen of them, eight per side, and clamped down against the inside of the spacecraft. They wore sealed armoured battle suits, consisting of a complex array of armoured plates and nodes fitted over a fully sealed inner line; that itself contained an armoured outer layer capable of withstanding stabs from blades and small calibre weapons.

"Now!"

Captain Thompson couldn't breathe as the breaching lander slammed into the ship's superstructure and forced its way inside several more metres. The craft was small, with most of its structure made of an armoured wedge, along with powerful thrusters front and back. And then it was over as quickly as it had begun. Some of the newer marines moved their hands to release their clamps, but Captain Thompson shook her head.

"Not yet."

She tensed her body and counted down until the breaching charges detonated. Even though it was a controlled explosion, it still sent a shockwave back into the heavily armoured body of the breaching lander. When she looked ahead at the smoke, she could see nothing but darkness in the distance and the innards of a ship.

"We're in. Let's go!"

Each of them released the clamps holding them in position and pushed away from the ship. They floated through the craft and past the breached hull to move inside. Captain Thompson was first through and floated into what appeared to be a weapons battery control room. Three bodies floated about, and bloodstains marked the walls.

"She's depressurized," said Sergeant Hammond, "These outer compartments have all been vented."

"Keep moving, and record everything. We've got just minutes in here."

She reached forward, grabbed the sides of the compartment, and pulled herself forward. There were grab handles on all the surfaces, much like her ship, though the internal layout was quite different. She pulled herself into the next passage where it moved back into the ship, with numerous blast doors along one side. Most were sealed shut, but some were open and filled with floating debris.

"She looks dead to me," said Corporal Lutz.

He reached for one of the open bulkhead openings and pushed his head inside, letting the dual beams on his shoulder light up the interior.

"Looks like bunk space to me. No crew."

As he turned back, the other marines moved in closer. They were well armed, with the majority carrying the ever-reliable Kousar T9 assault carbine. One in four also carried heavy demolition packs on their backs, each capable of destroying a small ship if positioned in the right place.

"Which way?"

The Sergeant turned back and then pointed ahead.

"Our schematics show passages here...and here leading towards the energy storage array."

As he pointed off into the darkness, the tagged locations appeared on Captain Thompson's visor. Faint dotted lines marked the expected position of passages, shafts, and other areas of interest, though much of it was incomplete.

"Good. Increase the pace!"

They moved through two more compartments, and then approached a large hexagonal hole directly ahead. The marines clustered around the entrance, like camels around an oasis as they looked over the edge and down into the blackness.

"This must be the primary engineering deck," said Captain Thompson.

She looked back and signalled for her tech specialist to move forward. He was armed and equipped much like the others, though on his back he carried an additional array of sensors and equipment. His helmet was different to the others, with an ocular assembly fitted above one eye and connected via cabling down to the pack behind him. He activated the unit, and it moved into position, granting him various scanning modes.

"Yes...the energy cores are close. We need to move through the engineering deck towards the stern."

"Follow me," said the Captain.

She pushed off through the hole, slowly and silently through the shadows. Her lamps cast long shadows as they scanned the vastness of the interior. The place was massive, with tall bulkhead barriers creating a solid structure to work inside. They dropped down, clunking against a wide metal gantry. As they looked about at the interior, they were greeted with something incredible.

"This place. It's nothing like a ship."

"More like a fortress," said Sergeant Hammond.

The walls looked more like stone, with arches rising off into the corners. Hanging from fixed points on the walls were the massive insignia of the Vrokan Empire, a design harking back the centuries to a time long forgotten, as well as a portrait of the war hero Luther Maximillian, now dictator and their charismatic leader.

"Or a cathedral to that monster."

One of the marines took aim with his carbine and was quickly stopped by the Sergeant.

"That's not what we're here for, lad."

"Wait," said Captain Thompson, "I saw something move."

Sergeant Hammond stopped speaking and each checked every crack and crevice they could find with the lamps. And then without warning, Sergeant Hammond slowly drifted back towards her with globules of blood floating after him. With no atmosphere remaining in the ship, there was nowhere for the sound to travel, leaving him to die in silence.

"Contact!" Captain Thompson shouted over the comms network.

Lights flickered as a myriad of small arms opened fire on the marines. Half of them were still at the hexagonal entrance and fired down to support their comrades, and gunfire crashed throughout the interior of the ship. Captain Thompson breathed harder and harder as she looked for her foes. Then the guns fired again, and she saw them just a few metres away, pointing their guns right at her. They were big, larger and bulkier than the marines. They looked like they were wearing medieval armour, with exaggerated edges and plates to make them look sharp and dangerous.

"Push them back!"

Her Kousar T9 assault carbine shook violently as she sprayed them with short bursts. The weapon was far from subtle and hit the enemy with a barrage of armour-piercing, explosive slugs. Puffs of light marked the impact along their bodies. One lost the contact from his magboots and floated up and away from the fight. A second fired back, and the rounds hammered past Captain Thompson. One caught her below the knee and knocked her leg back without managing to penetrate the plating.

"Captain!" Corporal Lutz shouted.

Her boots detached from the ground to save causing her major injury, and she floated upwards, striking the nearby bulkhead. The boots automatically reattached her to the metal plating and left her standing on what would have been the wall, and at ninety degrees compared to the others. She looked for her attackers, and then her finger moved to the trigger. The gun fired again, this time a series of short bursts.

"Keep moving. I want those charges set…now!"

More of the marines pushed through the hexagonal opening, while others followed the Captain to the end of the gantry and a single massive blast door. It was open and led into a room filled with red light.

"Is this it?"

"I think so," said the tech specialist as he moved to the

Captain's side.

"Good. Stay right behind me."

Captain Thompson took a one step inside, and then stopped as she spotted seven or eight crewmembers in sealed environmental suits, as well as a trio of Vrokan marines. She took aim with her weapons and opened fire. She hit two of the marines before they could respond and then leaned back to avoid the return fire. More of her people floating in behind her, with two walking in as they used their grav-boots so they could remain upright.

"Captain…we've got a problem," said the tech specialist.

Markers appeared on her helmet visor, and as she looked more closely, her eyes opened wide.

"No," she muttered, "you're sure?"

"Those are detonators. They're going to skuttle her."

Gunfire from nearby struck the bulkhead to her side, sending sparks cascading towards her and lighting up the marines. She returned fire and then turned to the others nearby. "She's rigged to blow. Everybody off the ship…now!"

One of the sergeants from the second squad to board waved to the others following right behind, signalling back in the direction they'd arrived from.

"Marines, get back to the boats…we're leaving!"

* * *

Commonwealth Heavy Cruiser 'Norfolk'.

Three massive detonations ripped through the innards of the mighty star dreadnought with such massive force the ship's hull visibly deformed under the immense pressure. Seconds later, great plumes of light burst through holes and cracks in the outer armour as if the energy from a decaying star now struggled to break free.

"Good God!" Rear Admiral Wake-Walker said, "Captain…Get us away from her, best possible speed."

"Yes, Admiral."

He looked on, entranced by what he could see. The ship visibly shook as the light struggled to escape from deep inside her. Then one of the main turrets burst free from the hull, and behind it tall plumes of light from detonating ammunition blasted out into space.

"Just look at her. She's falling apart. I've never seen a ship take what we've inflicted on this day…Hood was gone in seconds. But this monster…"

"Her crew fought like demons," said Captain Phillips, "No matter what we've heard of the Vrokan, we cannot deny their skill and bravery in this fight."

Lieutenant Madeline wiped her forehead for the third time in the last ten minutes and then leaned in closer to her displays. There on the main screen was the massive shape of the Bismarck, her hull now surrounded in broken pieces of metal, broken drones, and the flotsam of battle. Her engines were either offline or destroyed, and all but a handful of the secondary guns dormant and silent.

"Cease fire," said Capt. Phillips, "She's done for. No need to waste more ammunition on her. Let her die in her own time."

The heavy cruiser's main drive activated, and the ship began to turn away from the fight for the last time. The two Commonwealth battleships were already clear, leaving just the cruisers and destroyers moving around the burning carcass.

"There's no need to…"

Captain Phillips stopped and almost choked as three batteries of secondary guns opened fire. They were barely visible as fires spread around them, with smoke clouds masking their armoured turrets from view as they blasted away. The shots were wild, with most missing. But then they fired again, and this time the shots slammed into the port-side stern bow armour of the heavy cruiser.

"Breaches in the forward compartments," said Alethea, "A battery is offline, and we have fires near the magazines. Reports of light casualties."

Captain Phillips kept shaking his head as he looked to his superior.

"I'm sorry, Captain. We have fresh orders. We and Dorsetshire are to finish her off with torpedoes and then withdraw as fast as we can."

"But, Sir. They're burning. The ship is a hulk. Nothing more."

"This comes from the top," he said sadly, "We're to make sure she is never recovered."

"What of her crew?"

Lieutenant Alethea Madeline used the gunnery scanners and moved in closer to the heavily damaged vessel. She moved quickly along its massive hull, picking out markings in the Vrokan language.

"No signs of lifeboats," she said in surprise, "Maybe they're all dead."

"Then who's firing the damn guns?" asked the Admiral.

To emphasize the point, several more shots came perilously close, with one managing to rip away the antenna from the dorsal communications array. Alethea watched as it tumbled away into space with sparks cracking at the severed base.

"Why won't they stop?"

"The Vrokan have been indoctrinated into the belief that they are greatest race to have ever settled the stars. They show no mercy, and today we cannot afford to be any different," said the Admiral, "They will not surrender, and Bismarck, or whatever they call their damn ship, must be eliminated. Lock onto her hull and fire one last spread. We can't take chances…not now."

Alethea gulped and looked to Captain Phillips, who grudgingly nodded.

"Yes, Sir."

If Alethea had any doubts, she would never have moved her fingers to the controls. But as wretched as she felt, she knew that if left intact, Bismarck would be back in a matter of years, and she might succeed where this time she had failed.

"Launching now."

The rattle and thud of the auto-loading mechanism was unusually vacant this time as the last of the torpedoes speed away from Norfolk. There were no interceptor drones left, and the last few guns reached out under manual control to try and stop them. There was no chance at this range and speed, and they soon hit, each striking almost a hundred metres from the next. By the time the second struck, another volley loosed away from Dorsetshire.

"Farewell." The Admiral removed his hat and placed it under his arm. One by one the others did the same as they watched the warheads slam into the great warship. Alethea did the same and watched in silence as the explosions spread through the ship.

"I don't believe it," said Captain Phillips, "She's still standing."

"Our orders are clear," said Admiral Wake-Walker, "We cannot stay here a moment longer. The destroyers will pick up any survivors they can, and then we must move, pronto. Jaeger ships will be here within the hour."

"Helm," said Captain Phillips, "Push the engines as hard as you can. Maximum burn away from this place."

"Aye, Captain."

* * *

The flight of battered and scarred Swordfish burst out of the fog and to a sight none had ever seen before. Debris and tiny fragments of metal drifted about in vast clouds. Sections of ship, large pieces of armour, and thousands of chunks of expended ammunition floated about as a deadly hazard. Small destroyers and lifeboats circled the area as they hunted for survivors, while blue streaks marked the course of the retreating heavy cruisers. Three more of the fighter-bombers moved in from the clouds to the right, with the distinctively marked Swordfish of Lieutenant-Commander Coode leading them.

"Good to see you, thought we'd lost you back there," said Stewart-Moore.

"So did I," chuckled his friend.

He moved slightly ahead, taking up the lead position and command of the flight as agreed. They were positioned in a wide V formation, with those carrying torpedoes now moving to the front.

"Where is Bismarck?" Coode asked.

The flight whooshed through another bank of white clouds and was forced to swerve away as the broken remnants of a light cruiser blocked their path. Half of the Swordfish cleared the area, but the others ploughed through the smaller fragments, creating a series of white puffs and flashes. One suffered engine damage, and smoke began to trail behind it.

"I'm okay," said the pilot, "Clearing the blockage now."

Blue flames flashed around the engine, and the smoke vanished as quickly as it had started. They moved on past the debris, and then without warning, a flicker of yellow lit up in the distance and a massive bank of debris and smoke. As the lights flashed, they could see the silhouette they'd been hunting for. There before them was the shape of the dying monster, that great grey brute, surrounded by fire, and flickering like a star in the distance.

"Bismarck sighted," said Lieutenant-Commander Stewart-Moore, "This is it, chaps. Time to end what we started."

Each armed their warheads and waited for the command.

"Let's move in closer," said Coode, "No sense in taking chances, not now."

Onwards they went, directly at the star dreadnought. Lieutenant-Commander Coode looked to his sides and to the other Swordfish as they made their serene move through the battleground. He'd never seen the aftermath of such a battle in outer space before, where parts of ships were left to drift for an eternity. But even stranger was the lack of gunfire. Bismarck looked to all intents and purposes little more than a hulk, and then to his surprise, he spotted flickering lights along her upper hull.

"Good God. There're still people aboard her. Take evasive action!"

The fighters rolled away as scattered fire from small turrets hidden throughout her burning hull tried to pluck them from space. Bursts came close, though nowhere near enough to hit the Swordfish.

"Regroup, let's get this done."

The fighter-bombers turned back to face the ship, though now in three separate groups. More shots came for them, but it was clear the gunners were firing manually, making it almost impossible to hit even a cruiser at this range.

"On my mark…"

A single white light grew from the centre of the ship, and then continued until the entire ship was engulfed in the expanding energy wave. A moment later, another followed, and then another. The light soon faded, and this time parts of the ship ripped apart into an expanding cloud of wreckage travelling in all directions. The main hull remained intact, though her turrets were gone, along with the stern and half of the bow. Most of the central hull and superstructure remained in one piece, spinning slowly away from the explosions.

"Good God," said Lieutenant-Commander Coode, "It's done."

"The show's over, chaps," said Lieutenant-Commander Stewart-Moore, "Time to get back to the Ark before she leaves. We're done here."

They waited a short time, each looking to remains of the ship, and then ever so slowly the formation of fighter-bombers moved away in a long, slow arc. As they left, the carcass adrift in space, Stewart-Moore lifted his right hand in a smart salute.

"Farewell."

Half a kilometre away, Lieutenant-Commander Coode did the same while slowly shaking his head.

"You died as you fought, on your feet and with guns blazing."

His hand moved back down, and the ruined ship began to shrink behind him. The monster was barely visible, as the burning inferno of what little remained ripped apart in an apocalyptic blast, scattering its metal hull to the stars in a shower of minuscule fragments. The Vrokan Star Dreadnought, codenamed Bismarck, was gone.

"And so dies the beast."

THE END

Printed in Great Britain
by Amazon